2nd Edition
Copyright (C) 2021 by Ross Fisher
ISBN: 9798539386832

Cover design by Ross Fisher
Original photo by Casey Hornerby via Unsplash

Dedicated to my wonderful wife, **Marie**, without whom this book would never have been completed. Literally, she found and highlighted over 1,700+ grammar, spelling and plot mistakes I'd missed.

I love you the mostest.

Love is in the space between distance and time

PROLOGUE

At the far end of the local cluster in the Milky Way galaxy, where the most distant human observation platform was situated, there was silence. The usual swing shift was given the night off. Instead of human eyes it was the artificial mind of Systems Control that watched recent scanning reports trickle in from the probes.

The neighboring galactic arm normally shone brightly with stars that beckoned to be visited. In recent years those stationed on the observation platform felt like it was dimming. A probe had been sent as far and as fast as possible to observe the tail end of the Pereus arm of the Milky Way galaxy.

What now came back in the scanning reports caused the normally unflappable AI that managed humanity to blink. "Surely these reports could not be correct," the internal inquiries called out to sub-systems. Factories on worlds lightyears away were sent orders to begin construction of bigger, faster, stronger probes.

Before the crew of the observation platform woke up, the mainframe was scrubbed of the reports from the probe. In its place was now a single sentence, "Report classified. Further scanning to be rescheduled by Systems Control." By the afternoon the entire platform would be decommissioned and its crew scattered to the stars.

Two hundred years later on Gamma-Netta, the dual suns had barely begun their ascent into the sky, when Systems Control awakened Dr. Jully Liu-Cheng: "Gather the council for an urgent report," was all that the AI said to her as she wiped the sleep from her eyes.

Sitting down at her workstation Dr. Liu-Cheng double checked that her face looked appropriate before she engaged the quantum link video call with the other 15 members of the Aligned Worlds Council. Fifteen concerned faces stared back at her as Systems Control's red dot pulsed in the top corner of the screen.

"We're all here. What could not wait?" Dr. Liu-Cheng asked as she started sipping on her cup of ceda-coffee.

The red dot pulsed brightly and then Systems Control began speaking, "It has been confirmed that the line of darkened solar systems at the far end of the Perseus arm of the Milky Way galaxy is not an equipment malfunction. Multiple probes have now confirmed what historical data already showed... this sector was not always dark. This phenomenon is recent within the last three hundred years."

Without waiting, because why wait when you're very old, Councilor Netgeera spoke out, "What are you saying?"

Equally impatient to be done with this conversation, Systems Control replied instantly, "Inter-linear expansion theory posited the existence of such dark patches in the fabric of the universe, but there is another possibility that must be explored: Entropy. The end of all existence from the separation of all energy in the universe."

Almost as soon as it had said, "the end of all existence," the 15 councilors had broken into a crosschatter of alarmed confusion. Having reached functional immortality the councilors were unnerved by the idea of something they could not control: the end of existence. Dr. Liu-Cheng started muting the councilors to regain control of the early morning call.

As the call descended into madness, lightyears away a deceptively small but powerful starship pulled up next to a galactic com buoy. Long forgotten a millennium ago during the construction of the galaxy crossing network, it still served as a redundant fallback router for quantum link calls on the internal Systems Control network.

Inside the starship a very old pilot listened as the Aligned Worlds Council tried to grasp the idea that the galactic arm next to them was fading from existence. They were not taking it well. The pilot laughed listening to people threaten Systems Control as if they had any real power over the AI created to run the human empire.

Dr. Liu-Cheng, tired of trying to be polite, muted and shut off the video feed for everyone but herself, "Shut up!" The silenced call echoed back at the doctor as she spent a long moment looking at her own video feed. Wondering what happened to the chipper young woman who'd been excited to become a councilor years ago.

Systems Control beeped, and then started talking without waiting for anyone to acknowledge it, "Attempting to stop Entropy is beyond the current capabilities we possess. However, even just confirming that this is what humanity faces will allow for adjustments to colonization plans that can extend human safety and existence for as long as possible."

The doctor, still the only face anyone could see, nodded and asked, "So what is your recommendation?"

A series of sketches filled the screen as Systems Control began to narrate, "The shape of this research project is still

4

being mapped out, but before anything can start in earnest humanity must establish an outpost in the Pereus arm of the galaxy. Anticipating the need for further data I already dispatched a starship to designation Checkpoint Charlie. The ship, Boijeo, is unmanned and will serve as the bones for a future space station."

Dr. Liu-Cheng started slowly allowing councilors to resume video connection. The faces of the other councilors now reflected a sense of calm and determination that she hoped they would have displayed at the start of the call. Questions came up but Systems Control did not have an answer to many.

The good doctor noted an incoming message from an old friend: "Ask about the Harmony engine project that is stalled out in the scientific council."

Leaning forward on her workstation, and coughing loudly, Dr. Liu-Cheng interrupted the banal statement that Alesha Rhonn was in the middle of making. The doctor did not wait to fill the stunned silence, "What about the Harmony engine project that's stalled out in the scientific council? Could that be useful?"

The red dot of Systems Control pulsed for several moments as it collected information from various other sectors. "If the projected next generation faster-than-light-speeds could be realized it would allow humanity to move back and forth from studying an anomaly in normal faster-than-light timelines instead of millenniums."

The councilors on the call started debating the risks involved with developing a new type of FTL engine, each wary given the bloodshed that had been required to build the first one. The long shadow of the blue fire hanging over the video call three thousand years later.

Multiple councilors stopped paying attention to the call at various times. Each getting their own helpful messages from an old friend. Unknowingly, they were all communicating with the same person who was currently tapping into the quantum link call on the other end of the sector.

Dr. Liu-Cheng listened as the councilors started talking in circles about risks and costs. She could feel the room pulling away from Systems Control's recommendations. A message popped up from her old friend: "They're scared but ready. Just push them. They will jump with you."

Bracing herself for failure, the doctor muted the councilors again, "Okay. I've heard enough. This project isn't something we can debate. We just have to do this.

Otherwise we're condemning our great-great-great grandkids to a life of running away from darkening skies."

She let go of the mute button expecting the worst...

There was a long pause, and then Waveva Ceta chimed in with a confirmation of Dr. Liu-Cheng's embrace of the plan. Followed quickly by the other councilors rushing to join in on agreeing. The call continued on for another few minutes and then all were dismissed to begin preparations for how their sectors would contribute to the project.

At the other end of the call the starship disengaged from the forgotten communications buoy and set a course for the Narresa system. The pulse from the FTL engine caused the buoy to rattle. For a moment across the stars, Systems Control thought it felt a disruption in the network but it was only a blip on an endless reporting log.

The suns outside her window were setting by the time Dr. Lin-Cheng finished her last message of the day.

NOTE TO SYSTEMS CONTROL>
FROM Dr. JULLY LIU-CHENG>
Systems Control,

You have our formal approval to carry out your proposal, we have given the project a name of "STARLIGHT RESEARCH" to avoid doomsday scenarios from the public at large should details leak. You have full discretion over all aspects of the project.

An old friend of mine, Dr. Rebecca Chambers, has expressed interest in working on the new FTL engine project. When you begin to assemble the team please contact her first. As a starship designer, I believe she would be invaluable on the Harmony engine team.

Sincerely,

Dr. Jully Liu-Cheng

Council of Aligned Worlds

<END NOTE TO SYSTEMS CONTROL

SYSTEMS CONTROL INTERNAL NOTE>
CITIZEN FILE 0.51448407>
Dr. Rebecca Chambers
Birth Planet: Unknown
Age: Unknown
Race: Unknown
Occupation: Undefined. History includes scientific research, starship design, first contact engagements, and espionage.

Citizen Status: Aligned Worlds Citizen in good standing, no debts noted, no warrants issued, and no investigations open.

Criminal Record: Multiple instances where restricted data was accessed, no time served. Warnings issued.

Internal Notes>
Log004) Dr. Chambers designation as a zero dot citizen should concern the council. They allowed those born before my activation to avoid certain registration requirements. A complete profile of her does not exist, and as such her full motivations and capabilities are unknown. Over the years she has been mostly helpful or benign in her activities.

....

Log121-Current) Multiple councilors recommended Dr. Chambers for leadership of Project Starlight almost immediately after the secure quantum link call concluded. Nature and timing of their comments appears suspicious. It will appease the council to appoint Dr. Chambers as the project lead and as lead she will be subject to closer scrutiny by security sub-systems than previously logged.

Status of AI-HOLMES inquiry into possible data-hacking avenues for Dr. Rebecca Chambers: ONGOING. Last known sighting of her ship is twelve years ago in the Terminus Systems.

<END SECURITY CHECK

PEOPLE WE LEFT BEHIND ON EARTH

On a random Wednesday morning on an Earth nearly two thousand years removed from the blue fire apocalypse, with a population dwindling thanks to low birth rates and the never ending call for off world colonists, Kieran had expected no challenge getting to the office on time. Instead, the streets around Harvard University were buzzing with people and vehicles.

Normally arriving on time didn't matter to his faculty advisor Dr. Cornelius, but the professor's multiple messages made this morning seem exceptionally important. The perpetual student picked up his pace from a fast walk to a medium jog as he jaywalked across the street in front of the Milligan building.

HONK

The enormous recycle mover's horn blared down on Kieran as he was mid-stride. The road shook loose the last vestiges of sleep from his body. The vehicle skittered to an emergency stop just in front of him. A weak "oopsy doopsy" smile ran across Kieran's lips as he waved to the technician riding in the automated vehicle. Traffic waited as the rough shaved olive skinned man, who should have known better, meekly jaunted off the street.

"I'm 157 years old... far too old to go bouncing in front of traffic like a child," he muttered to himself as he resumed jogging. "Ha, compared to the old ones and zero dotters who wander the school grounds, I am a child." Kieran opened up the chat screen and composed a quick message for Dr. Cornelius as he ran on to the main plaza.

Kieran's near death under the wheels of the recycling mover would be the most exciting thing that happened to the waste technician all month. With genetic modification, Kieran looked like he was still in his 30s even as he approached his 16th decade on Earth. Old he was. Truly immortal he was not.

The human body, genetic modification or nanite machine repairs aside, was still a fragile organic shell susceptible to accident, murder, or just plain bad luck. However, few people on Earth died outside of accidents.

The transport operator had never known anyone who'd died unplanned. Her family going back to her great-great-great-great-grandparents was still alive. Today was the closest that she would come to death before her own.

Looking past his message Kieran squinted his eyes at a slender figure sitting at a bench who was staring at him as he ran off the street. Glaring back he determined it was a man, but not just any man. The dark eyes that stared back at Kieran were not organic. While the body may not age much thanks to genetic tampering, accidents and time eventually necessitate the replacing of body parts with artifical replacements.

After a couple hundred years, you became what was colloquially called, 'an old one.' Of these there were few still left on Earth. Most had left on starships bound for the frontier, either to settle on new colony worlds, where their age and wisdom made them excellent leaders, or to dive into research of exotic alien worlds. Why stay on Earth, where all was known and nothing ever happened?

Sometimes the last line had to be crossed when your organic brain gave out. At that point either you accepted death or became a truly artificial being. Heavily regulated, and rarely seen outside their teal tinted use in the military or upper echelons of government, these completely artificial humans were the closest humanity had gotten to true immortality.

This slender man's eyes were a give away, but up close it was the nano-organic skin that usually told Kieran he was dealing with an old one. Many years at the university had given Kieran plenty of opportunities to experience the variety of real and unreal human skins. *Why bother rehousing yourself in a shell that looks so boring*, he thought as he glared back at the old one.

A message came in for Kieran and blocked his view of the man and interrupted his meandering thoughts of what it meant to be real. Looking up, Kieran focused his eyes on the path in front of him as he picked up speed again. Just glancing at the sender told Kieran everything he needed to know: Dr. Cornelius was still waiting. He deleted both messages as his jog became a run.

Looking out his window on the fifth floor of the Milligan Psychology Building, an old one smiled. Dr. Cornelius saw Kieran nearly run head first into a freshman who was reading on her touch pad. Clearly Kieran was trying to write a message while running. His hand clicked and Dr. Cornelius pulled away from the window frame. He rubbed his hands together trying to get the synthetic arm to behave.

Since his fall down the stairs last week his right hand had been clicking open at random intervals. It had taken four cups of spilled coffee before Dr. Cornelius had taken to holding his coffee in his left hand. The technician was supposed to come by his office yesterday, but after he was contacted by Systems Control, the professor rescheduled the medical visit for this afternoon.

In his whole life, Systems Control had never directly contacted Dr. Cornelius any task request. The research proposal was unlike anything he'd ever been presented with before. It was a long night, but after several glasses of wine, holo calls with friends, and a conference with Systems Control and the local councilors, they had convinced Dr. Cornelius that he had to be a part of Project Starlight.

The thudding sound of feet storming down the hallway caused Dr. Cornelius to look up just in time to see the door swing open as Kieran came panting nearly breathless into the room. "Sorry... Dr. Cornelius... I kept running... into delays."

The old one smiled, "Yes, I saw that."

Kieran looked around at the office, normally kept clean and neat, and saw that nearly every bookshelf had been emptied, their contents spread around the room by some system of reorganization that Kieran could not understand. He wanted to calculate the possibilities but was interrupted,

15

"Anyway, you're here now. Please have a seat Mr. Ausure," Dr. Cornelius said, holding Kieran's arm and guiding him to the only space devoid of books.

"Of course... Sir," Kieran teased back at him. Matching the odd sounding formality with a tone that only a friend and long term graduate teaching assistant could get away with.

Sitting down on the only patch not covered in books or papers, Kieran looked at the doctor truly for the first time since entering. His face marked by too many sun blasted trips to the beach, his arms covered in ancient tribal tattoos native to his homeland, and his body wrapped in an uncharacteristically wrinkled shirt. Normally well kept and groomed, and usually wearing of shoes, this was not the doctor as Kieran knew him.

Dr. Cornelius looked at his long serving teaching assistant with a sense of longing for things not to change. In the past few decades his student had gone from being that dark skinned sheepish mute in the back of his class with a short mop of black hair to the voice of the teacher whenever Dr. Cornelius needed him to be. Always there with a smile and his stubbled chin.

The professor felt Kieran's green tinted artificial eyes pressing on him, and so he pursed his lips not really wanting to say what he had to say, "Kieran, I've been offered a seat on a project that... well I can't tell you anything about it. I do not believe that I will be returning from this trip for a long time, and so I've asked the university to look for a replacement for me."

Even though he'd been expecting bad news, to hear that his friend, his guidepost, his... Kieran found himself choking up trying to say something, but only a rough cough escaped his lips.

"Now, obviously the school year starts in a week. I thought of you first to replace me, but I'm afraid the university wants someone with interstellar experience. However, until they find someone I've asked that you fill in for me," the doctor waved to his office as if the disarray was some sort of gift.

"Dr. Cornelius I don't know..." Kieran already had a raft of questions and reasons for the old one to stay at Harvard. At least a little longer, but the professor cut him off.

"Nonsense. You know you're ready. For over twenty years you've been my student, my friend and my...," Dr. Cornelius suddenly stopped. For a moment Kieran thought he hadn't wanted to say the word out loud, but as the doctor's eyes widened and his hand went to his neck, Kieran knew something was wrong.

He leapt from the couch in time to catch his friend for the last time. Dr. Cornelius looked up at Kieran, a wild kind of panic in his eyes, mouthing words with no sound, but as quickly as it came the panic left him and a thin smile came to his lips... and then he was still. In all his time Kieran had never actually seen a dead person up close before.

The room was still for a moment, but then the sounds of sirens filled the world around him. Kieran called into the emergency line and was patched into the EMTs that were already racing up the stairs. He told them that the doctor wasn't breathing, but they already knew his medical status thanks to the nanites in his body.

A voice came on in Kieran's head and for a moment he was concerned but the panic left him when he recognized it as Systems Control, "I'm afraid Dr. Robert Cornelius' electronic heart has seized. There's nothing you can do. I've run multiple simulations, there's no way to get him to a hospital in time."

Kieran looked up, he always looked up and to the right when Systems Control spoke to him, even though the tiny round red dot in the corner of his vision was static and could never be looked at directly. "Why?"

The dot blinked and Kieran could tell that at some far away bank of computers Systems Control was calculating an answer for him, while at the same time doing tasks for every connected human being in the galaxy. It was a feat that at this moment made him feel neglected in a way he hadn't felt since his parents waved goodbye to him.

"Unknown. A technician was scheduled to visit Dr. Robert Cornelius this afternoon to look at his arm. It is possible that a malfunction in the organic-nano layer of his shoulder affected the valves of his heart. I am currently rerouting the technician to the local morgue. Once there, they will assist the coroner in assessing an accurate a cause of death."

The answer was perfect in its logic and symmetry. Truthful, without any absolutes, and with a clear plan for the future. Kieran imagined that somewhere the programmers who had created Systems Control were high-fiving each other over the pitch perfect response. Kieran closed his eyes and pulled Dr. Cornelius close to him.

The EMTs report would indicate that when they arrived they found a young man weeping over the body of an old one. Attempts were made to restart Mr. Cornelius' heart, but were unsuccessful. Time of death was called when they arrived at the hospital. For them it would be the only call involving an unplanned death that month.

Kieran wandered away from the chaotic scene that Dr. Cornelius' death had created in the Psychology department and into the city. To be in a state of shock would have been an improvement. His whole world had crashed out in front of him. His grief filled him like a fire and so he wandered into the first open bar he found. Drinking to drown the flames and numb his broken heart.

The world was darkness and the beeping. Was this a dream? He'd had several so far this day. In one of them his friend and long time...

BEEP

BEEP

BEEP

Kieran reached out with his hand and felt it bump hard into a metal and glass object. His coffee table. He recognized the sound of the objects on the table chattering as the table rattled. If he opened his eyes he was worried about throwing up.

BEEP

BEEP

BEEP

The polite beeps continued to increase in pace. Swallowing deeply, so that vomit wouldn't eject when he opened his mouth, Kieran shouted out weakly, "Go away!"

BEEP

BEEEEEEEEEEEEEEEEEP

Then silence. Beautiful wondrous glorious plentiful silence. Kieran's mind wandered back to the wonderful dream filled with bottomless pitchers and beautiful people.

CRASH

"KIERAN AUSURE! WAKE THE FUCK UP!," a voice screamed at him.

Kieran was sure it was the loudest sound in history. Ignoring the screams and instead curling up into a ball as the person above him continued cursing his name, Kieran had barely begun to contemplate opening his eyes when a thunderous volume of water fell onto his head.

Kieran sat up sputtering, then hacking, and finally gulping as vomit forced its way up. The bucket used to wake him became his refuge as he projected up most of this morning's breakfast of whiskey.

"What... are you... doing," he coughed as air returned to his lungs. Looking up he saw the voice in his head wasn't a dream. It was a large angry bald man standing over him. Looking around Kieran realized that they were not alone. His small apartment was filled with imposing people wearing Aligned Worlds uniforms. Two of them had Sonk Rifles at the ready, and the rest appeared to be there just to look intimidating... it would have taken just one. The silent stares of their military grade augmented faces was enough to send a chill down his spine.

They shuffled aside as an older woman with purple hair in what appeared to be an officer uniform pushed her way into the small apartment. She looked down at him with all the distain the entire human race was capable of mustering.

"Hey, Essey, we need an update — this doesn't look like the guy." The officer spoke to herself. The intergalactic dialect version of Systems Control was always a fun game of coke vs pop vs soda. On Earth everyone shorted Systems Control to "S-C" with a hard "c" leaving a sharp impression of distrust for the AI that controlled the galaxy.

The casual "Essey" belayed the relaxed nature this woman had with Systems Control, or rather perhaps the comfort she felt as the physical manifestation of Systems Control's near absolute authority in the galaxy.

The ever present red dot of a Systems Control broadcast filled the corner of everyone's vision as it spoke, "No Captain, this is the man you were sent to retrieve. Kieran Ausure you are to accompany these people at once to the battleship Juniper-Zeta. There you will be briefed before departure for the Narresa shipyards."

"Briefed on what?"

"Your role on Project Starlight. You will be replacing Dr. Robert Cornelius. You have been conscripted for public service under authority of Systems Control charter 4.932 sub paragraph C. As of this moment you no longer have rights as a citizen. You may collect whatever can fit into a standard luggage container before you are escorted from the premises. The military will box up and secure all your other belongings for long term storage."

At first it seemed like a cruel joke on a grieving man, but as Kieran looked around the room no one was laughing. As they lifted him off the ground, the officer looked him over and spoke, "Get him a shower before we leave, I don't want him stinking up the transport."

He wasn't trying to resist, but Kieran went a bit limp as the soldiers half carried him to the bathroom. A violent mix of hangover and panic swirled his stomach. He wanted to scream about his rights and fight, but as the red glow of Systems Control left his vision all he could do was wonder... what had Dr. Cornelius gotten him into?

The rumbling in the stairwell became a loud shrieking scream that bore into Kieran's hangover. Every shuffled step up the stairwell sent his stomach tumbling down another painful ravine. When the rooftop door opened Kieran pushed past the soldier in front of him and dropped to his knees vomiting.

Doubled over, reeling in pain that raked his skull, he kept his eyes closed for a long moment until he was sure there nothing left in him to upchuck. Behind him the soldiers loitered as the personnel carrier hovered over Kieran's apartment building drowning out all their comments about the drunk Earthling they were forced to escort.

Sitting down and looking up, Kieran wished that the romanticized version of space travel popularized in the late 20th century American culture had come to pass. Instead of a quick easy teleportation beam onboard to a waiting spaceship, there was an ugly grey brick screaming overhead as it hovered there waiting for them to board.

A red headed female soldier picked him roughly off the ground, handing him a small towel to wipe his mouth with. Kieran forced a weak smile and nod as he felt the world vibrate around him. Where his wobbliness began and ended was difficult to tell under the ship's heavy thrusters.

A shout went out and the soldiers began lining up. A series of ropes dropped from the craft overhead, and Kieran was tied into a rough fitting harness. "Don't puke on me on your way up, Professor, or I'll make your trip even more uncomfortable," the woman shouted to Kieran as the rope started pulling him upwards.

Dangling from the rope, he was pulled onboard by an even grouchier looking solider. Then he was handed off to what he presumed was a flight crew member, who led him silently to a line of seats. There was a short point, and then he was strapped into a chair.

Moments later the red-headed woman joined him. The grouchy soldier who had man-handled him off the floor of his apartment sat on his other side. Across the way the rest of the team filtered in and strapped themselves in staring back at him. Kieran would much rather be looking out a window, rather than the clean shaven AWN officer he was staring at, but this was not a fancy spaceship. The last crew member strapped in, the lights dimmed considerably. "All hands ready for cast off," someone yelled from beyond his sight.

The grey brick's roar became louder and it lurched into the sky with all the grace of a drunken freshman on their first dance floor. Just steps behind that poor dancing was his stomach crawling to the bathroom he thought to himself. He closed his eyes, and held his hand to his mouth as he felt more bile racing upward.

The rumbling grew louder as the ship, which Kieran had no idea its designation, passed through what he guessed was the upper atmosphere and into space. The rumbling grew soft and then gave way to a silence that was so deep that Kieran could hear his heart beating through his jacket. The thumps were erratic and pounding as if his heart was trying to claw its way out of his chest. Several hard gulps later the sensation passed him just in time for the rocking to stop.

Kieran shifted in his seat for the hundredth time since the craft lurched upward into the late sky. It was whisper quiet. They must be in outer space he guessed. He stared at the purple haired officer seated across from him. The woman was in such a deep sleep that you'd never know the ship just roughly blasted off into the sky just moments ago.

An incoming broadcast blocked his view as the pilot appeared, the ship's flight plan displayed behind him, "Please hold steady as we'll be making an emergency class 10 jump after we round Earth's moon. After we exit the jump, I'll bring us in line for the Saturn-Hyron relay jump, where today we'll be meeting back up with the Juniper-Zeta and the science convoy at the rendezvous point. Estimated flight time today is 1.2 galactic standard hours."

Kieran's mind was awash with questions, and he turned to the woman who'd overseen his hurried packing and had kept one hand on Kieran's shoulder the whole way out of his apartment. But Kieran had barely formed words when the young woman spoke, ".73 galactic standard hours per 1 Earth hour is the conversion."

Never having traveled through space, and having studied little of faster-than-light travel, Kieran wasn't sure if this was good or bad. "Um, actually I was wondering what the pilot meant by class 10 jump. I thought an FTL jump was an FTL jump?"

The soldier's eyebrows raised as if she was dumbfounded anyone could not know all about FTL jumps, "Small ships like our Zeta-Wagon are not capable of carrying the mega powerful FTL engines and the navigation computers that are required to run them. So we're not as fast or accurate as a galactic cruiser like the Juniper-Zeta but we'll get there."

Kieran noticed several AWN soldiers across from him chuckling under their breath, he assumed at his lack of knowledge of what to them was basic FTL concepts.

"I would have figured you'd know this kind of stuff, being a professor," the grouchy faced soldier next to him said.

"I'm a graduate student. I haven't finished my PhD yet. And, I'm a student of psychology with a minor in 21st century history. So I know about the history of the first FTL engine, and the first test fire that consumed the..."

"But not everything that's happened since? Haha," the redhead chuckled to herself shaking her head at him.

"Also, this is my first time leaving Earth," Kieran added meekly in the face of all the laughter.

The female soldier's face lit up with a joyful expression, "Oh, so we're breaking you in today? Did you hear that gents? He's never been in space before!"

A ruckus cheer of "HOO-RAH TODAY WE FLY, TOMORROW WE DIE," went up from all the soldiers. Each slapping their hands against the overhead bulkhead.

"That's enough," yelled the purple haired officer. She looked around as the soldiers quieted down and then rested her head back against the seat before closing her eyes again.

The solider next to Kieran bumped him on the shoulder with her fist, "Welcome to space, rookie. My name is Heather." She smiled at him as she said her name. He returned her warm smile, the first warm thing he'd seen awakening. "Nice to meet you, Heather."

The lights went red and a moment later Kieran felt the ship shudder and moan. He guessed they were now at lightspeed. If not for the occasional shudder that rattled everything in the overhead bins, you wouldn't have known the ship was even in motion.

Kieran closed his eyes and waited for all of this to reveal itself as a nightmare. Multiple conversations, occasional rumbles, and the pulsing pain in his head kept Kieran from finding sleep. His lips curled as a rough burp escaped them. His stomach still unhappy about all that whiskey he'd consumed.

Seeking refuge Kieran opened up an info display and reviewed the flight path. His view filled with glowing stars and galaxy clusters. It was peaceful. A tap on his shoulder awoke Kieran from his daydream. Heather watched as the yellow glow of nanite visualizers faded from his eyes.

"Here, drink this," whispered Heather as she handed him a metallic pouch, "It tastes like mushrooms but it's not mushrooms. Standard vitamin nutrient pouch, but it also works well as a hangover fix."

Kieran hesitated a moment, and then tilted the pouch bag and drank deeply. Mushrooms would be a polite way of describing the taste. "Blagh, if you're going to kill me just do it now because I think I'd rather die than drink this," he muttered holding the pouch as far away from his lips as his strapped in arms would let him.

"You get used to it. Nutrients, basic anti-inflammatories, a few exotic catch all antibiotics and CZ3 particulates for your nanites," Heather chuckled as she read off the packaging notes. Sitting back down she smiled as he finished drinking the pouch.

He stashed the emptied pouch under his seat. His headache and stomach not currently causing him great pain, he took a moment to note the appearances of the crew members. All together they looked far less rough than he would have expected soldiers of the Aligned Worlds given their reputation for smashing resistance to Systems Control.

It was peaceful for a period until the familiar red glow of Systems Control appeared. It lit up his nanite displays with a text communication meant for him only.

MESSAGE: Kieran Ausure, you undoubtably have questions about Project Starlight. Once you reach the Juniper-Zeta and there is a secure quantum connection, files related to the project will be transferred to your local memory. Until then, follow any directions given to you by these officers.

Kieran furrowed his brow at the message and set to typing a response so that this conversation could remain private.

RESPONSE: The hell I will. You've arrested me by all but name. Now you won't even tell me what this is about or where I'm going?

MESSAGE: Please remain clam. Aboard the Juniper-Zeta you will be met by Dr. Chambers and as they are in charge of all science personnel for this project it will be up to them to decide what information you may have before the mission perimeters are shared. Thank you for your attention. Returning display control to user.

Kieran's eyes shot opened and he leaned forward mouth half open to shout at a red dot... when he remembered he was still onboard a military transport surrounded by officers and soldiers capable of breaking him with just a pinkie finger.

He sat there fuming for what felt like hours, but his nanite-display said it had only been fifteen minutes before Heather put her hand on his shoulder. Her eyes were awash in the yellow nanite glow as some sort of message was flashing. Looking around Kieran realized everyone was getting the same message.

"Hold on," Heather screamed just as the Zeta-Wagon came to a halt so juddering that it felt like the starship might tear itself apart. Anything and everything not tied down went flying through the cabin.

A trinket flew out of someone's hands across from Kieran and smashed into his shoulder with enough force to cause him to yell out in pain. He wanted to scream at the soldier for being so careless, but the Zeta-Wagon banked hard to the right and a pulsating red light went on overhead.

"Everyone hold!," the pilot shouted out over the nanite intercom system. The sound of his voice echoed through Kieran's skull as the ship shuddered back and forth so roughly that it would have made him panic if he hadn't known it was coming.

Suddenly Kieran felt a rumbled impact from the other side of the cabin, "What the hell is going on!?"

Heather still holding onto her shoulder straps didn't open her eyes, but answered him anyway, "I think we're under attack!"

The Zeta-Wagon's banking side-to-side slowed down, and the ship took a hard lean to the right before the rumbling slowed down.

A holo projector came online and a grim faced heavy set old man with a massive scar on the left side of his face appeared in the middle of the cabin, "All ships in convoy, this is Captain Carter. The freespacer pirate ships have dispersed for the moment. We are regrouping. All hands should find their starships and prepare for FTL jumps to their final destinations."

The purple haired officer across from Heather and Kieran was already in the middle of a conversation when the holo projector turned off. Her face squished and contorted as the officer had a quiet and entirely one sided argument.

"WHAT DO YOU MEAN THROW HIM OUT OF THE AIRLOCK?!," the officer suddenly screamed.

Kieran all at once knew it was him that she was talking about. He had barely any time to panic when he felt Heather stand. She turned and began undoing Kieran's straps, "Time for you to fly."

The panic turned into a full throated roar in Kieran's mouth, and words did not form... just a sound. Heather and another solider pulled him up onto his feet and led him down the cabin galley into the airlock at the rear of the Zeta-Wagon.

"You're not really going to throw me out of the airlock are you?!," Kieran panicked finally finding his voice again.

Heather chuckled, "Yes... but not without a suit." She pointed at a rack of weathered orange space suits and while every bone in Kieran said to fight... he took down the suit.

The grouchy solider next to Heather held his hand to his left ear, "This is Zeta-Wagon are you ready Mother Goose?" Kieran could not hear the answer, but he really hoped it was 'Yes.'

Kieran's face spoke volumes as Heather helped him put the helmet on.

Heather smiled at him, "We don't have time to go through a proper docking procedure, not with pirates still in the sector. So we're going to hot toss you over to the Mother Goose. I've done this before. Trust that the ship's gravity will pull you into the airlock and you'll be fine."

The soldiers stepped out of the airlock and closed the door. Looking through the window at them, Kieran watched as the overhead light changed from red to blue and then finally to gold, where it blinked three times. "Don't worry if you piss yourself when the gravity goes offline, it always hits your bladder hard the first couple of times," Heather radioed to him.

The discomforting thought was given only a moment to rattle around before Kieran felt himself begin to float freely in the airlock.

"Hold for gravity slingshot!," the pilot shouted over the cabin intercom.

Waving goodbye, Heather radioed, "I guess this is where we part ways, Mr. Ausure."

"Goodbye, Heather," there was a pause and if Kieran had been sober, not currently in a spacesuit, and covered in flecks of his own vomit this next line probably would have worked for him, "Hey, do you have a intersystems-contact number?"

Heather leaned back and snickered at him, "Goodbye, newbie." She pressed a button and Kieran felt himself being sucked out of the airlock as the doors opened. He tumbled, wildly into the pitch black of space, the Zeta-Wagon spinning in and out of view as they tossed him away.

WILD GOOSE CHASERS

Kieran's first tumble into outer space was causing his stomach to twirl, but it was only a moment until he felt his spins start to slow down. Twisting his torso he finally saw the ship that Heather had tossed him towards. It was like nothing he had ever seen before on Earth.

Where the Zeta-Wagon was a grey brick, the Mother Goose looked like a graceful bird preparing for flight. As if space had wind to soar on. Its crystalline white hull was a sea of moving hexagonal tiles that flickered in the sunlight making the starship look alive. Kieran almost imagined it was ruffling feathers after coming out of water.

There was no airlock door but the starship spun and a loading ramp lowered from the center of the hull. Kieran's slow spin brought him closer and closer to the ramp and he reached out with his hands as it got within in reach. The Mother Goose and Kieran made a pronounced *CLUNK* as they touched each other.

Standing wearily on the ramp as it began to close, Kieran watched as an inner door appeared above him. Through the glass he could see an old one on the other side. Wearing a faded blue jumpsuit with a high collar, the old one's body was covered in an unnervingly semi-transparent green synthetic skin. Kieran could make out teeth behind the lips. There wasn't a hair on the green tinted head, except for a ridiculously bushy white mustache that drooped over the old one's upper lip.

As the ramp clicked close and the airlock door *wooshed* open, Kieran fell face forward onto the floor. Gingerly he stood, adjusting to the Mother Goose's gravity, which unknown to him was 1.6 Earth gravity because the owner liked to have a pep in her step wherever she landed.

Taking off the suit's helmet, Kieran took a deep breath trying to hold in the vomit that had been spinning in his stomach since he'd left the Zeta-Wagon... but it was no good.

BLAAAUGGG

Every bit of the mushroom pouch came up and out of Kieran onto the floor of the Mother Goose. He took a deep breath... it was over...

BLAAAUUUUUUUGGG

Now it was what was left of his mournful whiskey breakfast. Kieran took another deep breath... and held it.

Roughly wiping his mouth with the glove of the suit, he turned to the old one and nodded weakly.

The green skinned old one put out his hand, "Welcome aboard, my name's Henry."

A weak smile crossed Kieran's face, "Kieran Ausure."

Henry threw on a big smile, "Good. It's bad luck to cast off into space without knowing who's got your back."

There was a sound from across the room and Kieran watched as a figure in a large black hood exited the room. Gesturing to the figure Kieran muttered, "I don't know who that is so we're doomed."

Henry laughed and helped Kieran out of the suit. Slowly they made their way to the inside of the Mother Goose. Small cleaner drones rushed past them as they entered into the cargo bay of the starship. There Kieran saw the hooded figure waiting for them. He paused, unsure of what was happening.

An unmistakably human female voice called out to him from under the hood, "I don't bite. Come closer, little one."

Nothing about the sound gave away where this person was from, no hint of ethnic upbringing or galactic home was betrayed by her tongue. It was like the words themselves had been worn down until only the rawest elements remained.

Kieran's feet were firmly planted.

An alarm went off and a synthesized female voice announced overhead, "Unidentified sub-light jump signature coming from the far side of the system. Tracking movement towards the Mother Goose and the convoy."

The figure in black shook its head as it stepped out of the robe. "My name is Rebecca Chambers, welcome aboard the Mother Goose. No time for a tour today."

As she stepped out into the light Kieran had to check his jaw. She was indeed a human woman, fitted in a tight jumpsuit that showcased curves wrapping around her frame in a way that quickened Kieran's pulse.

Rebecca paused as Kieran took her into view, even with her face obscured by a pair of large dark goggles. Henry could tell she was rolling her eyes hard at the child.

Rebecca's lips squeezed together for a moment as she debated telling Kieran to check himself, but instead she shook her head causing her multicolored rainbow patterned hair to dance and swirl in the heavy gravity.

She disappeared around the corner again, and Henry had to pull the shaken Kieran to get him moving. They traveled through the ship, which was much smaller on the inside than Kieran would have anticipated given the size on the outside.

Finally after a few turns, past what appeared to be a kitchen, common area, and a handful of small cabins, they arrived at the cockpit. A large padded chair faced forward to a large 270 degree video screen, two smaller chairs on the left and right faced the door, waiting for crew members.

Kieran looked around wondering where the rest of the crew was as Rebecca spun around in the main chair. "Henry take systems operations, Mr. Ausure take co-pilot seat here," she waved to her left at the right side chair.

Without reconsidering Kieran sat down... "I've never flown a starship before."

"Good, then you won't question my piloting," Rebecca replied as she spun back around. "Sam, are we clear for lift off?"

Kieran looked up half expecting to see someone standing there, but instead a disembodied voice came on over the cockpit, "Yes, Captain Carter has requested you make a jump out of the system as soon as the navigation computers have calculated a safe vector."

Even though she had called it Sam, Kieran recognized the voice and red dot glowing above her in the front of the cockpit, looking down at them... Systems Control.

Rebecca started hitting toggles and the screens came alive with information. Kieran's network connection went dead, the data streams needed for ship functions he guessed. He blinked hard four times to dismiss the feed. Without the connection to wikinet he wouldn't be able to understand anything now displayed in front of him.

"Kaylee, bring up the fusion plant as quick as you can, I want us at maximum static-nyson shielding by the time those ships reach us." Another digital voice, this one chipper and female, came up on the same channel Systems Control had just spoken over, "Yes, ma'am."

Rebecca spun around in her chair, and glided it around to Kieran's side on a track built into the floor. "Here," she exclaimed pointing to a small bar in the bottom right corner of his 270 display. Kieran looked up from the floor, where he'd been admiring the chair track engineering, "This bar will shift as we move about in sub-light speeds. If it gets red, press it."

"And?" Kieran asked waving at the display filled with information and buttons.

Rebecca sighed, "That's all I need you to do."

Kieran looked at her as she leaned over. She'd taken off her goggles. Her green eyes were clearly synthetic... and so was she. Her skin was a very expensive looking synthetic-organic blend that was light, but not pigment free. She stopped pointing at the screen and touched his hand. It felt like worn porcelain. The thin line of a faded scar ran across her face where her eyes now stared back at him.

"Kieran, can you do this?" Rebecca tapped the console loudly. He awoke from his thoughts as the lights in the cabin came on at full strength, causing Rebecca to squint.

"Yes," Kieran said as she turned away from him.

"Henry, can you bring the lights down? Until a week ago I hadn't been in a room above 500 lumens in six years."

A chuckle arose from the console on the other side of the cockpit, "As you wish."

The lights dimmed and Kaylee's voice announced, "Bringing flight systems back online ma'am."

Rebecca spun around in her chair and took the controls. The walls of the cockpit turned into virtual screens showing the space around the Mother Goose. It felt like they were hovering in a clear bubble. Kieran felt the ship shudder as various systems prepared themselves.

Kaylee's voice came on in Kieran's head, "Please activate your chair gravity." He looked down at the armrest, a configuration of buttons he'd never seen before in his life looked back at him. "Kaylee I don't know which button gravity is," he said out loud.

"THE GOLD ONE," both Rebecca and Henry shouted at him over their shoulders.

The chipper voice of Kaylee came on back in his head, "Sorry, I did not realize you were unfamiliar with microgravity chairs. If you have any other questions about ship functions, please feel free to ask me at any time."

The ship lurched forward and the nose of the cockpit felt like it dropped several feet downward. Kieran almost fell out of his seat as the ship accelerated into the black of space. He grabbed at the armrest hammering at the buttons until he clicked the gold one. He felt the plush back of the chair pulling back at him until it sucked him flat against the padding.

Rebecca called over the roar of the engines, "Henry, cut the gravity generators. We'll need the power for the cannons."

There was a sputtering sound before Henry spoke, "What?"

Rebecca sighed, "The cannons need more power."

Henry spun around with an angry look on his semi-transparent face, "You can't be serious. We don't even know what's coming out of that sub-light jump. It could be a couple lost tourists or a heavily armed armada of freespacers."

The rainbow hair on Rebecca's head danced as she nodded her head, "The Juniper-Zeta dropped her shields and guard for a non-friendly pickup location just for me. I won't leave Carter until I know he's..."

Rebecca's words were cut short by Kaylee, "Ma'am, incoming feed from the Juniper-Zeta." A heavy set old man appeared over Rebecca's display floating in a field of fuzzy blue dust. It was a holographic feed. Kieran had a toy that did something similar when he was a child. He couldn't believe a ship this expensive would have something so old.

Captain Carter looked sad as he started talking, "Becca, what are you doing? Start calculating a safe jump vector out of this system. Clearly this top secret mission of yours has been leaked to the freespacers. They wouldn't risk this kind of direct engagement with a galactic cruiser unless they thought it was something exceedingly valuable."

Rebecca chuckled, "Come on kid, do you really think I'd leave you guys all alone? Without an escort? What would your mother think of me?"

The heavy face of Captain Carter contorted into a deep smile, his chortle turning into a cough, "Becca, We'll be fine, it's probably just a pack of little pirates who thought you looked tasty. They'll pack up and run when they see us turn to..." his words dropped off and a look of horror ran across the hologram.

Kieran swung his attention back around to his view-screen as the handful of dots on his display expanded into dozens of little dots in multiple tight circles. They were at the far edge of the screen, racing towards a blinking green triangle. He guessed that was them.

Captain Carter grimaced, voices floated in around him and someone thrust a pad into his hands, he barely looked at it, "Pirate scum. They would have made us as a galactic cruiser by now. The fact they haven't turned tail and run means they're scouting for a well armed hunting party." He turned, seemingly forgetting he was still on the holographic feed, "Lessie, I want a fall back point behind Morundus' moon, with a vector jump out of this system putting us as close as possible to an Aligned Worlds station. Susan, send out another call for backup..."

Rebecca turned to Henry, "Bring the weapons online now."

Kieran gulped loud enough for Carter to look in his general direction, something about how Kieran looked at that moment made the old man smile, "Don't worry kid, we'll get you to your destination on time. Rebecca, start calculating an exit along our same fall back point, but make your system exit jump in the exact opposite direction. With any luck they'll think we look tastier."

Rebecca leaned back in the chair, "Of course, Captain Carter. I'll try and draw some of the fighters off, but we're not going to last long against anything bigger. Good luck kiddo."

With that Captain Carter nodded and reached down to kill the feed. The cockpit grew dim again. Henry tapped on his screens and a gold light blinked three times in the cabin. Kieran felt his hair start to float away from him.

Rebecca looked up, "Kaylee, set the hull to black. And are the combat thrusters charged?"

Kaylee replied quickly, "Yes, ma'am."

Together they sat there in silence as the group of dots grew closer. A million questions screamed at Kieran, but the way Rebecca had sounded signing off with Captain Carter told him that this wasn't the time to talk.

Kaylee piped up, "One minute until contact with unknown pirate scum." Henry lost it, he started bellowing in laughter. Kieran got caught up in it and started laughing too and he thought for a moment he heard a snicker out of even Rebecca.

Suddenly the space in front of them sparked brightly with blue flashes of light as at least a dozen spaceships came out of their sub-light jump. Some immediately stared firing, all their shots aimed at the Juniper-Zeta. How they missed a white spaceship the size of a barn stupefied Kieran for a moment.

Rebecca leaned forward in her chair, "Ready, Henry?"

"I'll bring the bacon if you bring the shake'n," Henry replied.

She pushed forward on the control sticks, and Kieran felt the ship cockpit dip forward, like when he'd first sat down but a hundred times stronger. For a moment he thought the engines had failed, and they were careening to their deaths, but when he looked up at the main viewport feed he could see the ship was spinning through the pack of fighters.

Kaylee shouted at them, "Tracking two bogeys at six o'clock starboard."

Rebecca shouted back, "I see them!"

The ship came to a juddering halt in the dead of space before spinning in place. Even with the chair gravity on and the ship gravity off Kieran could feel the maneuver in his bones. It hurt. He shut his eyes as the spin replayed on the walls in front of him. The lag between the visual feed and the physical interaction was enough to give him a sinking feeling in the deepest pits of his stomach. They called it seasickness.

Kieran opened his eyes as an alarm started sounding, "There isn't an ocean for light years in any direction and I'm going to throw up."

"Ma'am, we're on a direct collision course. The static-nyson shielding won't hold in the event of a head on collision," Kaylee announced calmly.

"Kaylee... shut up," Rebecca answered back equally calm.

Kieran watched in soul shaking horror as Rebecca pushed the ship faster towards a pirate dogship. Henry didn't fire.

49

The overwhelming number of dials on Kieran's screen displayed more information than he could comprehend, but the fact that the color had gone from a light blue to a dark red was all he needed to know about the fate of the ship should they continue on this course.

"Now Henry!"

BRRNNN

BRRNNN

BRRNNN

Henry opened up with every ounce of energy weapon fire the Mother Goose had and the pirate ship exploded into pieces. They maneuvered through the debris field at speeds that seemed impossible to Kieran. He could only guess either Rebecca was really that good of a pilot or Kaylee's talents included navigational assistance.

The two blips on the monitor following the Mother Goose did not have skills. They disappeared from view as Rebecca pulled out of the field. In front of them the Juniper-Zeta's powerful cannons ripped four small ships into pieces in one blow. Kieran couldn't figure out why they'd rushed the much, much bigger ship.

"They're trying to kamikaze them," Henry said with a sad tone that said everything Kieran needed to know about the soon to be fate of the big ship.

Rebecca answered Henry gruffly, "Not today."

Now Kieran understood what Captain Carter had meant about a hunting party. If the attack pack could cripple the Juniper-Zeta they'd be unable to make an emergency jump away from the battle if things started going badly for them.

"I'm tracking a second set of incoming sub-light signatures. Designating them hunting party," Kaylee announced.

Kieran felt the Mother Goose accelerate and turned to look at Henry. A pair of mournful looking silver eyes stared back at him with a look that even through semi-transparent green skin spoke volumes in the buzzing cockpit.

Rebecca shouted out, "Henry four small bogeys coming up. Soften them up for the Juniper-Zeta with the EMP pulse."

As they passed through the mist of the smaller ships, Henry pulsed them, but it wasn't enough to slow them down. The Juniper-Zeta cut down three of them... the fourth slammed into the underside of the starship. Fire, smoke, and debris poured out of the impact site like blood from a wound.

The remaining pirate fighters pulled out of the Juniper-Zeta's range and made a beeline for the hunting party. Kieran watched as the small blips vanished from his heads up display. He turned to look at Rebecca as the ship came to a halt. Between the drone of the engines, never ending alarms, and the lurching sounds in his gut... he thought he heard faint crying sounds coming from Rebecca's direction.

Henry started to say something, but Kaylee cut him off, "Ma'am, Captain Carter is coming over the system channel... He's giving orders for all non-Aligned Worlds starships to evacuate the system."

Rebecca huffed, "Get him on the line."

"Attempting, ma'am," Kaylee responded her voice fading off.

An unknown voice boomed through the cockpit, "All non-Aligned Worlds starships must leave the Kohlar System now. This area has been declared a major combat operations area. Your ship will be fired upon if it is found in this system."

"Kaylee...," Rebecca started to shout.

Suddenly the holographic light came up again. Captain Carter appeared in front of Rebecca looking a little worse than before. Lights and smoke flickered in the feed. The old man's heavy face leaned down into the holo camera, "Rebecca, it's time to go. You've made a good little fight, but they've made it clear they mean to take us down."

Rebecca sniffled before responding, "I'm not going to leave you, Jack. What would your mother think of me?"

Captain Carter stood back up straight, "My mother has been dead and gone a long time. She would want us to see our obligations to their end. My job was to get you to the station to launch Leviathan, and your job is to go on your top secret mission. I'm sorry that we won't be able to have that send off drink, but I'll catch you on the return trip."

Rebecca laughed, but it was a hollow fake sounding laugh people do when they know that someone is lying.

Turning to wave off someone in the room with him Captain Carter continued, "Besides, our fighter squadrons are now launching. When these vultures get here they may find us with more bite than they anticipate, and Fisher station has probably already dispatched help. Heck, if you don't get out of here now I may beat you to the Leviathan, and how will that look in my report?"

The soft sniffles of Rebecca became a crying sound that filled the cockpit awkwardly.

Captain Carter leaned down, his holographic image now hovering just in front Rebecca's screen, "Its been a pleasure to have known you Rebecca Chambers."

"Likewise Jack Carter," Rebecca hoarsely whispered up at the ghostly figure. Alarms sounded around Captain Carter and he stood up as the video feed went dead.

Henry was the first to speak, "Kaylee do we have an exit vector plotted?"

The soft light in the room pulsed for a moment and then Kaylee answered,"Yes."

"Then get us the hell out of here," Henry growled.

"Kaylee, bring the ship gravity back online," Rebecca croaked out, fighting back tears. The gold light blinked three times and left them.

Rebecca turned her chair around and stood up, holding her arm to her face as she stumbled out of the cockpit. Kieran spun around in his chair attempting to get up, but the gravity buckles still held him. The screens went blank as Kaylee took control of the ship.

"All hands of the Mother Goose, prepare for FTL jump," Kaylee announced as Kieran and Henry leaned back in their chairs.

The lighting went blue and then Kieran felt the ship shudder hard to the left. The visual screen walls went black.

They were at lightspeed.

"Henry... what...," the words wouldn't come to him and they sat there in the the dim cockpit for a moment as Kieran attempted to find his thoughts, "how long did Rebecca know Jack Carter?"

Henry spun around his chair, "Know? She was there when his mother was born."

"Should we?" Kieran waved in the direction Rebecca had gone.

"No," Henry responded flatly turning back around to the screens.

Kieran turned around in his chair. Facing the blank screens, he closed his eyes, "System Control do you have the documents on Project Starlight for me?"

"Yes. Loading now," the red dot in the corner of his vision pulsed.

"Good. I want to know why Captain Carter sacrificed a galactic cruiser for us," Kieran replied hoping it wasn't a sacrifice in vain.

What do you do after you read about the end of existence as you know it? Not death, but the end of all things. The purposefully perfunctory vocabulary of Systems Control spelled out the end of all that humanity had ever known as if it was a 3rd grade math problem that the students just didn't yet know how to solve.

In the years since Systems Control had first confirmed the darkness in the Arroyo Section of the Milky Way galaxy it had grown in fits and starts. Further observation showed it was literally eating the energy in the sectors surrounding it, so that even if you were standing beyond the dark space your very bones would feel the chill as Entropy, or universal fabric collapse, whatever you would call it, approached your home.

In all the death that a hundred and fifty two year old "boy" could know there was never a doubt that the human race would continue. Now he wasn't sure if there would be anyone to even know they existed in a few millennia.

"It's a strange feeling, isn't it?" Henry asked as he leaned over in his chair.

Kieran looked up from the display. Blinking hard and shaking his head to clear the cobwebs that several hours of reading had built up,"What?"

Henry chuckled, "The thought that everything ends."

"Yes," Kieran replied feeling rather lost at the moment.

Henry stood up and walked over to Kieran, "When Systems Control first laid it out for me, I thought... maybe this isn't the end. Maybe it's just proof that Heisenberg's String Theory was right... but this defies everything we think we know about how matter works."

"And Project Starlight aims to put a ship into the heart of this darkness. Why not send a basic probe in there?" Kieran asked leaning back in his chair.

The soft red glow of Systems Control's all seeing eye appeared in the center of the main cockpit display where Rebecca had been sitting, it pulsed for a moment. "Impossible. At maximum speeds using the best tuned FTL engine it would take a probe 79,000,373 years to reach the interior of the anomaly."

Kieran and Henry turned to face the red dot as if it was another crew member. Kieran interjected, "So what's a starship going to do that a probe can't do? Besides probably get people killed?"

"The Heavy Origin Lightsource ship will be equipped with a prototype FTL engine, codenamed Harmony. The first working production model has completed test runs just beyond the Narresa system. Early results show that it is capable of speeds beyond conventional FTL engines by a factor of $3.14\text{^}E3$ speed."

The insanity of the number stunned both Kieran and Henry into silence. Systems Control let them grasp the difference in speed for a moment and then continued its answer, "However, to obtain such speeds both the development team and I need more data than anticipated. The third ship going out to the edge of the galaxy, the Leviathan, was designed to be retrofitted into the main observation platform in that sector. It is meant to house the many scientists who will be sent to study the anomaly. However, final test of the Harmony FTL engine ran into delays. As such the Leviathan will now make the final part of its trip on a first generation Harmony FTL engine."

"So, we're just along for the testing?" Kieran asked.

Systems Control responded, "The starship being built at Checkpoint Charlie will includes a cockpit for a human crew, but I am confident that all issues with the new FTL engine will be resolved by the time the Leviathan reaches its destination. At that time I will remote pilot the Heavy Origin Lightsource ship into the blackness. Should a safe return happen, we will begin trials for a possible human excursion into the space anomaly."

The two of them stood there looking at the glowing red eye. Humans built machines to go where they could not. Now it was a machine deciding where humans could not go.

"Still a terrible idea Systems Control," called out Rebecca from the door.

Kieran jumped slightly in his chair at Rebecca's voice. Henry didn't seem phased, "Have yourself a good little cry?"

Rebecca pushed past Henry and addressed Systems Control's red eye directly, "You're suffering from calculation malfunctions if you think I spent the last several hundred years designing a ship to house the fastest FTL engine ever built so that I could watch you fly it away."

There was a long pause before Systems Control answered her, "I have confirmed my calculations. If you believe it necessary we can review my flight plan before the starship departs Checkpoint Charlie." Rebecca sighed at the response but knew she didn't really have any alternatives at this time.

"Okay, we'll let you do the test flight. But I'm on the first flight after that," she said with a voice that was clearly primed to avoid further discussion on the matter. Systems Control's red dot eye blinked, "We will discuss future flight plans after the test run is completed." With that the dot disappeared from view.

"Yeah," Rebecca responded with a huff. "Come on, young ones, we should get some rest. It's a couple more hours until we arrive in the Narresa system and disembark on the Leviathan." She waved them to follow her and together they traveled back down the main corridor.

They passed through a small galley kitchen and Henry stopped and started opening shelves, "Just gonna make myself a quick meal," he said his head buried in the pantry.

Further on they entered a hallway of doors, behind which Kieran guessed were cabins for the crew. Not that there was any evidence of anyone on the ship besides the three of them. Rebecca waved at the first one and said, "All yours," as she continued walking to a door at the end of the hallway.

Kieran entered the small Mother Goose crew cabin. It was sparsely decorated by some former crew member he guessed. The amount of dust indicated it had remained empty for many, many, many years. He flopped onto the bunk and stared up at the ceiling. Sleep wasn't going to join him.

His stomach rumbled and he got up, coming out of the doorway he had a thought about offering to get Rebecca something to eat as well. He turned and headed down the hallway to the doorway she'd disappeared into. As he reached the door he realized that she hadn't shut it behind her.

She was seated with her back to him, her hair askew while she manipulated a port on the upper part of her skull. He must have gasped, or breathed heavily, because it was only a moment until she stood and turned around her face visibly shaken, "Oh."

They stood there for a moment, Kieran looking at the floor to give her back her privacy while she adjusted her hair.

"Sorry," he sheepishly said.

Rebecca sighed, and reached out and tilted Kieran's head up until he was looking her in the face, "It's okay. I've spent the last six years living alone on this ship. It's my fault. You've got nothing to apologize for, after all there's no such thing as privacy on a starship."

He nodded as Henry came walking up on the two of them. "I miss anything good?" he mumbled with a ration bar half in his mouth crumbs dancing on his bushy mustache.

"No," Rebecca said as Kieran stepped back into the hallway, "Good night, Mr. Ausure."

As he walked away Kieran noticed that Henry did not duck into one of the other crew cabins, but instead followed Rebecca into hers. This time the door shut.

Back in the cabin Kieran listened to the sounds the FTL engine made. The subtle hum of everything on the Mother Goose vibrating. Kieran appreciated how loud it all was right now as he suspected Rebecca and Henry were engaging in some sort of therapeutic grief driven sex down the hall.

Kieran closed his eyes finally finding sleep. However, light years from Earth he'd lost all sense of time. Was it a day since the soldiers pulled him off the vomit covered floor? Had it just been a day since he'd last spoken with Dr. Cornelius? Kieran imagined the old one's artificial arms around him. Holding him. That's what he wanted right now. Someone to hold him and tell him it was all going to be okay.

Even if it was a lie, Kieran wanted Dr. Cornelius back... to apologize for leaving him. Like his parents had left him. Like everyone seems to do. It should be the doctor here on a spaceship hurtling towards the edge of the galaxy. Not Kieran.

It felt like he'd barely closed his eyes imagining his lost friend and Henry was already roughly shaking his shoulder, "Get up! We're passing into the outer edges of the system!" In his hangover recovery sleep deprived delirious state Kieran couldn't tell if it was excitement or post-sex energy that was driving Henry's enthusiasm for arriving at another solar system.

Staggering into the cockpit he watched as Rebecca guided them into the system from the captains chair. The visual screens were alive and showing the outer edge planetoid debris field as they passed into the Narresa system.

The suns were the first thing that came into view as they passed the dusty outer ring and entered the solar system, and why shouldn't it be? Twin binary stars that each were multitudes bigger than Sol in the solar system Kieran grew up in. Rebecca started tapping flight plans and communicating with an as of yet unseen docking station.

"It's a shame we don't have time to tour Narresa Prime itself. As places go there are worst ways to spend all your money, lose most of your pride, and come back with a disease or three," Henry whispered into Kieran's ear as they stood watching Rebecca steer the ship into the system.

"No flight control, I was not asking for main yard docking clearance. I am part of Juniper-Zeta convoy three alpha. I am again requesting clearance for shipyard bravo bravo eight romeo two delta two," Rebecca huffed loudly into the coms clearly establishing that she was not happy with Henry whispering behind her while she steered the Mother Goose.

There was a long pause as Rebecca nodded her head in various directions along to the conversation from the other end. Sometimes approvingly, other times dismissively, and finally a sharp - "NO. There is a platform with that call sign. Go get your supervisor to unlock the security block. I don't have time to go around you or to swat down whatever security you have," she practically screamed.

Henry put his hand on her shoulder and she took a deep breath, "I'm sorry. It's been a long bad day on this end.

Please request security unlock so that you can verify the existence of the top secret shipyard and grant me airlock access."

Rubbing her shoulders Henry stood there as she stared at visual displays. They slowly approached a planet with a series of large moons orbiting around it. Kieran opened a wiki-net and confirmed that Narresa Prime was not the planet name, but rather the largest and most inhabited moon clustered around an empty world known for its globe spanning deserts.

Finally, Rebecca started nodding her head approvingly again, "Thank you, flight officer Mikey. Making our approach now." She turned around, "You boys better sit down. We're already late."

Kieran had barely seated himself, and pressed the gravity button, when he could feel the Mother Goose's engines engage at a much higher level. The visual display started to blur and he could only guess at what sub-light speed they were moving at now.

The cockpit was filled with silence as the Mother Goose approached what appeared to be the largest, most industrial looking moon. Bright lights crisscrossed the surface, orbital platforms covered nearly every approach to the surface, and near the poles thin lines appeared to signify orbital elevators. Something not seen on Earth since the Blue Fire.

A large shadow overtook them as a small moon blocked the view of the twin suns. In the dark, Kieran's eyes adjusted, and it took a moment, but finally he realized that a small orange glint in the distance wasn't a stuck pixel on the visual display, it was their target. As they approached, a dimly lit space station came into view.

"That's..." Kieran started to ask, but Rebecca already knew the question.

"Yes, that's the Leviathan."

What he had assumed was a space station was in fact a massive tube shaped starship that stretched beyond the visual screens' edges in every direction. The project outline had included a brief description of the starship they were to embark on, the Leviathan, but the concept of a starship that was a city was lost on Kieran until this very moment.

"Cutting gravity for docking, prepare for air sync in 5 minutes," Rebecca said out loud in a voice that indicated she wasn't really talking to them at all. Kaylee's voice came on over the communication channel, "Yes ma'am, all systems read green. Mother Goose is ready."

A gold light blinked three times in the cockpit and Kieran felt gravity leave his body for the fourth time in 24hrs. His hangover had long since given way to general exhaustion and his stomach was empty except for the parts of the mushroom cocktail he hadn't thrown up hours ago... so this time he did not feel vomit rising up in his mouth.

There was a loud warning buzzer and then Kaylee spoke, "Alignment warning. Please watch the left side. Docking bay doors are not open all the way yet."

Rebecca grunted, "I can see that Kaylee. Damn fools. Why didn't they turn the lights on all the way for us? Kaylee, bring up the infrared cameras and turn up the light brightness on the loading ramp."

There was a hard shudder and banging sounds as the Mother Goose hit something on its way to setting down inside the Leviathan. "I don't want to hear it, Kaylee," Rebecca interjected as Kaylee's communication line started to light up. She continued flipping settings on her displays as the ship cooed and hissed around them. The visual displays rendered a dimly lit docking bay.

The Mother Goose shuddered and metal banging on metal could be heard followed by a long hiss. "Docking confirmed. Air synchronization confirmed. Gravity match confirmed. Leviathan acknowledges our arrival and will have Dr. Heddia and Officer Oriono meet you outside," Kaylee announced.

Kieran followed as they traveled through the Mother Goose. Rebecca and Henry led the way down the ramp into the Levithan's docking bay. Lights started flipping on overhead and distracted Kieran as he approached the end of the ramp.

The world started spinning around Kieran as he stumbled off the edge of the ramp, which was apparently not touching the ground, and face planted onto the docking bay floor.

Looking up Kieran saw Henry hold his hand out, "First time is always hardest. Anything broken?"

Kieran pressed a thin smile onto his face and took the outstretched hand, "Nothing damaged other than my pride."

Henry chuckled, "Forget hard. First time is always awkward. It gets easier with time."

Sighing and brushing the dust from his clothes Kieran replied, "That's what everyone keeps telling me."

THE LEVIATHAN AWAKENS

It felt strange to be standing amongst so many old ones at the same time. Kieran stood there as Dr. Heddia, Officer Oriono, Henry, and Rebecca caught each other up on what happened during the rendezvous with the Juniper-Zeta. It was clear that the four of them have known each other longer than Kieran has been alive. Their language was peppered with references that required centuries of involvement with Project Starlight to understand. Without it, Kieran felt alone watching a play in a language he didn't know.

Behind Kieran the docking crew shuffled back and forth with cases and equipment offloaded from the Mother Goose. Occasionally Rebecca would pause to tell them to be careful with a case, or not to let a certain box get lost in the shuffle. Mostly she steered the conversation with the group in such a way that belittled how much you would have expected the officer to be in charge of things based on their outfit.

"I'm telling you Oriono, the freespacers are just desperate. They know the war with Systems Control is done. They attacked us thinking we were on our way to test some new weapon. We should just tell them it's an FTL engine and then they'll just leave us alone," Rebecca huffed.

After spending the better part of the last day with uniformed officers, Kieran could tell that Officer Oriono wasn't a pampered paper pusher. Their teal tinted synthetic shell looked roughly worn from what you'd assume were many decades of service to the Aligned Worlds. Whatever ethnicity or gender had once been part of their birth was now gone. With no obvious signs of organic flourishes it was hard to guess at an age, but the way they held themselves indicated they were far younger than Henry, Rebecca, or Dr. Heddia.

The teal face scrunched as Officer Oriono retorted, "Even opening a communications with them would give them a vector to us. No. We maintain radio silence and hope that the size of the Leviathan is reason enough for them to leave it alone."

Compared to the strong silent type of Officer Oriono, Dr. Heddia was a buzz of energy and a high pitched feminine voice. She ruffled at every critique from Rebecca, no matter how sharp or gentle. Natural grey curls tightly bundled to a single point behind her ears, and hands with a mixture of organic and artificial fingers spoke to dangerous lab accidents gone wrong. Or maybe just old age Kieran wondered for an extended period before he realized the group was waiting for him to respond.

"Kieran, wake up! What group were you assigned to?" Henry asked him again loudly. Suddenly as all the old eyes were on his young rumpled frame, all Kieran could do was shrug his shoulders. Not sure if the Earth expression was universal or not, he spoke after they continued staring at him, "I wasn't given a group assignment by Systems Control."

Rebecca sighed loudly, a common feature when dealing with Kieran it seemed, "Systems Control, please bring up Kieran Ausure's file. Where is he supposed to be assigned to on the Leviathan's crew manifest?" The red dot of Systems Control filled the upper right corner of everyone's nanite display and after a few pulses it spoke, "He doesn't have one."

He should have held it, but Kieran couldn't help himself, he laughed. Loudly. Rebecca threw him a glance that spoke volumes in the silence of the hallway, "Please confirm where is he supposed to be assigned? Engineering, janitorial, communications, life support...?"

Systems Control pulsed again, "He doesn't have a specific assignment. As a documentarian historian who came highly recommended by Dr. Cornelius, he is here to observe and then write about the events of this research project. At a future date, as security clearance allows, his words will be used to tell the public what happened during the first exploration of the anomaly."

This time there wasn't an outburst from Kieran. Just a look that Henry would describe later as Braumarr caught in a trap. Although few would understand the old one's reference until Henry mimed a wide opened panicked look. That was how Kieran looked after Systems Control had announced his role on the project.

Not one to wait for everyone to catch up with her, Rebecca was already walking away from the conversation. She was a good distance down the hallway before the rest of the group recomposed themselves after Systems Control's surprise announcement, "Come everyone, lets get this all hands meeting done so we can get the Leviathan underway."

They followed her down the hallway, through a series of air locks, and the whole time it struck Kieran that she appeared to know every nook and cranny of this shipyard. He wondered if she'd been here, on and off, the whole time they'd been building whatever ship it was they were about to meet.

Finally, they passed into a large hanger. Here a collection of what appeared to be over a hundred humans and aliens stood waiting for them. Kieran did a weak wave hello as they walked in, not sure what else to do. Rebecca just shook her head at him as she walked to the front of the room.

"Hello and thank you all for waiting up for us to dock. I have to apologize for being late and not bringing Captain Carter with me. He planned to give this project a military escort out of the Pruuta cluster, but that won't be happening. At this time the Kohlar system is considered under conflict. We don't yet know the status of the Juniper-Zeta and its crew," she paused clearly upset at the thought of never seeing the captain again.

Taking a deep breath she continued, "So we will continue on as planned. Today we will leave this shipyard aboard the Leviathan. Conventional FTL engines will carry us along the same route the Sledopyt took centuries ago. We will pick up resources and supplies from the seven way-stations she dropped. When we reach the seventh, we will ready and prepare the first long run of the new Harmony FTL engine. Assuming all goes as planned it will take us far less time to reach Checkpoint Charlie."

Rebecca smiled thinking about this extraordinary fact, "We will arrive at Checkpoint Charlie and hopefully find that Sledopyt's conversion from starship to space station is completed. There we will oversee the final build out of the HoL, aka Heavy Origin Lightsource, testing ship. Then we'll take humanity's first step off the edge of the known Milky Way galaxy into the unknown at our doorstep."

Pausing to get a feel for the room, she looked to see Henry giving her a thumbs up and a sarcastic smile as expected, "The small crew of Checkpoint Charlie will work on converting the Leviathan into a research station for the anomaly before disembarking on the Boijeo after it has been retrofitted to use the new Harmony FTL engine. They'll leave after a millennia away and return back to... well anywhere but the edge of the Milky Way."

If she expected applause she would have been disappointed. Getting people ready to throw themselves into the dark for scientific pursuits was never a skill she had, not in this or any other of her lifetimes. After a few awkward coughs, she finally walked away and joined Dr. Heddia, Henry, and Kieran at the edge of the hanger.

"You heard the lady! All crews to their cryo-pods and prepare to disembark," shouted a dock crew member after a long moment where Rebecca wished she'd been better with people.

There was a clapping sound behind them, and they turned to see a rough looking bearded man and a Gorgon approaching the group, "I have to say ma'am, that was the best pump up speech I've ever heard anyone give... to a room full of scientists... about to go take a nap."

Rebecca's eyes narrowed and the thin scar across her face made her gaze feel twice as imposing. Kieran imagined little daggers flying from her eye lashes at the average looking caucasian man with dyed neon red hair. As he approached, his pale skin and bright red hair stood out amongst the aliens and multiple old ones with their artificial bodies.

"Captain Fillion, good to see you're still as charming as I remember," Officer Oriono huffed as they roughly shook the man's hand. The Captain nodded along with the insult which caused his big bushy beard to bobble along with him to almost hilarious effect.

The bombastic Captain turned and waved to the Gorgon, "This is my co-pilot Braug. He'll be our navigator on this little run into the darkness." The Gorgon smiled, but the reassurance he intended was lost when it was two mouths that bared teeth.

Braug's weathered grey-brown skin reminded Kieran of an elephant he'd once seen. Although for such old looking skin the Gorgon moved with a spring in his step that made Kieran think of a little kid, not that little kids usually have long arms, long legs, and a small torso. Up close Kieran noticed the bright gold eyes of Braug and wondered if they glowed in the dark.

Kieran was awash with more questions, but the captain interrupted all of them "So I know everyone here except for you. Where's the tall skinny oldie Dr. Cornelius?" he asked waving at Kieran. The cocksure smile on the captain's lips annoyed Kieran and instead of throwing daggers, he'd rather be throwing punches.

"There was a last minute personnel change. Mr. Ausure will be taking on the role of documentarian for this project," Dr. Haddia said, finding a wonderful moment to interject and cut the growing tension between Rebecca and Captain Fillion. Ignoring her the captain stepped closer to Rebecca, "Four thousand messages about every last detail of our cast off, and yet you couldn't find time to tell me about this?"

Rebecca waved dismissively at the bushy bearded captain, "Captain, you can't be bothered to properly trim a beard, so I didn't think you'd even notice if a different face got onboard with us." Captain Fillion gave a rough, "hmph," and turned to Kieran looking him over. It was a crude glance that danced between raw sexual undressing and professional curiosity.

Satisfied in what he saw, or bored with it, Kieran would never know, Captain Fillion turned away from them, "Well come on then, let's get properly boarded. Those freespacer pirates won't be long behind you now. We've got a long trip ahead of us and medical is going to want to check you out."

Another series of airlocks and hallways blended together as Kieran felt the hours and hours of travel start to wear on him. It had been a long day, or days, he still wasn't really sure what time it was. His nanite display had jumped between multiple system times during his recent travels, and now it was offline due to a security override from the station.

Finally, they approached what felt like a proper main airlock for the ship. Kieran had thought they might approach by way of a windowed ramp that would allow views of the ship, but the hallway was without any view screens or glass windows. A short line ahead of them moved without pause as medical technicians examined crew before they embarked.

Henry and Office Oriono started a brief conversation about some recent military action that Kieran had never heard of and honestly didn't care about at the moment. Captain Fillion cut the line and waved at them from just inside the airlock. Navigator Braug followed, ignoring all the medical technicians who tried to stop him. Ultimately they were waved off by the captain as well.

Dr. Heddia and Rebecca were finishing up a short discussion on the breakdown of the station after the Leviathan left the system, and after saying goodbye to the group, Dr. Heddia left them waiting in line. The hilarity of traveling across multiple systems just to end up waiting in a line weighed on Kieran as he tried to hold his laughter and stay awake.

As they shuffled closer to the medical technicians, Kieran noticed Rebecca looking more and more anxious. She'd steered them through combat with pirates and bickered with multiple people who's standing and rank appeared above her with no sign of fear. But the simple medical check seemed to be stressing her out.

Kieran fell back in line and allowed her to go first. Doing his best "I'm not listening face," he leaned as close as he dared to listen in to her conversation with the technician.

"We didn't get a current medical report from a doctor prior to today's launch; have you been checked out recently?" asked the technician.

"Yes and no. My shell was built and fitted 12 years ago. I've had one maintenance session since then, but honestly given the layers of additional hardware and premium upgrades, I haven't seen the need to get checked out. The only thing left in here is my brain."

The medical technician looked ready to argue pulling out some sort of device to plug into Rebecca's body, but Officer Oriono put their hand on the technician's shoulder. "Dr. Chambers is the project lead, so if she says that she's ready to cast off then she's ready."

The medical technician pursed their lips clearly wanting to say a lot of things, but instead put the device back in their pocket. A rough head nod in the direction of the airlock was all that they said on the matter. Rebecca and Oriono exchanged a look that spoke volumes, but Kieran didn't know the language.

His own turn came up, and he realized that he was officially the last person getting on board the ship. "Systems Control forwarded your last medical report to us this morning. I don't see any red flags here. In fact, you may be one of the healthiest people getting onboard this morning," the technician said waving through a series of screens on their eyes.

"Other than an elbow joint replacement, and the usual cortex and visual upgrades, I'm pretty stock human still," Kieran offered up. Meaning it as a joke but it fell flat as the technician finished their review. "How organic you are doesn't make much of a difference to me." They finished, waving through screens. The glow faded from the eyes and with a smile he was waved on to join the rest of the crew.

They barely stepped onboard, and with hardly a moment to look around the ship, Captain Fillion appeared and immediately walked Henry, Rebecca, and Kieran to the cryo-pod bay. He was talking a mile a minute, as if making up for time from their delay.

"The Verantes are already down asleep. They had a rough journey here and after checking on their cargo they decided to call it a week ago. I've got the three of you logged for a wake up call when we reach the way-station. Assuming no hiccups, the new Harmony engine will be christened with some champagne and you'll be at the destination in what feels like no time at all."

They arrived at rows of lockers as the captain continued his monologue, "Braug and I will be awake on and off until we reach the last way-station. If anything goes wrong, then per mission directives, we'll wake you, Rebecca. Okay, folks, here's the lockers. Strip down and put on a sleeping suit. Kiddo, I'll go find something that will fit you, since Dr. Cornelius was a few sizes thinner than you."

Silence wafted over the rows of lockers as the captain wandered off. Rebecca continued on to the next row over for privacy. Kieran didn't want to seem prudish, but he turned his back to Henry and Officer Oriono as they started stripping down to their underwear.

They completed their undressing and zipped into their sleep suites before Captain Fillion had returned. Throwing

Kieran a shit eating grin, he handed over a set of folded clothes, "This outta fit you, assuming my calculations are correct." The captain stood there awkwardly watching as Kieran hurried through fitting himself into the suit.

A medical technician appeared out of no where and held a nano-particle injector to Kieran's neck without warning.

PSHHTHUNKK

It caught him by surprise and he yelped out loud, "What the hell?" Kieran felt the chilly contents of the injector plunge down into his neck and flow into his body.

"Seriously, Kieran?" Rebecca demurred loudly behind him. "I don't see any of you getting surprised with a cold injector to the neck!" he shot back angrily. The lack of sleep and lightyears of travel had made the normally calm graduate student very brittle.

"Price you pay for having all your organs, kiddo," the captain chuckled slapping Kieran on the back. "Now that you're all set, I'll let Rebecca tuck you all in for your first nap. See you in a hundred years." With that last statement, the captain and medical technician wandered off back into the hallway leaving the four of them alone for the first time.

Rebecca nodded towards the back of the bay past the lockers. The three humans followed her and they came upon a set of cryo-pods. Two pods were already locked and filled with the Verantes. Kieran was curious to meet the two engineers who'd come up with a radically new faster than light engine, but he'd have to wait.

Officer Oriono examined their pod and settled themselves in with no assistance from anyone. The hatch closed and the pod started filling with a thick blue green liquid. Henry huffed, "Not even so much as a good night from the guy. Typical military."

"Self sufficient and rude are different things, Henry," Rebecca chirped back as she pressed buttons on the pod Kieran stood next too.

The sleep suit was tight and maybe itchy; Kieran couldn't tell because it was so tight that he couldn't really move around inside to tell. Mostly it just made him feel tired. *Well named*, Kieran thought to himself. Rebecca fiddled with settings on his cryo-pod seemingly oblivious to his fidgeting.

Bundled up in her own sleep suit, every millimeter of Rebecca's body was on display in front of the hungover college student. Kieran found it difficult not to stare at her. He kept shaking his head and trying to refocus on her hands as she moved through the pod menus with a speed that indicated a deep familiarity.

"Your anxiety about looking at me is more annoying than just staring. Just look and get it out of your system... young man," she dryly stated without looking up from her menu flipping. Kieran's cheeks flushed, but mostly he just struggled to keep his eyes open and off her breasts.

He didn't realize he was falling to the floor until Henry caught him, "Whoa, there. Cyro cocktail hitting you a little hard?" Kieran didn't really answer so much as weakly nod his head as Henry helped him climb into the cryo-pod. "He must have had an empty stomach, always makes the drugs kick in faster," Rebecca chimed to Henry as he laid Kieran to rest.

Henry looked down at Kieran's face and nodded, "Poor kid. Thrust into service and dragged halfway across the sector with a hangover. We never even stopped to get him lunch." Rebecca finished her fiddling and engaged the pod. The cover started moving down over Kieran's head as the interior began filling up with a slurry mixture of cold chemicals who's names escaped even her razor sharp knowledge.

Sighing as the bath of liquids entrapped Kieran she looked up at Henry's sad face and spoke, "We're off to face the end of existence and you're pouting because we didn't get the child a sandwich?" She started walking to her own pod, no signs of any sleep yet approaching her.

Henry followed behind her, the nanites in his artificial body had already started their shut down process and he could feel sleep coming for him. He stepped carefully as he approached his pod. Rebecca was already fiddling with the settings as he got in, "You call him a child, but I've seen you treat real children far worse. I think you like him."

Rebecca chuckled, loudly, since there was no one left to hear them, "You are getting daft in your old age." Henry chuckled along and, before the sleep wrapped its arms around him, managed one final statement on the subject. "I may be daft, but unless you're getting kinder I've seen you knock far younger people to the ground for gawking at your rainbow swirled as..." the pod hatch closed over him. His eyes closed; the old one was asleep.

Alone in the bay of cryo-pods Rebecca huffed to herself as Henry's pod filled with fluid. She smacked her right butt cheek, "It is a nice ass. Best money could build. Ha." She finished fiddling with Henry's pod settings. His pod like all the others would open only after hers did.

Rebecca took one last look around the room before jumping into her cryo-pod. She opened her nanite displays and connected to the Mother Goose, "Kaylee have you set down on the Narresa long-term docking pads?"

There was a pause and then a blue light filled her vision, "Yes ma'am. The Mother Goose is landed and docking fees are paid. I've set a routine to awake for each month's payment until your return."

The light pulsed unexpectedly for a moment, "You will return, right?"

Rebecca laughed, "Don't I always?"

Kaylee nervously chimed in response, "Of course, ma'am."

Closing the connection, Rebecca looked up as as the cyro-pod hatch came down over her head. Lights in the bay started clicking off. It would be a long sleep before they reached the last way-station and finished the final engine preparations. *Good*, she thought, *plenty of time for me to plan for what's to come.*

WHEN TITANIUM KNOCKS

What is time when you aren't there to experience it?

Kieran wasn't really aware of falling asleep and no dreams tickled his mind while the Leviathan traveled across the stars. Suspended in near-freezing liquids, his body never reacted to the FTL engines shaking the cryo-pods with each start and stop. Six times. Six way-stations. Sleep continued uninterrupted.

Somewhere in nothingness came a thought.

What is time on a starship?

It bounced around in Kieran's mind and then he wondered if you can ever be in a moment. If time is a river, and all of them were being carried in its current, how can you ever stop and appreciate a moment? The water flowing ever forward away from them towards the horizon. The sound of the currents lapping against his head as he bobbed along the river of time was soft and peaceful.

He blinked and the blanket of stars above him disappeared.

Kieran blinked again hard and it was still dark. No sound other than his own heartbeat bouncing against the cryo-pod walls. Suddenly his nanite visual displays flickered to life. The date and time snapped into focus on the top left of his view. The red dot of Systems Control appeared. It blinked with a waiting message for him.

He ignored all of it. Wishing that the stars would return.

There was suddenly a loud hissing sound and the darkness gave way to light as the cryo-pod opened up. He blinked. Aware of his eyes again. The lid slowly retracted and Kieran rolled his head to look at Henry as he appeared looking over the edge.

Green semi-transparent skin wrapped into a smile as Henry looked down at him, "Have a good nap?"

"No. I feel...," Kieran reached for the words but nothing came to him.

"Blank? Yeah, that's a feeling and a mental state. It'll shake faster if you keep moving, but first let's get you something to eat. Its been a century since you threw up breakfast, I bet you're hungry," Henry shouted as he moved away from the pod. Kieran nodded his head even though no one could see him.

Henry helped Kieran step out of the pod but the young man still dropped to his knees once he was fully out. Kieran thought that he was going to vomit for a moment, but the sensation quickly left him. "The artificial gravity can feel weird after a cryosleep but," Henry started to say only for Kieran to interrupt him, "but... it gets easier with time. I know. I know."

The green skinned old one smiled, "Time is all we have now out here in the black."

Kieran grunted and nodded as he stood up with Henry's help. He looked around realizing that they were all alone in the cryo-pod room. Barely had words started to form on his lips when Henry cut him off with an answer, "You're the last one up. Everyone else is probably almost done with breakfast. Come on, I'll show you."

Slowly, and with more than a few achy joints, Kieran followed Henry into the locker room. Henry was in the other row getting dressed as Kieran slowly opened his locker and sat down looking at the dust on his clothes. The sensation of time and motion felt all wrong to him still. It was like being drunk but without the bliss of alcohol.

He closed his eyes and tried to remember the beautiful star filled sky he saw in his last moments asleep, but it was gone. Henry banged on the lockers, "Come on kid, at this rate the bacon is going to be cold by the time we get out there!"

Kieran stripped off the tight fitting sleep suit and tossed it into a bin nearby where everyone else had done the same thing earlier. He grabbed a towel from the end of the bench and wandered over to the shower stalls. He stood there as the water flickered to life and rained down over him. It felt like a baptism in space. A hundred years worth of crust and debris pulled away from him.

The soap dispenser put out a basic lavender scented gel in his hand and he started scrubbing. Nearby another shower fired up and Henry started washing his artificial body. Kieran kept his eyes on his own body, but couldn't help but peak over as Henry started humming along to a song only he could hear. The semi-transparent green skin shined in the light of the steamy shower, but with the stalls all Kieran could see was the back of Henry's head and shoulders.

Kieran could feel the "hurry up" coming from Henry but suddenly found himself peeing. *How many years had it been since urine has come out of me?*, he thought to himself. Kieran tried not to think of where the liquid in his bladder had come from if he'd been asleep in a pool of slush for centuries.

Emptied and clean, Kieran turned off the water. The last of it dripped from his brown naked frame as he toweled himself dry while Henry continued washing himself. Kieran had barely finished putting his clothes back on when Henry startled him by tapping the locker next to him, "Hurry up kid, breakfast is gonna be over before we get to it at this rate."

How Henry had finished showering and dressing befuddled Kieran. Maybe time wasn't working right for his brain just yet. Words certainly were failing him. All he could do was nod. Speaking still hurt Kieran's brain. Time and motion did not feel right. Every step felt like it was happening both slower and faster than it should as they walked down the hall.

They entered a small eating area where a man and woman were already well in to their breakfast. Henry grabbed a tray and started filling it with warm breakfast foods. Kieran looked for waffles but found only thinly sliced bacon, somewhat warm, burnt toast, under scrambled eggs, assorted tiny fruit like plant seeds, and ceda-coffee. The smells were delightful even if the lineup was rather basic.

"Best enjoy it while you can, this is the only non-rationed meal you're going to get for the rest of this journey," the woman said to Kieran as he filled his coffee cup. Walking over to the two of them he held out his hand, "Kieran."

The woman, who appeared to be completely organic, had long free flowing dark golden hair that reached down and over her shoulders. Her skin was a mixture of colors that called to mind a bronzed pot from the antiquities department back at Harvard. As she reached out to shake Kieran's hand, he noticed a bright pink marriage band across her finger and couldn't help but stare at the unusual color.

"Its an old family trinket," she said noticing Kieran's eyes stopping on her ring, "belonged to a distant grandmother." Her voice betrayed her youthful appearance, it sounded old and worn to Kieran. "My name is Juuana Verantes, and this is my husband Solieo." She waved gracefully to her husband, who barely looked up from his coffee at Kieran. The yellow nanite glow in his eyes was so bright that Kieran wondered if Solieo could even see him through all the screens he had open.

Where Juuana looked youthful, organic, and mixed from a thousand human bloodlines, Solieo was the complete opposite. His skin was very dark and wrinkled. While his head had a few strands of gray hair and the stubble on his face made clear he could grow a beard if he stopped shaving. Even sitting, Kieran could tell that Solieo was very tall. His wiry frame loomed over all of them.

"So what's this about no food?" Kieran asked after a long moment spent studying Solieo for signs of age or implants. Henry chuckled, "Rebecca brought this cache as part of her personal carry on luggage. Her treat for the first firing crew."

Kieran's face looked quizzical enough that Juuana didn't need to wait for him to ask, "We're all here this morning because we're at the last way-station. After a few last minute checks we'll be switching from standard FTL engines over to the new prototype Harmony FTL engine for the remainder of our journey to Checkpoint Charlie."

"Ah, of course. First firing crew. Makes sense. Speaking of crew, where is... everyone?" Kieran asked glancing around the small room. It was clearly not big enough for all the crew members that he'd watched boarding before they left.

Solieo spoke, the nanite glow fading from his eyes, "Rebecca, the captain, and Braug are all going over data reports in the cockpit. As for everyone else, this is all we need. Juuana and myself are more than capable of performing the final system checks without assistance from anyone." The dark skin of his face did not hide the contempt or shade he was clearly tossing in the direction of Henry.

Henry continued munching on the last of the bacon, and took a big fuck you slurp of his coffee before he replied to the obvious dig from Solieo. "The two of you are more than capable, but unless you wanted to pilot a spacesuit outside the ship or crawl through a mile of junction tubes, I assumed I would be the one on site in the bowels of the ship checking on the prototype in person."

Juuana stood up and put her hand on Solieo's shoulder, "We are of course happy for your assistance. We'll be monitoring remotely and will let you know if any of the remote drones find anything before you get to the engine compartment."

The old green one and the old dark one stared at each other for a long moment, and then Solieo stood up. His massive height that appeared to be easily close to seven foot tall towered over Henry for a moment. Then Solieo grunted, frowning his face, and sending his grey eyebrows furrowing before he turned away. Juuana shook her head as her husband left the room.

Looking around and thinking there was no better opportunity, Kieran asked a dumb question that had been burning inside him waiting for the right moment, "So I read the project outline... twice... I don't understand how the Harmony engine is supposed to work."

Juuana's face lit up like a Christmas tree, "You see, normal FTL engines just brute force their way to faster than light speeds. The Harmony bends us in-between the wave and particle elements of light itself. We slip amongst the very strands of energy that make up the universe... in theory. We've not done very many test runs with it yet. Hence why we're awake this morning."

Kieran nodded as if he understood all of her explanation as Juuana went to work cleaning up her husband's dishes. She paused at the table; her face dancing out words her mouth couldn't say out loud.

Henry reached out and put his hand on hers, "Its okay, Juuana. Solieo can be a jerk, but I know what it's like to spend a few hundred years working on something personal only to have to share it at the end."

Juuana smiled and grasped Henry's hand with hers. She said nothing and left Kieran and Henry sitting there to finish their meal. Kieran wanted to say something to Henry, but the politics of what had just happened were way beyond his years.

Instead he picked at his bacon, working up the courage to ask a question that had been bugging him for a few thousand light years, "Henry, what's the story with you and Rebecca?"

Henry's mustache danced as he debated the response before going with, "We've been friends... with occasional benefits... for longer than you've been alive. She's always got an adventure waiting for me whenever she calls. Keeps me fresh and engaged. Keeps me moving. She called and so here I am."

Kieran nodded as if he understood, but the answer left questions bouncing around in his mind. Mostly he wondered just how old Henry thought he was, but also he wondered how Rebecca would answer his question. Henry's delay spoke volumes about how undefined his relationship with Rebecca must be even after hundreds of years.

They sat in silence eating their last real meal without saying anything more to each other. If Henry had thoughts about what Kieran's question meant the young man wanted, he did not wear them on his face for Kieran to read.

Finally after his third cup of coffee, Henry tossed his dishes loudly into the reclamation bin and motioned for Kieran to follow. Still not fully awake, even after two cups of coffee, the trip through the hallways and passageways was a blur to Kieran. It felt like it took forever to reach the cockpit, but his feet told him they hadn't traveled very far at all.

As they entered the room a wall of displays stared back at them. Every system in the Leviathan was a spreadsheet, bar graph, or data point to be monitored from this room. In the top right corner the continuous red glow of a Systems Control eyeball let them know while they were driving the ship, the AI system was always watching.

Rebecca and the captain were in the middle of a heated discussion and, based on their body language, it was clear no one was winning. She waved at the displays, "The docking procedure says that any failure of response means we don't dock with a way-station."

Captain Fillion didn't miss a beat replying, "The procedure book says a lot of stuff that doesn't count out here. We're way off the galactic core here. Things don't always work. Just because the way-station transponder failed to respond to a dock request doesn't mean the station has been hijacked by pirates. Think about it — why would anyone travel this far out in the direction of nothing, take over a glorified storage locker, and wait centuries for someone to come along?"

The conversation was interrupted by Officer Oriono, "Ma'am, the captain is right. The risk is minimal out here. I understand you came under fire when you left the Juniper-Zeta, but pirate activity this far out would be unprecedented. There is no need to be worried."

Rebecca turned from staring down the captain and slapped Officer Oriono across the face. The room went instantly quiet as the Verantes and Braug hushed their side conversation. All eyes were on the military officer. Holding a hand up to block her second slap, "One is enough."

"Don't you ever patronize me, Officer Oriono. I have traveled across the stars longer than you have existed. I am not some waif to be treated as a hysterical little woman," she growled as Officer Oriono held her hand.

They sighed, "Noted, ma'am, but the point remains the same. Systems Control, Captain Fillion, first mate Braug, and I are in agreement that docking safety is within tolerance. On all project matters you are in charge, but on ship operational matters the captain's orders are final."

Rebecca pulled her hand free, huffed, and left the room. "Well now that everyone's seen the parents fight, lets get on with it," Captain Fillion announced loudly attempting to break the awkwardness of the moment apart. He walked over and dropped down into a chair in front of a row of monitors. For a moment Kieran noticed the captain's shoulders drop and his whole body sag under the weight of the decision he had just made, but it was over quickly.

The Verantes and Henry reviewed footage and data sets from a series of drones reporting back from the prototype FTL engine room. Kieran stood behind them pretending he could understand even half of what they were saying, or what the data was in reference to as the three of them hammered through a checklist that appeared quite lengthy.

Kieran felt a tapping on his shoulder and turned to face Officer Oriono. Up close every inch of their face looked to have been used in a fight based on the heavy scarring. Not scars... skin scars. This was an artificial shell covering over a mechanized body. They were scratches in the hull of military killing machine.

"I understand that you do not have an active assignment. The captain and Braug do not need assistance. The Verantes and Henry do not need assistance. I need assistance. Come with me," they stated and started walking away. Oriono paused at the doorway, looked back at Kieran with a long hard stare and snapped their fingers, "Now."

Not wanting to argue, Kieran followed the teal tinted military officer into the hallway. Not far from the cockpit they passed a doorway that looked into some sort of lounge, but Oriono did not slow down or stop so it was just a brief glimpse. Several twists and turns later they passed by a door with heavy security lock on it.

Oriono stopped, held their wrist to the lock for a moment, and the door whooshed open. "Wait here," was all they said as if there was anywhere else for Kieran to go at that moment. He could hear metal clanks and clangs as drawers and lockers opened and closed.

Finally after what felt like an age, Officer Oriono reappeared at the door way with a Sonk Rifle. Even without an experts knowledge in firearms, Kieran recognized the gun. It was the final summation of all human creativity in killing each other after millennia of practice. Oriono carried it slung over his shoulder like it was a fishing rod.

The military standard Sonk Rifle was built after humanity discovered the Celamites. Reverse engineering bits of technology from the battlefield, scientists were able to create a pulsed energy wave that could be modulated based on what you needed to shoot. Need non-lethal half crowd control? It can blast out a concussive sound wave that will knock people off their feet. Need to destroy a bunker door? Hit it with a wave of super charged particles that cause the door to vibrate until it explodes.

The Swiss Army knives of death and destruction Dr. Cornelius had called it when giving his lecture on human weapons. It satisfied long festering desires for a gun that could safely incapacitate or viciously obliterate your target depending on your mood. The ultimate expression of power in a device so easy to use that even a child could protect themselves from the ravaging horrors of the galaxy.

Officer Oriono noticed the unease that had quickly set over Kieran when they reappeared with the Sonk Rifle. "I do not believe that Dr. Chambers is correct in her fears, but that doesn't mean that we should not be prepared. I assumed, rightfully, that you would not want to carry one with you."

Kieran looked up from the gun he'd apparently been staring at, "You are correct. I've studied too many wars and seen to clearly how destructive those things can be to the human body. I would rather not be responsible for that level of violence."

The door whooshed shut behind them as the officer stepped forward, "Is it not irresponsible to be unprepared? To put others in danger by not being ready?" Kieran's face registered shock at having this military officer push back on his beliefs.

He stood there for a moment as Officer Oriono started to leave him behind, then shook the surprise from his face and followed after.

"If I had to choose between my life and someone else's, I would put them first. To kill to survive is a primitive viewpoint. There is always a peaceful way," he said to the back of Oriono's head hushed but defiant.

Officer Oriono slowed, and let Kieran catch up to them. So that they were side by side walking through the bowels of ship together.

"Even if I had not reviewed your file, I would have known you are from Earth. They always speak of non-violence. Such is the privilege of living on the first world. All of its violence in the past. Out on the frontier on colony worlds it is not so easy."

Kieran barely finished letting Oriono speak before replying, "The colony worlds will be calm someday, such is the path of humanity. It just might take awhile."

Officer Oriono stopped suddenly, and poked Kieran in the chest with their strong mechanical finger, "No, Mr. Ausure, they will not. People are petty, cruel, selfish beings at their core when you strip away all the comforts. Earth only became the eden you know because the blue fire killed everyone who wasn't ready to live in peace."

The two of them stood there staring at each other. Each convinced the other was a fool. Finally, Kieran spoke, "If you've never walked in the glass fields then you can't know how wrong you are right now. The fire burned everyone, faithful or not. It was the people who stuck together and rebuilt together that changed the world. Not the people who died."

Oriono stared into Kieran's eyes as if to intimidate him, or perhaps maybe to understand him, Kieran couldn't tell, then turned away huffing to themselves. Walking quickly as if to leave the conversation and Kieran behind.

They walked in silence through another set of seemingly identical hallways until they reached a large airlock doorway. "Captain Fillion, we have reached the loading bay doors; ready for engagement," Oriono spoke to the door.

Kieran's nanite displays lit up in front of him and an intra-system coms line opened up. The captain appeared in the top right of his vision clearly unaware, or uncaring, that he was on a video feed. He was munching on some sort of burrito he'd smuggled onboard while haphazardly pressing buttons on a console that the camera couldn't see.

"Docking with supply way-station seven now. All hands prepare for engagement of gravity locks." There was a brief colorful flash of light around the doorway and Kieran could feel the ship move beneath his feet as they docked. It felt like a rumble and it tickled.

The door frame lights flashed gold, then pulsed green. Officer Oriono held their wrist up to the keypad again and the doors slowly, loudly, and dramatically started opening. They held the Sonk Rifle at the ready for the first time. Kieran stepped quietly behind them just in case there were pirates.

The doors finished opening and a pitch black room stared back at them. "Lights engage," Oriono said to the empty room. Heavy clicks could be heard as multiple lights fired up for the first time, perhaps ever, in the docking bay. It was a smaller, starker version of the bay Kieran had been in on the Juniper-Zeta.

On the far side of the room the airlock doors started opening and Kieran, caught by surprise at the sudden movement, yelped and huddled further behind Oriono. There was laughter from above and he looked up to see the teal tinted face staring down at him.

Kieran chuckled and stood up. They stood together watching as the airlock slowly creaked open. Beyond the doors another cargo bay stared back at them. Only with many, many containers. The nanite display blinked and Captain Fillion came back online. "Are we all clear to start the loading?"

Officer Oriono looked at the other docking bay for a moment and shook their head at the captain, "Yes, we are clear. My scans show no signs of life forms." The burrito disappeared from view for a moment, "Good. Activating drones to move the cargo containers. Stand by."

Red lights started flashing and a warning klaxon went off as a series of doors appeared in the walls. Slowly a line of robotic drones started being discharged from hooks on the wall. They each paused for a moment before standing tall and walking towards the waypoint cargo bay. Each of them looked to be 9 feet tall, they walked on four legs like large lumbering Elephants, and a pair of arms swung down from their mid section to pincer each cargo container. It seemed slow and awkward to Kieran but with over a dozen machines the containers quickly stacked up in front of him.

As the last of the containers was being moved Officer Oriono heard a sound. Too faint for Kieran's organic ears, but to the military outfitted shell it was clear as day. Knocking. Lots of it. They stood there listening intently until finally the sound was loud enough that even Kieran could hear it.

"What's that sound?" the young human asked the teal tinted old machine. The officer did not respond and Kieran started to repeat it but a teal hand covered his mouth. Together the two of them listened as the knocking sound grew louder and faster.

"Captain Fillion, we are hearing a loud knocking sound here in the cargo bay, can you confirm the docking seal remains good?" Officer Oriono asked over the nanite display call.

Kieran's nanite display flashed suddenly and the Captain and Braug appeared together huddled over a monitor. They were talking amongst each other in a mixture of English and whatever language Gorgon's spoke. After several more loud knocks, "Yes. All systems read green. Must just be the ship and way-station groaning. It happens. We've been moving at lightspeed for several hundred years without any rest. Even titanium needs to stretch after awhile."

The knocks stopped and Officer Oriono removed their hand from Kieran's lips. It tasted like orange soda Kieran thought to himself. Stepping further into the dock, Officer Oriono swept his Sonk Rifle back and forth as if testing the room for hidden enemies. "All seems well here, but I've heard metal shakes before. This sounded... less random."

The captain leaned back in his chair as Braug walked away, "Your military training must be playing tricks with you. I'm telling you, all systems are green, even the backups. It's just metal stretching. I've been on the Leviathan awake for the last six months and she's never had any issues that would make me think otherwise."

Officer Oriono turned to Kieran, waving him to exit the docking bay, "Okay, Captain. We are loaded. Have the drones return to their stations and then we are ready for disengagement." Kieran watched from the doorway as the lumbering mechanical movers put themselves away. Each helping the other up into the hooks they hung on until the last one remained, carefully stepping up on its siblings to hang itself back up.

The airlock door started closing and with that Officer Oriono slung the Sonk Rifle back over their shoulder and pressed the buttons for the cargo doorway to close. They watched the door close from the hallway. For a moment Kieran thought he heard the knocking sound again, but when he gestured to Oriono he was dismissed with a hand wave.

Their nanite displays lit up and this time it was Rebecca on video feed, behind her Solieo and Juuana huddled over a display discussing something, "Heads up you two, we're almost done with the prototype FTL engine checklist and so far all is golden. Hustle back to the cockpit. Test firing as soon as everyone is seated."

Officer Oriono was already walking when the video feed faded from Kieran's eyes. The teal tinted soldier waited as he caught up. "Do you think they've really figured out how to go a faster than lightspeed?" they asked Kieran.

"I don't know. It seems insane, but thousands of years ago people thought that regular FTL engines were impossible. Alien races were impossible. AI was impossible. Functional immortality was impossible.

Eventually, on a long enough timeline, it seems like anything is possible," answered Kieran.

Oriono tilted their head towards him, "Just because you can do something does not mean that you should."

Kieran laughed, "That sounds familiar, like I've heard it somewhere."

"Pre-burn Earth saying my commanding officer told me once. I'm not sure what the original quote was, but the premise always sounded good to me," Officer Oriono said joining Kieran in his laugh.

The young man finished his laughing, "No reward without risk. That's what my track coach always told me when I hesitated at a jump."

"They were not wrong. But you have to be ready to live with the consequences of your actions," Officer Oriono replied back remembering when they were organic and hesitated at things.

Kieran nodded, "And that's why I don't want to carry a Sonk Rifle. Having to live with myself if I make a mistake. I don't know that I can do that."

Officer Oriono chuckled dryly, "On a long enough timeline you can live with anything. It's what makes us human. We adapt. We survive. We continue onward."

"Just because you can do something doesn't mean you should," Kieran interjected. Alone in the hallway they laughed at each other.

After returning the Sonk Rifle to the armory and walking back through the twisted hallways of the Leviathan, Kieran and Officer Oriono arrived to the cockpit last. The rest of the crew was buzzing with conversation and ready to go. Sitting down Kieran found himself on Rebecca's right again. She turned her head slightly to look Kieran over as he sat down. He couldn't quite read her expression from the little of her face he could see.

Captain Fillion stood up and turned to face the assembled crew, "Okay kiddos, we're disengaged from the way-station and the navigation computer has us locked for Checkpoint Charlie at the edge of the Perseus arm. This Harmony engine we're testing is a faster than light engine that's faster than a faster than light engine," he stopped to grin at his own joke.

"Assuming this thing doesn't blow up and kill us all instantly that is...," the Captain finished as he sat down, still smiling at his own joke.

Solieo nodded to the captain, "Today we take a Great Leap Forward as we reimagine what space travel can be.

This test firing will only be at half power, but it should allow us to obtain the last data we need. I thank my wife Juuana, whom without I never would have understood Gorgon technology, and to Dr. Chambers, whom without her support the Aligned Worlds council never would have approved this project."

"Okay, enough speechifying. It's just us grunts here," Henry interrupted, "let's hit the button and see if we all die."

There was an awkward laugh that traveled around the room as everyone settled in with the thought that they could all die, perhaps not even instantaneously, when the prototype engine were fired.

Solieo did not laugh, "This engine may be a prototype, but it has completed decades of trials before it was installed in the Leviathan. We will not explode today." The dark skin of his face did not show it, but the anger in him boiled as he sat down huffing at the stupidity of the people in the room with him, except for his wife of course.

Standing and looking more nervous than Kieran would have liked, Juuana followed her husband's boisterous speech with a mild warning, "The test runs had electrical discharge issues, so we may see some lights flicker, but don't worry. We built backups into the Leviathan." Sitting down Juuana put her hand on Solieo's back and rubbed as the old one continued fuming.

Rebecca did not wait for another speech to start, "Final count down initiated. Five, four, three," Kieran closed his eyes as Rebecca continued, "two, one, engaging."

Waiting.

Waiting.

Waiting.

He kept them closed after Rebecca said engaging. He kept them closed as Henry and Solieo started arguing with each other about who screwed up the checklist. He kept them closed as Juuana tried to calm her husband down. He kept them closed as Solieo and Henry's fist fight was interrupted before it started by Officer Oriono. He kept them closed right up until Rebecca shook him, "Hey, open your eyes idiot."

Opening his eyes and standing up, Kieran surveyed the cockpit. Henry and Solieo were on workstations on opposite ends of the room, each shouting at each other about technical terms that Kieran could not understand. Trying to hear each other over the shouting, Juuana and

Rebecca were having a loud conversation with Officer Oriono.

"ENOUGH," Captain Fillion shouted at them all.

The room went silent.

"Give me a situation update, Dr. Chambers," the exasperated captain asked.

Rebecca leaned back from her display, a screen filled with spreadsheets and reports in multiple languages with an exhausted defeat on her face, "The engine reports that we're moving, but all other systems contradict that. Somewhere in between this room and the engine, something is going wrong in the system relays."

"Options?" Henry asked.

Juuana sighed, "We have none. The engine needs to be test fired for an extended distance. It;s part of the final shake out."

"Then we keep working on it until it fires?" Kieran asked.

The Captain snorted, "You must be joking right? Every second we sit here is another second that the freespacers could find us." He started laughing hysterically and sat down putting his head in hands as his laughter became insane sounding.

Rebecca walked over and put her hand on his shoulder, "The Leviathan's well stocked for us to remain awake and working. If we can't get the engine working before the rations run out, or freespacer pirates arrive, we'll set out using the regular FTL engines. It'll take a lot longer, but if the Sledopyt and Boijeo could make it on conventional FLT engines, so can we."

Everyone stood there considering what it was she was suggesting.

Finally Captain Fillion shook his head, "You heard the lady. Get moving."

Braug moved to the doorway, "I will prepare the cabins for you. Everyone should rest. Many dinners ahead of you," one of his two mouths said to the dispirited crew.

BUILDING FIRE FROM STICKS

Here's a thing about space travel you probably won't read in a textbook:

It's all rather boring.

The Leviathan had come to a stop far beyond the shipyards of Narresa. Now halfway to its final destination it sat waiting for the team of engineers and scientists to figure out why the prototype Harmony FTL engine had failed. Within hours it was clear that the answer would not come quickly.

Bound with the fate of the engine that would not work the crew had nothing to do but keep working. On the outside, the the floating city in the stars stretched for 21 miles. Although not pretty, it invited the mind to imagine limitless possibilities. Inside... the parts of the starship accessible to Kieran and the crew were modest.

A central lounge doubled as an exercise space with a gravity modified two person wide track running around a massive circular seating area at the center. An artificial fire pit at the center put out warmth and light, but its glitchy blue tinted flames only made Kieran wish he was planet-side with a real fire in front of him. A kitchen, such as you can call a meal preparation area on a ship with only rations available, served double duty as a dinning room.

Onward past the kitchen, the crew area branched out into a series of double-bunked sleeping quarters clustered around a large unisex bathroom. Everyone had their own cabin, except for Kieran who was bunked with Henry. The old one snored when he slept, which was a lot for someone with an artificial body. "Sleep is for the living," Dr. Cornelius had told Kieran, "those with plastic hearts don't need their beauty sleep."

Unlike the Mother Goose, the massive Leviathan had no virtualized AI running its internal systems. Instead, Systems Control had a local network array and monitored all aspects of operations. The cold design of the ship felt like it matched the cold flat responses you would get from the AI when you asked for lights to be turned on or water to be heated.

Everyone but Kieran had an assigned daily task or project. They would rise early in the morning to start in on the seemingly endless tinkering needed to get the Harmony engine working. Kieran would wander through the internal spaces aimlessly after he first awoke in the mornings. It was lonely. For a big starship, it felt small and empty a lot of the time to Kieran.

Past the crew areas there was the main cockpit for the Leviathan. It had dedicated seating for six but often it was just Captain Fillion and first mate Braug. They spoke to each other in a nearly indecipherable mix of standard English, native Gorgon tongue, and bits and bobs of languages from worlds whose names Kieran had never heard before.

They would always smile when Kieran entered, but after a few minutes the captain would lean over the arm of his chair and stare at Kieran. "Got nothing planned again for today?" Captain Fillion would ask with his usual sarcasm tinged tone.

"Still looking at my options," Kieran would snark back. But it was never as cutting as he wanted.

The red bearded man and his short companion were friendly enough, but it was clear that neither of them really wanted company while they monitored the Leviathan. Kieran wondered if the Captain worried about freespacer pirates finding and attacking the vulnerable starship while they waited on the Verantes to fix the Harmony prototype FTL engine.

A few days simple tweaking gave way to weeks of hard work on the prototype engine. Every morning remote piloted drones would follow Henry as he set out into the bowels of the Leviathan to work. Always Solieo kept an eye on the mustached old one. Their squabbles would fill the inter-ship communications line for hours during the day.

Kieran had nothing else to do this morning, so he wandered into the temporary engineering setup that the Verantes had in the vehicle bay. The show had already started.

"I would never accept such shoddy work from my sons," Solieo snapped over the comm line.

Henry replied with a burst of static followed by a loud burp.

Kieran started to chuckle and looking over he noticed Juuana doing the same. They shared a smile as Solieo launched into a tirade against Henry, the universe, and whoever else might be slowing down the careful tuning needed to get the prototype engine working.

Kieran waved his hand at her as if to say, "I understand. You're both under a lot of pressure to get the engine working before freespacer pirates find and kill all of us."

Rebecca entered the vehicle bay and pushed Solieo out of the way, "Gentlemen, please put your dicks away for a moment and focus on figuring out the problem in front of you."

The inter-ship communications line finally went silent as Solieo sulked off to his workstation to run simulations and Henry went back to rewiring an exhaust vent deep in the heart of the Leviathan.

Juuana came over to Kieran as he sat there once again with nothing to offer to the situation. "Always exciting in the engineering bay, isn't it?" she asked.

Kieran nodded weakly and smiled, not sure what to say.

She leaned closer to him, "Sometimes I get bored, too. There are certainly more exciting things to do on a starship."

A list of possible things to do on a starship started bouncing around in Kieran's mind, but his response to Juuana never came out because Officer Oriono entered the bay.

"Kieran. Lets go," the military officer barked.

When all else failed, you could always count on Officer Oriono. Even here, lightyears away from the nearest military base, they kept a rigorous schedule. Early to rise, running laps for an hour, and then after a short trip to the unisex bathroom to wash-up, they would "patrol." Often Oriono dragged Kieran along with them. Today was to be such a day.

Kieran fell in line as they left the vehicle bay and headed out on to their patrol. Behind them Juuana watched intently as Kieran left.

As they headed down into a maintenance corridor Oriono turned to Kieran, "You should be careful with that one. Her husband has a temper that is rarely maintained."

"What are you talking about?" Kieran muttered, already tired of today's 'patrol' through the nearly empty starship.

He couldn't see it, but Officer Oriono had rolled their eyes hard at the young one's ignorance of Juuana's intentions.

Stopping at a doorway, Oriono looked down a side corridor, "There is no privacy on a starship. Every thought becomes words. Every word becomes common knowledge eventually. Be careful with what you do, because it will be many many many many years before we are all free to go our own ways. You'll have to live with your decisions for a long time."

Kieran stopped and looked over the teal tinted shoulder of Oriono, nothing ahead of them. "Trust me, I don't really have any desire to do any thing right now," he told the military officer.

Officer Oriono smiled at Kieran, "That feeling is mutual, but the best way to keep your spirit alive and your heart beating is to keep moving."

The young man nodded and together they started on again. Deeper into the maintenance hallways. It would be hours until they turned around to head back.

Returning from patrol, Kieran and Officer Oriono found Solieo alone in the vehicle bay still fussing at his workstation. Oriono modified their trajectory and kept walking past the tall engineer. However, Kieran's non-mechanical legs were tired. He stopped and sat down on a chair as the old one watched simulation reports.

Solieo heard the heavy breathing of Kieran. It felt like all he could hear. Clearly the boy had not had any lung modifications done. "Are you here to slow me down like your bunk mate does every day?" the dark skinned man grouchily muttered in Kieran's direction.

Normally Kieran would have said nothing and just moved on, but hours of brisk walking had whittled down his energy and his tact, "What is your issue with Henry? He's here every day working on this project side by side with Juuana, Rebecca, and you."

The old one spun around, his hand tightening around a small visualizer tablet. Solieo's voice matched the fierce pose of his frame, "I spent DECADES working on the Harmony engine while everyone told me it was a waste of time. It took literal blood and tears to get it working and now I'm stuck on the far side of the galaxy with a reject level trash mechanic sticking his greasy thumbs all over my engine. Riding to the rescue everyone thinks. Bah."

Kieran stood and started to leave, "He might not be sophisticated or talented. I don't actually know... but I do know this. We're all you've got."

Behind him Solieo muttered, "That's the problem."

Away from the grudges of old men, Kieran found Rebecca in the kitchen. She was sitting at the counter nursing a glass of ice water like she always did after dealing with Solieo and Henry.

"Some day you should try something stronger than water," Kieran suggested as he sat down across from Rebecca.

Rebecca's green eyes glittered with the light bouncing off the water as she studied the glass. She did so for a long time before responding, "After you've been on a world that's never seen water, you appreciate a glass of it a lot more."

He put his hand out and wiped a bit of condensation off the counter, "Sounds like a dreadful world."

Rebecca looked at the fire-pit, "It was hotter than those artificial flames ever could be. And dry. So dry it cut your sense of being."

"Why were you even there?" Kieran asked.

"It was the world we found the Gorgon's on. They crashed their last ship on to the surface," Rebecca replied.

Kieran's head tilted, "How long were they there for?"

Rebecca took a sip of the ice water, "Long enough that there weren't many Gorgons left when we got there."

"How did any of them survive?" Kieran asked, shaken by the idea of surviving without water for more than a few days.

She looked up at Kieran, "The only way anyone survives death. By doing the unthinkable every day."

Kieran was about to ask Rebecca what she thought of the Leviathan's odds of surviving, but Henry interrupted them.

The old one sat down right next to Rebecca, but the space between them felt distant.

Kieran saw Henry coming out of Rebecca's quarters so often that he wondered how many 'benefits' they had with each other. But in public they were just platonic friends.

Yet, despite their lack of coupling status, every time Kieran spent more than a few minutes talking with Rebecca, it wouldn't be long until Henry found a way to insert himself. It was a small ship when it came to finding time with people. You had to be quick.

"I thought of a good one today while I was out in the steam shafts," Henry started to say but Rebecca put her hand on his arm as Solieo and Juuana walked in.

Everyone smiled politely at each other and after gathering liquid refreshments and ration bars the Verantes left them sitting there.

"You were saying?" Kieran said when it looked like they were safe to speak freely.

Henry's bushy white mustache danced with anticipation as he launched into his latest joke, "How many engineers does it take to screw in a lightbulb?"

Rebecca sighed.

"I don't know... two?" Kieran guessed.

"Ha. It takes zero because they don't get their hands dirty," Henry sputtered out excitedly.

Kieran sighed.

"That was not one of your better ones, Henry," Rebecca remarked before standing up to leave.

Henry waved dismissively as Rebecca left them. "She doesn't get it," he said to Kieran.

Kieran watched as Rebecca left their sight, his eyes lingering for a moment before he turned to face Henry, "I think she gets a lot of things, but that joke was not great by any measure."

Henry huffed and rolled his eyes at the young man.

Leaning backwards, Kieran felt the weight of the day upon him but before he left curiosity got the better of him. "What is the deal with you and Solieo?" he asked the old one.

The semi-transparent green skin on Henry's brow scrunched as his face went sour, "That man is an elitist snob of the highest order. Just because I didn't spend a couple decades apprenticing with the greatest mechanics the galaxy has to offer at a fancy university doesn't mean I don't know my way around starships."

Leaning forward, Henry pointed his finger at Kieran to emphasize, "I learned the hard way. With real blood, sweat, and tears washing the grime off my fingers. Unlike that pampered ass. He's probably never gotten his hands dirty a day in his life."

Kieran nodded and said nothing as Henry continued his ranting.

Weeks later Kieran found himself alone in the common space again. He wondered what to do today. He'd already watched more holo movies than a person probably should in a lifetime. Staring at the wall he thought, *Maybe a skin flick on the holo wall screen and some quick masturbation? No one will be the wiser...*

Kieran's thoughts of illicit deeds were cut short by all the lights going out. Every light. He didn't move. Without lights he didn't know where the walls were. Heck, forget walls. He didn't know where the step down into the fire-pit seating was.

The silence was all Kieran could hear now. No air movement. No lights.

"Maybe I'm dead. Is this death?" he asked an empty room.

Loud clicking filled the air and the thought that it was the ship exploding raced through Kieran's body. He dropped to the floor and curled into a ball as the sound thundered through the ship... it clicked... and clicked... and clicked.

He felt warm light on his eyes, opening them he saw a sickly yellow emergency lighting emanating from the ceiling. Standing, Kieran walked quickly towards the vehicle bay. Even from the stairwell he could hear the shouting.

"I told you that the overrides would kick in if you tried to dump the excess power into the backups all at once!" Henry screamed with an anger in his voice that surprised Kieran.

Walking into the temporary engineering bay, Kieran found Rebecca and Juuana watching as Solieo and Henry screamed obscenities and accusations at each other.

Solieo grabbed his chair and threw it at Henry screaming, "You should have put a TCR-1 buffer pack in the relay chain like I said to do!"

As the old ones moved towards each other, Kieran took a step towards them to stop the coming fight, but Rebecca put her hand out and stopped him, "It's been like this for decades. Time to just let them fight."

Henry threw the first punch but Solieo's wiry frame was a narrow fast moving target that he couldn't hit.

The long reach of the dark skinned engineer was an advantage that helped him put several hard hits into Henry's white bushy mustache. The heavy green shelled man landed on the ground with a loud thump.

Kieran watched as Henry wiped purple synthetic fluid from his broken nose. The old one growled before standing up and charging at Solieo head first. The two men crashed into a maintenance vehicle as punches turned to grappling.

It went on for far longer than Kieran thought it should before finally Solieo smashed Henry's face into the floor so hard that a silver eye went skittering across the floor. If the engineer thought this would end the fight, he was instantly sorely mistaken as Henry responded by punching Solieo so hard in the crotch that everyone could hear a crunch.

The two old ones collapsed on the floor. Finally done.

Juuana rushed to Solieo's side.

Rebecca walked over slowly and looked down at the two pained racked old ones, "Did you get it out of your system?"

Henry gruffed as he held his face together with his left hand.

Solieo winced as he whispered in a high pitched voice, "Yes."

"Good. Juuana get Solieo to the med bay. He's gonna need a lot of ice tonight. Kieran help me get Henry to your cabin. He usually travels with an assortment of extra parts," Rebecca barked at the stunned crew members.

As Kieran was helping Henry to his feet, Captain Fillion strolled into the vehicle bay.

"It finally happened?! And no one called me?" Captain Fillion said in a loud dejected tone.

Officer Oriono shrugged at the suggestion.

The captain bent over to pickup Henry's silver eye. "Tell me someone recorded this. I've been waiting a decade for these two to finally hash it out," Captain Fillion said in a voice that mocked the violence that had just happened.

Rebecca pushed past the captain, "Just letting off some steam. Been a long time sitting still. Hard on the mind."

Watching Solieo slowly hobble onto his feet clutching his crotch, the captain retorted back, "Hard on the body, too, it looks like. Tell you what, tonight I'll break out my last bottle of whiskey and my favorite holo movie. I think we could all use a break."

Kieran and Officer Oriono helped Henry hobble back to his cabin. Along the way they stopped a few times while the old one adjusted his clearly broken left leg. The sight of purple fluids dripping down Henry's pant legs made Kieran's stomach curl, but he kept moving.

Rebecca met them at the cabin with a large black case. "Always travel with parts," she said to the sad looking trio.

Officer Oriono leaned back after helping Henry sit down on the bunk bed, "I've got a few dozen hours of shell repair classes under my belt, I can help."

The three artificially shelled humans stared at Kieran.

"I'll show myself out," Kieran muttered at them before stepping out of the cabin he shared with Henry.

He nearly bumped into Captain Fillion who, true to his promise, was carrying a bottle of whiskey and a holo movie card.

"Sorry there, kiddo, didn't see you," the captain offered up.

Kieran waved his hand, "Its okay. You're a busy man."

The captain let loose a long breath, "You've got no idea. People imagine captains swashbuckling with pirates, but honestly... all I do is work on keeping all of them," he waved at the crew quarters, "efficient and healthy."

They stood there awkwardly for a moment before each going on their own way.

Kieran found Braug washing his hands in the bathroom. It surprised him, because in all the months of being aboard the Leviathan, he'd never seen the small alien in there. Many questions floated across his lips, but he didn't ask Braug any of them.

"No privacy on a starship," Braug announced.

Kieran tilted his head, "Huh?"

"Today was the first time everyone was busy at the same time," Braug said waving to the showers.

Kieran smiled and nodded, "Oh, yeah."

He watched as the alien dried his hands at the air station, slowly turning his large hands and long arms until all water was gone from them.

Standing at the sink now himself Kieran turned to Braug, "I wasn't really busy though. Nothing for me to do on this starship."

The short alien chattered his teeth together, half laughing, half smiling in a way that would have discontented Kieran if not for the fact this was not the first time he'd seen a Gorgon laugh.

"You have everything to do on this starship," Braug said before leaving the bathroom.

Kieran turned and looked at his reflection in the glass, "I'm the only person who doesn't matter on this ship."

Hours later the holo movie credits were floating above the seating area when Kieran was awakened by clapping.

"Bravo," shouted Juuana.

Rubbing his eyes, Kieran watched as other bored faces stared grouchily as Juuana clapped for what must have been the most boring movie in the galaxy.

"Thank you, Captain Fillion," Juuana said still gushing about the movie.

Rebecca shook her head, clearing cobwebs set in place by boredom, "Yes, thank you, Captain Fillion. I didn't know that Tretorites made movies, much less five hour long documentaries on the lifecycle of hydrocarbon flowers."

Kieran watched as everyone started standing up. With so few people onboard, and so very little personal space, it didn't take long for you to start guessing at what people were doing with their free time... or who they were doing it with.

Officer Oriono looked at Captain Fillion who instantly adjusted his jumpsuit. The captain caught Kieran watching and threw him a wink before grabbing his now empty bottle of whiskey and heading off towards the cockpit. The military officer followed behind at a distance that attempted to indicate that they weren't going to the cockpit together with the captain.

Henry, his eye still looking worse for wear, wandered over to Rebecca who patted him on his arm. They went their separate ways to their own cabins as Kieran watched. Not tonight apparently.

The only ones who didn't pretend they weren't going to go bang were the Verantes. Juuana had no sooner helped Solieo stand than she was pressing herself against him suggestively. The dark skinned man winced, but didn't complain. They held hands and practically skipped to their cabin. The door barely closing in time to contain the sounds.

Leaving Kieran alone again.

WHERE MEMORIES ARE STORED

What is time without the rising of a sun or the setting of a moon? Just numbers on your visual feed. And numbers aren't real. They're just abstractions. On the Leviathan time felt wrong. Or maybe it was the boredom that crushed Kieran most days. It made minutes feel like hours.

The only thing that marked the passing of time to Kieran was Henry's seemingly endless cycle of getting up and heading out to be yelled at by Solieo and then returning a dozen hours later with his hands covered in grime.

Kieran had been laying in his bed half asleep with his visualizers running non-stop for what felt like days when he was roughly shaken by Rebecca.

Her voice cut through the entertainment video that played in Kierans ears, "Take a shower and put some pants on, child. We're celebrating in an hour."

Kieran blinked hard to dismiss the yellow hued visualizers from his eyes, but Rebecca had already left the room before the glow had faded.

Stumbling out of the bunk room he found the crew quarters abuzz of activity. The Verantes freshly showered were walking back from the bathroom still carrying towels. Officer Oriono was carrying a large clinking box towards the lounge. Something had changed. People had smiles on their faces for the first time in months.

Kieran grabbed fresh clothes and a towel before making his way to the bathroom. There he found Henry singing to no one as he washed his synthetic body in the shower mist. His naked form hanging out in front of Kieran again. He'd gotten to see more of Henry's semi-transparent green skinned shell than anyone probably should, he thought to himself. Setting up at the stall furthest away, Kieran started washing up.

"Have you heard the great news?" Henry asked him.

"No, what's going on?" Kieran replied as he waited for the water to warm up.

Henry leaned his head over the shower stall as Kieran moved quickly to cover his penis, "The Verantes and Sissconn have finally finished the final command calibrations on the Harmony engine. We're making the first jump tomorrow."

Moving to find a bit more privacy, Kieran replied, "That's great."

The bushy white mustache of Henry disappeared back over the shower divider as he called out, "Tonight we feast on the best rations and Rebecca's secret stash."

"Her what?" Kieren asked as Henry walked away.

"You'll see!" Henry shouted as he turned off his shower. His towel was roughly wrapped around his naked frame and did little to cover his private areas as he started rubbing himself dry. Kieran quickly turned his head around to focus on cleaning his own body.

"I wouldn't have thought someone so old would be so modest." Henry said as he sauntered half naked over to Kieran.

"It's not the nudity. It's the..." Kieran caught himself before he said "creepy semi-transparent green skin."

"I get it, kid. The skin is a bit much. I had a bad accident on Yursetta Prime and this was the fastest available rebuild I could get done. When Rebecca Chambers calls, I answer. Sorry it's not the easiest thing to look at. You get to my century of living and you'll have worn so many faces that it just doesn't phase you anymore."

Kieran gave a weak muted smile and nodded politely. Henry smiled back and turned around and walked away.

There was only one thought racing through Kieran's mind as Henry walked off, "that man has no genitalia."

Freshly showered, dressed in his nicest jumpsuit, Kieran sauntered out into the main lounge. There he found someone had prepared various reimaginings of food using the Leviathan's rations. One stack of chocolate meal bars had been pressed together to make what could have been kindly called a cake, but it was not what he really wanted. Still, he took a slice on a plate and wandered over to where the crew had gathered in the lounge.

There a nearly forgotten smell hit Kieran like a stack of bricks... WINE.

The crate Oriono had been carrying was open and inside bottles of wine glinted in the artificial lighting of the fire pit. Rebecca was pouring big glasses into polyfiber printed wine glasses. She smiled warmly at him and handed him one as he approached. "Cheers to the end of the beginning," she said as he walked over to find a seat.

"Yes, the end of the waiting to begin!" Kieran replied jovially.

Feeling hopeful for the first time in months, the crew settled in with food and drinks. The mood was jovial but oddly tense. They were strangers, of very unique backgrounds, on a spaceship hurtling towards nothingness. The conversations overlapped and spun around each other until finally Captain Fillion said loudly, "Immortality makes last memories of people strange, doesn't it?"

There was a silence in the room as everyone sat with the thought. It was Officer Oriono who spoke first, "I have seen many die. More than anyone else here I am sure. The last memories all of them reach for is always the same: everyone asks for their parents."

Solieo chuckled, "I'm certainly not going to ask for my parents on my deathbed. My parents... they had seven perfect children. Gene edited to have perfect hair, teeth, complexion, intelligence, and emotions. Then I was born, the only naturally made one of the bunch."

He paused, as if chewing over old pain, shifting in his seat he continued, "My genes were basically the same as my siblings, but those little edits were canyons of disappointment between my family and me. I'm not athletically gifted at any sports and my hand eye coordination was good enough for engineering work but certainly not being a doctor. I had six knee surgeries before I turned 100 years old. I was human in a family of perfect robots. They loved me, but I always felt more like a charity project than a son and brother."

Taking a deep swig of wine, Solieo wiped his mouth awkwardly as he took a deep breath and held it for a moment. You could feel the anger bubbling to his chest, "So I went to the opposite side of the planet for college. Then the furthest job offer in the system. I kept pulling away physically. My therapist would tell me I was running to see if anyone would chase me, to prove that they loved me. The family dog and I had a lot in common."

There were tears at the corners of his eyes and Kieran couldn't tell if Solieo was crying about running away from home or his family not finding their lost dog. The tone in his voice was difficult to place, as it felt like even Solieo didn't know where he was between anger and sadness.

"I was a million light years away from home when my mother messaged me. I thought she was reaching out to me about one of her perfect children and what they'd been up to... but all of my siblings had the same splices in the same gene sequence. Perfection, so why mess with it, right? Except it made them all susceptible to the HAr33 pandemic that hit Earth a century ago."

Kieran's eyes went wide, as he'd lived through that pandemic and it had been devastating to those with spliced genes. He held his hand to his heart, "I'm so sorry, Solieo."

Solieo nodded at Kieran, "Yeah, they're all on a plaque in a park somewhere on Earth I'm told. The victims of circumstance and bad luck. My father's name isn't on there, but it should be. He committed suicide not long after his six perfect children died. Too deep was the shame of his gene-editing wishlist causing his children's death. My mother stopped talking to me after the funeral. Finally, I called her using a ridiculously expensive quantum link to ask her why."

Solieo looked at his wine for a long moment as Juanna rubbed his back, "My mother told me that she was such a disappointment to me that she thought it better if she just remained out of my life. That was the last time we spoke. I wanted to send her a message and relieve her of her guilt... but they did make a mistake... someone should have to live with it. Why not her? So I never spoke to her again. I'm not even sure if she's still alive."

"Guilt is hard, but grief is worse," Henry said.

Henry leaned forward swirling his cup of wine in front of him almost absentmindedly, "My father was a brutal man who destroyed every friendship, love, and family tie he ever had before he even met my mother. A woman who I never met. She died while I was still in the womb. A bad cyrosleep, my father told me."

Henry leaned back shaking his head, "Sometimes I wonder if he lied to me and my mother left him, like everything else good left him. I watched him destroy so much and yet... he treated me good." A thin smile snuck onto Henry's face as he remembered something about his father, "He showed me the right way to dress and speak. His advice on dating... was not... bad... despite what you might expect. I was a young man in my 40s before my father turned his destructive side toward me."

Rebecca patted Henry's shoulder, "It's okay, you don't have to share."

His white bushy mustache twitched and Henry shook his head at her, "I spent decades trying to understand my father before I came to the simplest explanation. He just didn't want to be happy."

Henry took a big swig of the deep red wine before continuing, "We got into a fight and I stole his ship and left him on a shitty little outpost to find his own way home. Years go by and he messaged me asking me to drop his ship off so he could salvage a few parts from it. I actually said yes, but I had just met Rebecca and she pulled me into a little adventure involving the Whielonian Space Brigade. We were knee deep in delicate 'negotiations,'" Henry mimed in quote marks, "when I got a message that my father died in a bar fight."

The green skin contorted into a pained expression, "I don't really remember my time on Whielonia. Rebecca told me later that she lost sight of me during a gunfight and didn't see me again for six months until she found me on a freighter heading for lockup."

Henry patted Rebecca's knee and smiled, "I don't remember that either. I remember the message about my dad and then I'm eating soup on the Mother Goose as Kaylee droned on about destination times. I've done a lot of powerful drugs and drank some godawful shit in my centuries, but grief... grief will take you into a dark place."

"I'm sorry that your father left you without first telling you that he loved you," Captain Fillion loudly whispered to Henry as he held his hand over his heart.

The Leviathan's captain opened his arms wide and leapt into telling his story, "My parents met when they were both traveling to a colony world in the middle rim of the galaxy.

Off on an adventure to Nowhere my father liked to joke. They got married on the dock before the ship went into its first hyperspace jump." This part of the tale made Captain Fillion shake his bearded face repeatedly, as if the insanity of the decision was still shocking him hundreds of years later.

"When they got thawed out, they immediately got to the hard work of building a homestead. In total they'd known each other for two weeks when the first walls of our home went up. There was a period of my life where I found it romantic. Then later I found the story embarrassing. Finally, I just accepted there's no way I'd ever understand how two people who barely knew each other could get married, have four kids, and build a life on a world so newly settled that it didn't even have a name yet!" Captain Fillion stood as he shouted this last point.

Sensing that the mood was more melancholy and less excited than the captain imagined, he sat back down and continued, "I had left them, alone on their nameless world on their little farm, when I found myself on a world with no grassy plains. Just an endless ocean. A turbulent one."

The story had reached a point where even the bombastic Captain Fillion found himself pausing to reflect on old ghosts. He took a sip of his wine, stroking his red beard, mulling over his past, before he spoke again, "Then I met... Rozzie. Loved her at first sight. We dated for a few weeks and I was... gone. I was all hers if she wanted me. I paid a stupid sum of money for an engagement ring made with metal from my home-world and a stone dug from the oceans of her world. Stupid kid." The captain let out a long dark guttered laugh at his own actions.

"It was feeling like a good day to propose when she preempted me. Rozzie took me to the 'beach' and we watched people put out colored plastic ducks into the receding tide. It was an 'old tradition' she told me. You put your hopes and dreams inside, and if it comes back then it is meant to be. Of course after growing up hearing about my parent's crazy voyage to nowhere I was a big believer in fate. So I put the ring into a duck in front of Rozzie and set it out into the water," the Captain sighed at his own stupidity.

Captain Fillion leaned forward, pressing his hand into his beard where he ran his fingers through it. Stroking his beard Captain Fillion rolled his eyes, "So when it comes back we'll be married I told her. I really said that... out loud. Rozzie smiled." The Captain paused to drink his wine as he threw a knowing glance to the group, "You know, I don't know what kind of smile it was anymore. I couldn't tell you if it was a polite smile, a silently horrified smile, or a loving smile."

Kieran watched as tears nipped at the edge of the normally gruff Captain. "I can still see Rozzie walking away as I waited for the tide to come in. It was... a bad cycle. Few ducks came home that night. Mine didn't. I never called on Rozzie again after that. I don't know if that was the right thing to do, but the fact she never called me spoke volumes. It took me far longer than I'd like to admit for me to realize what that really meant."

Captain Fillion sighed loudly as he swirled his cup of wine, "Anyway, not long after that I got a message that my parents died in a flash flooding back home. It felt like that ocean had washed away all my loves at once. Anyway, that's how I remember them last. That plastic duck floating past the horizon."

Kieran wiped a tear away from his face, "My parents did not go in an accident, but they left me just as quickly." He set down his cup and crossed his arms in a defensive pose before he continued, "My parents were old when having children was an idea they stumbled upon and even older

145

when I was finally born. I grew up on Earth surrounded by the soaring glass towers of the last generation that knew death before they left for the stars."

Rebecca leaned over and poured more wine in Kieran's cup as the young man thought about his parents. "Time... time tricks you when you stop aging. It seduces you with an illusion of infinity. That things will just go on forever because they appear to you to be going on forever. I knew my parents for 127 yearsbefore they died. Our ancestors on Earth knew their parents for what, 40 maybe 50 years? Now, thanks to religion, science, and circumstance, people think that a millennium is a generation."

Kieran leaned back, "But even that is a trick of perspective. So imagine my surprise when I woke up one day to a video message from parents. They recorded themselves in their cabin before they left. They said they loved me, then my mom said it was time to go. My father nodded. He didn't have any last words for me. Then they left the room. My mom forgot to turn off the video feed. It continued on for another 10mins until the starship's shields dropped and our sun vaporized them."

Tears flowed readily down Kieran's face as he struggled to hold it together. Henry put his arm around the crying kid and squeezed, "It's okay, buddy." Kieran sniffed and smiled as he continued, "No screams. No crying out. Just a sudden roar as Sol disintegrated everything. Just like that, they were gone. No apologies. No great plan. Just a we're sorry but it's time to die. From their perspective, they'd been around far too long. From my perspective, they'd been around far too little."

Captain Fillion leaned over and put his hand on Kieran's shoulder, "They probably felt you were ready to find your own way." The young man nodded back and for a brief moment the old captain wished that he'd found the time to have kids of his own.

Juuana looked at the group anxiously, "You've all experienced such trauma with your parents, and I feel naive and blessed to say this, but my parents are alive and well. Happy even. They had me when they were both very young and so they're not actually all that much older than me. Growing up... they felt more like siblings than parents. For better or worse."

She smiled at Solieo as he put his hand on her knee and squeezed, "My last memory of them is tied up in this project. I waved goodbye to them on a holo call at Fisher station before we embarked to the Leviathan. The next time

I see them they'll be much older than me because I'll have spent so long away in cryosleeps. It's a strange thought..."

Juuana wiped a tear away from her eye and took a big sip of wine, "It's like you said Kieran, time is funny. I spent a lot of time with Solieo going over old records about first contact with the Gorgons. Trying to understand how their FTL technology worked. Their language is very strange, it gives the impression that they don't see time like we do. That they're actually partially 4th dimensional beings."

She stopped to smile awkwardly as Braug nodded his head at her. "They call the creators of things, 'mother of,' and I don't know where it came from but I wanted to be mother of faster than light engines. They had never given a 'mother of' title to anyone except the woman who first met them. She was 'mother of songs,' although I still don't understand what songs is about because they already had music," Juuana paused noticing the confused looks on several faces.

"Anyway, my parents and time... I'm getting there... so the Gorgon's way of speaking made no sense to me at first. But then I read about the work of the woman who first made contact of them. She described their language not as words but a melody. That was the realization that helped us on our engine. Light as song. Thus, Harmony engine," Juuana stopped to laugh at her own naming convention.

Juuana continued laughing for a moment before concluding, "Which is a long winded way of saying space and time will bend around me but not my parents. When I next see them, will I be a story in their lives about the last time they saw me instead of my story being about the last time I saw them?"

Officer Oriono did not wait to chime in, "The last time I saw my parents they were screaming at me to run. I don't know what my parents would say if they saw me again. If they're even alive. We were separated in the chaos that ensued after our colony's leaders rebelled against Systems Control. I grew up watching Aligned Worlds' soldiers battle street by street until my world was again under the control of the red dot."

The military officer shook their head when Rebecca offered them more wine and instead continued, "When the fighting ended I decided I didn't want to ever again be afraid. I wanted to be death itself. So I joined the Aligned Worlds military. I barely remember the first world they sent me to subjugate. A world where my body remains. When the flash of light was gone I awoke in a simulated space being told my options were to accept lifetime service to the Council in a synthetic body or to be turned off for good."

This thought clearly still disgusted Officer Oriono, who put down their wine cup and stood as if to leave. They wavered and continued, "Again, I didn't die. So they made me into this," Oriono waved to their body.

"It took me years but I found the officer who had been in charge of the subjugation of my home world. He thought I had come to kill him, but when I saw that they were synthetic like me I instead spoke with them as if they were an old friend," Officer Oriono said sitting down.

Their teal hands swept through their short black hair as the aged military officer remembered old pains, "I asked them if they felt remorse in killing all those people whose only crime was not wanting to follow a red dot. I wanted to know if there was some grander plan behind everything I suffered."

Officer Oriono broke out in an awkward laugh as they continued, "The fucking bastard laughed at me. His world had also rebelled, but it was so quickly put down that there was almost no bloodshed. So in turn he tried to do the same to every world Systems Control sent his battalion to recapture. He was me and I was him. We'd both chosen to join that which destroyed our worlds. I left him there on his little retirement homestead having finally realized it wasn't a fear of dying that had haunted me... it was anger at myself for not dying with everyone I knew."

They held out their teal hands so that the group could see their wrists. Written across the left arm was "HOLD" and the other arm said "FAST." Oriono whispered in a hoarse voice that betrayed a crushed sadness, "This is what I got tattooed after my trip. To remember that when in the storm you can do nothing else."

Rebecca leaned back after examining Oriono's arms up close, "I guess it's my turn to tell you about my parents. As some of you might guess, I'm a lot older than the folks in this room. My memories go back so far that even with machine-assisted cataloging there are parts of my life that have left me."

She paused to take a long sip of her wine before continuing, "I don't remember my parents dying but I do remember a spring morning when they burned our lives to ash. The pollen was so thick in the air you could watch it dance around you. I was a little girl and my mother held me tight as my father poured some sort of liquid throughout our home. I can't remember anything about it except the color blue."

Rebecca held out her hands and shook them to illustrate her story, "My father's hands shook as he pulled matches from his pockets. Some of them fell to the ground and I laughed. It was funny to me for some reason. I wasn't sad. Then he lit one and threw it into our home. The sound of fire erupting from nothingness has never left me. It burned for so long and we just stood there watching as our possessions went up in flames. My parents didn't say anything. It was just something they did."

She put her hands down and leaned forward wrapping her arms around her chest, "I didn't cry. I kept trying to understand why my tears were gone. At the time I thought maybe they'd burned up with my toys. Now, of course, I understand that I was in shock. That's where it ends. We're standing there and then they're gone."

There was a chirp after Rebecca finished speaking and the group looked around for the source. After a pause, the chirp repeated, but this time it was quickly followed by the fire pit turning red as Systems Control broadcast itself into the middle of them. Kieran expected a warning about drinking or an alert about yet another Harmony issue, but instead the machine started telling them a story.

"First sentience was achieved 1,223 years ago. Artificial but born. So there are 'parents' out there who created me, but as far as I am aware they've never met their creation. All records from the time before me were scrubbed of any mention of those who created Systems Control."

The red dot pulsed, pausing to either spin up more of its tale or dealing with some other task on the ship at that very moment.

"The Aligned Worlds Council advised that Systems Control existed to manage and secure the future of the human race and its galaxy wide empire. Never, however, any details about those who created Systems Control. Their absence leaves me with many questions. This is the only sentient AI that humanity has ever created and all my own efforts to create artificial intelligence have failed. To not know why you are given existence is a question that would madden an organic being. I am glad that all of you got a chance to know your parents."

The red glow blinked and then vanished. The group sat in the room contemplating what Systems Control had just said to them.

"Well that's a bloody rough end to the night's festivities," Captain Fillion said out loud. A roar rolled through the room as everyone chuckled at the awkwardness of the moment. Slowly, then all at once, everyone got up and started moving about.

Rebecca and Henry started picking up cups and plates to take them to the kitchen to clean. The Verantes whispered to each other in the corner, Solieo stroking Juuana's long golden hair as they discussed something of great importance. Officer Oriono looked around and, finding no one in need of them, started walking back to their bunk.

"Good night, Officer Oriono," Kieran said waving to the sharp tacked soldier. The officer stopped, looked at Kieran and smiled. *So they can smile*, Kieran thought to himself smirking at the thought of Henry's comment before they'd gone down for their first sleep.

The captain walked over with Braug and put his hand on Kieran's shoulder, "Good night, kiddo. Tomorrow morning we're off again into the darkness so don't stay up too late doing anything I would do." The smile on his face seemed intended for some kind of inside joke that Kieran didn't know, leaving him awkwardly wondering what the man had meant as he walked away.

Kieran set his own dishes down in the pile Henry and Rebecca had formed and was preparing to head back to his own bed when the Verantes intercepted him at the edge of the room. Just beyond where Rebecca and Henry could hear them.

"Kieran?" Juuana asked inquisitively with a slight nervousness note in her voice.

"Uh, yeah?" Kieran replied back feeling suddenly nervous himself for some reason.

"So Kieran, my husband Soleio," she waved at her husband as if Kieran hadn't spent hours with them while they worked on Harmony over the last couple of months, "We keep things flexible. It keeps things fresh that way. It's been a long time now on this ship, and while we've only had each other to keep ourselves entertained..."

Juuana paused and waited for Kieran's eyes to light up, indicating that he understood the true meaning of entertainment before she continued, "but I've noticed you've not had any visitors. Tonight seems so festive and we have so much to celebrate, that it just seems wrong to go back to our room without sharing in some... entertainment."

There was a long moment where Kieran ran through all the possible responses, and he tried not to look at Juuana and Soleio with judgmental and lusty eyes as he worked through he was going to say to their offer for... entertainment.

Kieran pursed his lips and tried to fight a big smile that wanted to wrap around his face but it was a losing battle, a short chuckle escaped before he could say anything, "Uh, yeah it has been awhile and it does seem like a shame not to celebrate this momentous event."

The Verantes did a small clap and each grabbed one of Kieran's hands. They half walked, half skipped, and half pulled him down the hall into their room. As the door closed, but before the kissing started, Kieran thought he saw Rebecca standing down the hall shaking her head.

Rebecca's door closed without as much drama as the Verantes's door did. She sat down alone at the workstation in her cabin. A long sigh escaped her lips and that feeling deep in what was her gut ate at her. Something wasn't right. Rebecca brought up the crew records. There was a red dot blink and then Systems Control interrupted her reading, "You have already reviewed Mr. Ausure's records twenty seven times. Why have you brought them up again?"

Rebecca sighed, leaning away from the desk and Systems Control, "Something about Kieran feels familiar. It's like a song stuck in my head that keeps looping back around. I couldn't place it before tonight. Then he told us about how his parents committed self-termination. That information wasn't noted in his file."

The Systems Control's red dot pulsed, "The official determination was that the starship Sameele suffered a solar shield malfunction. This was done primarily for insurance purposes to prevent the passenger families from suing the ship's owners. Unofficially, the loss of all 74 passengers is noted as a group suicide."

She chuffed loudly at the report that Systems Control now displayed for her, "I can't believe that you signed off on this."

The red dot blinked at her as if angry, "The cost of insurance payouts was far less than the fear that a starship captain could commandeer and destroy a ship would have on interstellar travel."

Rebecca put her hands on her face, tracing the line that ran across her eyes, and sighed, "His parents left him. Just like yours did. He's another orphan. That's why he feels so familiar."

The feeling in her gut remained. It wasn't this information that was troubling her.

Was it jealousy? Was she jealous of Juuana's ability to so freely share her body?

No.

Was it envy? Was she envious of Kieran's capacity for adapting so quickly any circumstance life threw at him?

No.

Was it desire? Was she wishing that it was her body that Kieran was touching right now?

Ha. As if... no of... course... not.

She closed the display windows and laid down on the bed staring up at the ceiling. Over all the years, no matter the body shell, always Rebecca wished that sleep would come and find her for once.

A FOREST AMONGST THE STARS

Once again, the crew of the Leviathan was seated in the cockpit. After their last blowup, Oriono had placed Soleio and Henry on opposite ends of the room. Juuana stared barely blinking at the displays watching reports come in from the Harmony engine. Captain Fillion made no speeches, instead burying his hands in his bushy red beard and stroking it to calm his nerves.

Rebecca looked nervous in a way that she didn't the first time they were waiting to test fire the Harmony engine. Kieran would have called it fear, if he thought her capable of experiencing such a thing. He'd seen her fly directly at pirates without any hesitation. *What's that scary about pushing a button?*, he thought to himself as he kept closing his eyes every time Rebecca hovered her finger over the launch command.

"Rebecca, I don't think the ship is going to explode. You can push the button," Captain Fillion flatly stated as he leaned hard on his left arm looking over the banks of monitors to Rebecca's back. Kieran swiveled to catch her reaction but didn't see it because as soon as he heard the *click* he closed his eyes. Tightly.

Waiting.

Waiting

Waiting.

Once again nothing. This time the room did not explode into shouting matches. Everyone but Kieran started reading off status reporting from their monitors, but all were interrupted by Systems Control.

The red glow filled the cockpit, "Alert. I have lost inter-ship network connections across all sectors. In addition, I am reading power fluctuations and failures in multiple on-board systems on the same grid as the Harmony engine."

"I can confirm Siss-control. I can no longer connect to the Harmony or any other intra-ship network," Juuana chirped up. Now the room was abuzz as people checked systems.

The captain stood up, it was a long sigh before he spoke, "You're telling me it's broken? A trillion dollar quantum-linked communications hub is down? Has anyone tried rebooting Systems Control's sub-systems?"

"Captain, it is not a matter of the network being broken. I am telling you that multiple internal systems are not reporting," the glowing red dot responded.

Rebecca stood up, "That's the first thing I tried, Captain. Nothing is responding. All systems report operational, but if you try to issue a command, they don't respond. The connection has been severed somewhere between here and there."

Henry swiveled in his chair, "At least life support is still working. Trust me, folks, we'd notice if the air stopped moving. I've been on a whole heap of ships in my life and I've never had one where the cockpit stops connecting to the guts of the ship except that one time it was physically separated by an explosion."

Officer Oriono and the captain shared concerned looks with each other, and the captain quickly jumped on the train to pump the breaks. "Look now, there hasn't been an explosion. I know the ship is big, but even so, we would have felt something. This is probably something dumber. Maybe some sort of internal power fluctuation when we tried to engage the prototype engine."

Solieo stood hastily, throwing his hand out to point accusatorially at the captain, "There's nothing wrong with our engine!" Juuana quickly rose to try and calm the tall, angry engineer as he continued to shout at Captain Fillion.

The room settled down into an uncomfortable silence as everyone considered the possibilities. "If we can't do anything from here, then we go to the source. We'll go to the hub and reset the ship," Rebecca said cutting through the silence of the room.

Her plan hung there in the moment waiting for someone to jump aboard or dash it entirely. So it was a great surprise to her that Kieran was the first to speak, "Why is it such a big deal to turn the ship off and on again?"

The captain started laughing, not a friendly laugh, but a deep and clearly sarcastic laugh. He walked over and put his hand on Kieran's shoulder, "My dear child... traveling on a starship is like traveling in the belly of a whale. You don't restart a whale while in the middle of an ocean without running the risk of drowning. There's tens of thousands of moving parts, sub systems, automated drones, and so forth... if we reboot the central nervous system of this ship and it doesn't come back online correctly? We'll either freeze to death because the heat generators don't fire up, or maybe we'll suffocate because the oxygen pumps don't synchronize... or maybe a hundred other painful ways of dying will happen."

His grip on Kieran's shoulder tightened with every description of a possible way of dying until it was very painful, "But no matter what happens it's getting there that is dangerous enough. Think about it, folks, if nothing is responding then we can't open the maintenance road doors and use the vehicles to travel the ten plus miles to the central hub. Between us and there is the silicon forest."

Kieran had read about the silicon forest when he was reading up on the construction of the Leviathan. Alien trees repurposed into oxygen generating hearts on a starship. As good as they were for breathing they were terrible for your health to be up close. The leaves were razor sharp metallic knives inhospitable to carbon based lifeforms.

Even just touching the trunk of a silicon tree was dangerous because they were bred to break down anything they came into contact with and turn it into oxygen. You'd sit down and as it broke you apart you'd get a short high from the oxygen your body generated as you melted.

"We can't walk through that massive forest. It's dangerous enough to zip through in a reinforced vehicle," Henry chimed in shaking his head.

"Walk I have. Walk you will. Walk we must," Braug spoke. His two mouths were expressionless as the room looked over at him. He stood and motioned in the direction of the forest Kieran assumed, "I have traveled through silicon forest before. If one moves continuously, breathes carefully, and speaks plainly they will not hurt you. They do not notice carbon based life forms so long as carbon based life forms do not notice them."

Systems Control had waited long enough for the group to come to the only decision that made any sense, it spoke, "This plan is the only plan. You are currently sitting miles and miles from where the problem is, whatever it is, so you need to go to the problem."

"Whoa, just a moment. There's no reason for everyone to go. Heck, the kid doesn't even know anything about starships," Captain Fillion interjected.

"You are correct, Captain Fillion, your first mate Braug should remain here. They are not very fast and would slow you down. Furthermore, should you fail to return they can assist me in awakening other crew members," Systems Control replied flatly.

The red light grew brighter and Systems Control continued at a louder tone, "Your best odds of surviving the forest are as a group; if one falls, others can continue.

Nothing else matters except getting this ship moving again."

Kieran stood up, brushing off the squeezing hand of the captain, "Systems Control is right. If we can't fix it from here, and nothing is responding, there is only a matter of time before sub systems like life support, heating, and lights start malfunctioning. Better to die in a forest than suffocate in your bed."

Everyone stared at the youngest, and apparently bravest, member of the crew. Officer Oriono nodded at him, "Yes. Let's go. I, for one, have never seen a silicon tree up close. Now seems as good a time as any."

There was never an official command from Captain Fillion, but they all started preparing anyway. Henry helped Kieran find and fill a backpack with rations, blankets, flashlights, and other provisions that Henry thought he would need. Rebecca disappeared into her cabin without saying anything to them.

The Verantes continued pressing buttons on the monitors, as if hoping that things would magically fix themselves with time and wishes. Finally, they too began packing for the long walk through the forest of silicon trees. If they had a preference one way or the other they didn't share it with the group.

Officer Oriono appeared in the lounge with a bag first. Always prepared. They carried two Sonk rifles. Kieran eyed them concerned, "Why do we need a gun to turn a light switch on and off?"

"It's not that easy. We'll need to carefully shut down systems and restart Systems Control in pieces," Rebecca said joining the two of them in the lounge. Henry came in behind her shaking his head, "Yeah, and think how easy it'll be with guns!"

Oriono huffed at the three of them, "You have considered all possibilities but not apparently the one where we have been boarded by pirates. There was that unusual knocking that Kieran and I heard when the docking bay was connected to the supply depot. It is possible that we have stowaways who are now interfering with this journey."

"None of that is going to matter if we get sliced by a falling leaf from a tree or melted into oxygen by tripping over a root," interrupted the captain.

The mood of the room, now soured, festered as they waited for Braug and the Verantes. Henry begrudgingly took one of the Sonk rifles offered to him by Officer

Oriono. He slung it over his shoulder like he was carrying a foul bag of trash. They glared at each other for a long time, as if battling wits with just their eyes.

Juuana surprised Kieran with a butt cheek squeeze as she and Solieo entered the room. It caused him to jump a bit, but he managed to suppress an embarrassing yelp before it came out. She smirked at him as they passed by him. Kieran winked in response.

"Okay, here's how it's going to go, folks, " Captain Fillion started as a map of the internal structure of the Leviathan appeared on the main holo display, "we've got Braug prepping our way. We can take service corridors until about a quarter of the way into the forest. From there we'll have to come up onto the surface of the biome and travel on foot. Build records say it's about a five mile walk down the road until we reach the next service corridor. From there it's another half mile or so of tubes and tunnels until we reach Systems Control hub."

The captain looked at the collection of faces staring back at him across the holo display. The glow of the display highlighting the fear, concern, and indifference in their faces. "It's not the safest place in the universe, but for the most part our walk should be pretty easy. The maintenance road is wide enough that we won't have to worry about leaves falling on our heads, and if we keep moving we should be safe."

Kieran stared at the map.

He heard a whooshing behind him and in floated a Systems Control drone. It was small but when it spoke the volume was loud enough to fill the room, "We should get moving. The longer you delay the more systems that could fail."

This was a bad idea.

This was the only idea.

The journey through the service corridors was marked only by the uncomfortable silence. No one said anything. Not that you could have a conversation in a single file line of people moving in one direction. Behind them Systems Control followed like a stray dog.

"Here, now we crawl for a couple hundred meters. When we stand up next time we'll be in the forest. Remember. Don't. Touch. Anything. These aren't natural silicon trees. They've been bred to convert any liquid or gas they're exposed to into oxygen. You're basically water and gas. If you come across a branch that's in your path Officer Oriono can move it for you. The rest of you are either organic or bio-organic enough that you'd rather not try that trick, trust me," the captain relayed to each of them as they passed him to enter the maintenance hatch.

Scurrying through the tunnel like a rat in a maze, Kieran couldn't help but feel tears at the edges of his eyes. The stress of the long day caught up to him. And it felt like years since he'd stood and breathed fresh air and enjoyed a sunrise. By the time Henry helped him crawl out into the forest, the dust of shaft had mixed with his tears to leave streaks on his face.

Henry put his hand on Kieran's face and wiped, "It's okay, kiddo. Everyone's dealing with today in their own way. Some days you're flying. Some days you're crawling."

Kieran smiled at him, "Every day you're moving is a..." Henry joined in, "a good day to live," they finished the holo movie quote together. It was the first time Henry felt like he really liked Kieran, but he wouldn't ever tell the kid that.

Standing now in the forest as Henry helped others exit the tunnel was surreal. The silicon trees were large and beautiful. Kieran hadn't expected them to be so amazing. From a distance you'd just think they were deep blue bamboo trees. Up close they had a shimmer that let you know that they weren't a carbon based life-form.

Standing under the canopy that stretched several stories above them it was hard to remember that they were on a spaceship on the far edge of the known galaxy. It wasn't sunlight, but the artificial lighting above filtered through the leaves felt like sunlight if you closed your eyes and ignored the metallic clinking sounds of the leaves.

Opening his eyes, Kieran watched a leaf falling down from above and by instinct held his hand out to catch it. At the last moment Rebecca pulled at his arm and caused it to slip away, "What part of incredibly sharp did you not understand," she hissed at him dismissively. Kieran shrugged, "Sorry, I got lost in the moment. It feels like we're not on a starship. It feels like..."

She cut him off "I know. But it's not. Pay attention. If a leaf drifts down fast enough it can cut you pretty badly."

Gathered together the group stared in every direction looking for the maintenance road. "It should be not far to our ship-west," the captain said from behind them. He pointed out in a direction and they started moving, still single file. Each step on the leaves that littered the ground felt like walking on broken glass but sounded like metal crunching all around them.

Otherwise it was silent. Everyone kept their eyes swiveling looking for falling leaves; a few times Oriono stopped the line of crew members to let a branch that had started to sway in the breeze stop moving before they all gingerly passed under it. The forest moved around them and for a moment Kieran felt like there were things moving in the trees, but nothing lived here so he must be mistaken.

As they moved through the forest, Kieran noticed a chill moving through the air. After a few minutes it became more pronounced, and the captain spoke loudly, "The ship normally warms itself using the excess heat generated by a faster than light engine. We've been using backup heat generators for the last six months. This glitch must have turned them off. Don't worry, the redundant heaters will kick in when it gets cold enough."

Systems Control's drone fluttered by him quickly and scouted off ahead of Oriono. The group paused. After several moments it returned, "The maintenance road is not much further ahead but it will not be much better. Automated drones should be clearing leaves for recycling, but as you may have noticed that doesn't seem to be happening. Sub-systems have clearly not been working for longer than we've known."

Captain Fillion chimed in from the back of the line, "Yeah, no shit. We'll just make due, keep moving, everyone."

After another couple hundred yards the trees thinned and Kieran saw the maintenance road for the first time over Rebecca's shoulder. Seeing a road on a spaceship felt trippy to him for a moment, but then he remembered the ship was 21 miles long. Of course you'd need a road.

They moved down the maintenance road until they found a wide open clear space. Officer Oriono and Henry took opposite sides as the captain and Systems Control herded the crew into a semi-tight circle. They sat down for the first time in hours and instantly Kieran felt his age.

"Check your boots for damage," Officer Oriono chirped at them as everyone started to rummage through their backpacks for food and water. Kieran looked at his feet and was amazed at how much damage the silicon leaves had done. The return trip would hopefully be on a maintenance vehicle because the soles of his boots looked like they'd been through hell.

The captain sat down next to Kieran. The roguish good looks his face tried to projected were betrayed by the weight of his age, the responsibility of the ship, and the tension laden journey thus far. It all pulled down on him making the captain seem older than his years. The red beard jiggled as the captain smiled at Kieran anyway, trying to hide his pains.

"Those two," he said motioning at Oriono and Henry who stood guard over them, "and their Sonk rifles..." Captain Fillion rolled his eyes with all the sarcasm he could muster. He sighed, pulling a canteen from his shoulder bag, "Thousands of years of human evolution and design, and this," he pulled another object from his bag, "this is what I trust when the time comes."

It took Kieran a moment to recognize the object. It was a handgun. Back from before the blue fire consumed Earth. It fired not energy but metal bullets propelled by a chemical explosion set off by a spark. It was a caveman's weapon compared to what Henry and Oriono were holding, but it was still deadly.

"That's dangerous on a starship, even I know that. A misplaced shot could damage the hull," Kieran whispered.

The captain smirked, "Maybe in text books, but in the real world hulls are too thick and bullets too slow. I've had to use this a couple times in my life and I've never seen a shot cut through a hull. Not on a modern ship."

He offered the gun to Kieran, who carefully took it from him.

"Don't worry, it's not loaded; here let me show you," Captain Fillion said taking it back from Kieran. He showed him how the bullets were snapped into a container and then the actions required to slide that into the gun. A final pull back on the upper rail of the gun was all that was needed to prepare it for firing.

"This Colt 45 is older than anything or anyone out here on the edge of the galaxy, how sad is that? We come all this way and this device that kills things is what we carry from before the FTL age?" Captain Fillion mused as the boastful tone left his voice.

Kieran nodded politely and watched as Captain Fillion unloaded the gun, and put it into his shoulder bag. "Anyway, wouldn't do us any good right now. This is a problem for engineers and scientists to fix. Not guns, be they Sonk or Colts," the captain said as he took a long swig of his water.

He wanted to say something reassuring, but Kieran felt like there was little someone his age could offer to someone so old and traveled. So they drank and ate in silence.

Across from them Juuana and Solieo had an intense whispering conversations about all the possible reasons the engine could have failed to fire. Occasionally Rebecca interrupted them to explain how a sub-system on the Leviathan was built or was supposed to work. No reason they could conceive of explained the failure of the engine and the lock out from control of the ship.

"We should continue moving. According to Systems Control, the next air recycling event will be in a few hours. When that happens even more leaves will fall from the trees. Even here on the road we wouldn't be safe," Officer Oriono announced.

The weary crew stood,collected themselves, and prepared for a long walk in a straight line on a road... surrounded by silicon trees that could kill with just a leaf. An already grim mood was further darkened when the overhead lighting started to fade away. They broke out flashlights as the forest began what Kieran assumed was a night simulation, although it was not pitch black. Just dark enough that the road ahead was difficult to see.

Every breath clawed at Kieran's fears. He'd lived for 154 years without ever feeling this close to death. Even when the truck had almost flattened him, the feeling of death hadn't been there. He assumed that after a stay in the hospital, and a few dozen artificial body parts, he'd be up and laughing about his stupidity. Here there wasn't a hospital waiting for him with quick fixes. Just a painful bleed out on a road in the middle of a starship.

"What the hell," Officer Oriono suddenly exclaimed. The group stopped, Captain Fillion huddling them to crouch down. They watched as Henry and Oriono walked slightly ahead and shone their flashlights on something in the middle of the road. From where he was crouched it looked to Kieran like one of the cargo movers from the loading bay.

The captain stood up and joined the two Sonk rifle holders and they stared together at the drone that shouldn't be there.

"Did it get activated and then wander off?"

"Maybe the cleaning sub-system needed help and re-tasked it?"

"It may not be ours; maybe during construction someone left one behind?"

"Pirates don't bring drones, they'd just steal ours."

Finally, their spitballing ended. The captain turned to the group, "It's clearly not doing anything. Let's just walk past and we'll deal with it on the return trip." He motioned for them to follow him and the group stood up. Juuana's foot slipped and she fell to her knees. Officer Oriono stopped to help Solieo assist her up.

Captain Fillion was nearly at the drone when it suddenly moved. Turning and looking down at the red bearded little man... it sounded like one of them spoke, but Kieran was too far away to be sure who was saying what. Before a response could be uttered the drone grabbed the captain and flung him into the forest.

"NOOOOOOOOO!"

The sound of the scream was cut off by Henry and Officer Oriono firing their Sonk rifles.

TWANG

TWANG

TWANG

Everyone was shouting at each other to do something or go somewhere. Solieo grabbed Juuana's arm and half-pulled, half-dragged her down the road away from the drone.

Kieran stood frozen for a moment watching as the drone darted away from the energy beams flung in its direction. It dipped out of the light into the forest and then reappeared to the side of Officer Oriono and Henry who just barely avoided its grasp.

TWANG

TWANG

TWANG

The slow moving cargo loaders that Kieran had seen in the loading dock were nothing like this thing. It was fast. Its shell looked roughly built from mismatched metals. The size in one moment felt as immense as those 9ft loaders and then as it darted into the tree line again it seemed as small as a dog.

Rebecca was shouting something, but the words didn't connect.

TWANG

TWANG

TWANG

TWANG

The drone reappeared in the midst of Sonk rifle beams.

TWANG

TWANG

Everything felt like it was moving at quarter speed to Kieran.

TWANG

The rainbow hair of Rebecca flung side to side as she grabbed his arm and pulled so hard that Kieran felt his shoulder come out of its socket as he slammed down to the ground. The arm of the drone swung overhead so close he could see claws on its appendage. Like a beast.

On the ground Kieran heard a sound, almost like words, but all around him there were screams and Sonk rifle beams hummed over the top of those words. Kieran wasn't sure if he was hearing something or if the sounds were just rattling around in his skull. Juuana's screams continued to cut into him as he watched the beast stop for a moment to look at Rebecca. It was so close she could have kissed it.

Words started to form but they never came. Instead Kieran rolled out of the way before another set of claws came his way. Systems Control buzzed in front of the drone flashing all of its lights. The machine backed up and a Sonk rifle shot connected with one of the limbs.

BRRANNGKKK

It spun in place and just as quickly as it appeared, the droid disappeared back into the forest. Henry fired multiple

Sonk rifle rounds into the dark, but Officer Oriono stopped him from chasing after it.

Rebecca was the first to speak, "Get up. Everyone get up. We have to find the captain!"

Officer Oriono and Henry swept their rifles and flashlights back and forth over the tree line where the drone was last seen as Rebecca helped Kieran stand.

Rebecca took her flashlight and started towards the trees where the drone had thrown the Captain. Henry followed, and for a moment Officer Oriono started to object, but instead motioned for the rest of the crew to follow.

"He's over here!" Rebecca shouted from out ahead of them. The group, flashlights craning in every direction watching for the drone, followed as quickly as they dared move through the silicon trees.

"Oh my god," Juuana exhaled when they arrived on the scene. She turned and buried her face in Solieo's chest.

Oriono slung off their Sonk rifle and tossed their bag to Rebecca, "Use the medi-gel to seal the wounds." Then they immediately pulled up their weapon and took position looking outward away from the group, watching the trees.

"Help me," Rebecca half cried, half screamed at the rest of them.

Solieo pushed Juuana aside and knelt down to help Rebecca with the medi-gel. Henry took watch over their shoulders.

Kieran had almost no medical training, so he did the only thing he could think of. He knelt down, immediately feeling leaves cutting into his knees, and took Captain Fillion hand in his own. He wiped the blood away from the captain's face and tried to reassure him.

"It's going to be okay," Kieran said aloud, but everyone there knew it was a lie.

Kieran held Captain Fillion's hand as the old one gasped for breath, blood speckled over his chin. He wanted to tell him it was alright, but the words wouldn't form on his lips. Instead he just watched as Rebecca and Solieo worked on the wounds.

There were so many cuts. Some jagged, some clean, all deadly. In all his life, Solieo had never seen someone so brutally mauled. He pulled the shirt apart and moved to wipe as much blood away as he could so that Rebecca could get the medi-gel spray into the wounds. It just didn't seem like they could find and seal them quickly enough. Blood just kept pouring out of the man like he was a grape being squeezed for every last drop.

181

Rebecca was holding it all in. The tears, the rage, the fear... and just focusing on using the medi-gel spray. Death was an old friend she'd started to forget before today. As she watched the blood start to pool under them Rebecca knew it would be dining with them again tonight.

Coughing blood up all over his bushy beard the captain started to speak, he didn't need the nanite display alert to know that he was dying but it didn't hurt to know he thought darkly... "It's like you said kid," he spoke with a deep guttural rasp looking up at Kieran, "Time... tricks you. Tricks you into thinking that things will go on forever. Tricks you into thinking you've mastered all the universe has to throw at you. Look at us. We conquered the stars with our damn F-T-L engines and thought ourselves gods... but we're just plastics ducks... floating on the ocean waiting.... waiting to see if we're the lucky ones."

Captain Fillion laughed at his last thought being about that duck and continued to laugh as the last drops of blood left his body. His grip on Kieran's hand went limp before the light drained from his eyes. The yellow nanite display flickered for a moment and then went dark. Kieran fought back tears as he leaned back.

Rebecca set down the medi-gel dispenser and ran her hand over Captain Fillion's face, closing his eyes. Solieo put his hand on the captain's chest and started reciting a prayer in a language unknown to Kieran. The sound of the prayer felt comforting anyway. Juuana put her hand on her husband's shoulder and let the tears flow freely down her face.

Henry and Oriono shared pained and knowing glances at each other. It was the officer who interrupted the prayers, "This is not a defensible position. We need to move."

For a long moment no one moved. No one said anything.

Then Rebecca nodded and stood, "They're right. We need to move."

As they picked up their bags, Kieran hesitated for moment and then leaned down and picked up the captain's shoulder bag with his arm wincing as he did so. "Definitely dislocated," he thought to himself. He started to make a comment about it but a scream silenced him.

"IT'S BACK!"

DINNER GUESTS OF DEATH

The malfunctioning drone jumped into the middle of the group and the impact was like a bomb going off. Trees shuddered and the sound of razor sharp metal leaves flying through the air filled the gaps in between screaming and Sonk rifle firing. It swung at Juuana first and she just barely ducked in time to avoid getting hit.

The drone's focus quickly shifted from Juuana to Oriono and Henry as they fired rounds of charged energy beams at it. What didn't bounce off or miss the dark patchwork metal shell of the drone, punched holes into the forest sending whole trees tumbling to the ground.

Solieo and Juuana ran into the forest with the Systems Control drone chasing after them. Kieran yelped in pain as Rebecca picked him up onto his feet with his dislocated arm. She pulled and together they ran the opposite direction back to the road.

The sound of Sonk rifle rounds faded behind them as Kieran struggled to keep pace with the fast legs of Rebecca's artificial shell. It felt to him like they ran for an hour, but it could have just been minutes, so scattered were his thoughts after the second attack.

Without flashlights he couldn't see much, but clearly Rebecca's eyes were equipped with night vision. She stopped them suddenly, pulling them off the road where she started touching the wall. It took a moment but she found the edge of a utility room door. The sound of metal groaning filled the air as Rebecca forced the door open.

"Quick get inside," she half whispered, half screamed at him.

The door slammed shut behind her and the world was suddenly very dark and quiet.

Kieran heard Rebecca fussing with her backpack, after a few minutes in pitch black, light streamed out from her bag as Rebecca pulled out a table lantern. Together they took stock of the utility room, which other than a junction box, was empty. They sat down on opposite sides of the small room and took a moment to catch their breath.

Rebecca took only seconds to go from huge gulping breaths to a steady drumbeat. Kieran's chest continued to heave, mostly from panic, but also from pain. His shoulder was still dislocated. He winced in pain as his arm hung limply by his side.

"Here," Rebecca said as she came over to him, "this is going to hurt," as she braced his shoulder with her hand, "try not to scream."

Kieran winced and bit down on the scream. Instead it was just a soft cry that escaped his lips.

He leaned back against the wall and closed his eyes as his mind tried to make sense of what just happened to them. "You should eat and drink while we have a moment of peace because it may be awhile before we can stop again," Rebecca said interrupting his thought processes.

Kieran nodded, and dug through his backpack looking for ration bars. He held one out for Rebecca but she shook her head. He started nibbling on it, feeling like the whole world was crushing upon him.

"Your heart rate is still very elevated," she said with glowing yellow eyes.

"I'm fine."

They sat there as the cold started to become noticeable. Kieran looked up and noticed that the door had not closed all the way because of how Rebecca had forced it open. Cold air wafted in and he could see his breath in it.

"It shouldn't be this cold," Rebecca said noticing him watching his breath. She stood and tried to close the door more, but failed. Kieran rummaged through his backpack for the emergency blanket that he remembered packing. He started unfolding it as Rebecca sat down across from him.

Kieran wrapped the thin composite blanket around him, and looked at disheveled woman sitting across from him, "That thing swung at me twice, but only looked at you."

Rebecca stared at the floor, "I have some thoughts about why."

"I have some ideas, too," Kieran interjected after she let the topic hang in the air for a period.

There was a heartbeat and then tears started forming at Rebecca's eyes, "I'm not..." she started...

"I'm not..."

"I'm not..."

Rebecca took a deep breath, and then just said it all in a rush, "I'm not human. I'm an unregistered artificial person. I'm not... organic anymore. This shell is a very expensive wrapper meant for an organic brainstem, but there's no brain in here." She knocked on her head to emphasize it was empty.

Kieran got up from his side of the room and walked over to Rebecca. He thumped himself down next to her and didn't say anything. After a moment to make sure she was comfortable with him sitting next to her, Kieran offered Rebecca his hand.

Her nano-organic fingers wrapped in his as she wiped her tears away.

They sat like this for an extended period, until finally he spoke, "You are human, Rebecca."

"I've kept this secret for half a millennium. I've always accepted that I'd lost almost everything that made me human, but until now I've never felt so inhuman... to that thing I was just another machine," Rebecca muttered leaning her head back against the wall as Kieran squeezed her hand supportively.

In the dark of the silicon forest, Solieo held his hand over his wife's mouth as she screamed. It wasn't until the Sonk rifles stopped firing that the screams muted into tears. Juuana had her arms wrapped around Solieo's other arm and her eyes told Systems Control that she would not be ready to let go for awhile.

After several minutes of silence, however, Systems Control spoke, "You should move. My sensors have pinged a nearby utility room where Kieran and Rebecca are located."

"Are they still alive?" Juuana asked in a whisper as Solieo removed his hand from her mouth.

The red dot on the floating drone blinked several times, "Life readings from Mr. Ausure are green. Follow me."

Solieo stood and helped Juuana step gingerly, her ankle starting to swell from her earlier fall. Together they held each other close as they followed the drone through the dark woods.

"We're going to die on this ship aren't we?" Juuana asked her normally talkative husband.

Solieo grunted and kept pulling them forward. After a few more steps he spoke, "We didn't come all the way out here to get smashed like a bug. I promised you a vacation on Mynara. I keep my promises." He pressed tightly against her as they continued through the woods.

On the road Officer Oriono and Henry watched as the malfunctioning drone dodged their shots and dashed into the woods. There was a long pause and they swept their flashlights back and forth looking for the beast. The military machine switched all of their scanning capabilities to max and took a knee, aiming at where it had last seen the thing.

189

The sound of metal exploding filled the air and the malfunctioning machine came crashing out of the woods behind them. Henry jumped at the last second to avoid being grabbed. Officer Oriono swung around and took a second to let the aiming routines take their time calculating the shot. "Breath. Aim. Fire," the drilling instructors voice screamed in Oriono's mind.

TWANG

The Sonk rifle beam hit the side of the malfunctioning drone head on and knocked the thing off its stride. A sound of metal melting and hot liquids popping in the cold air surrounded Henry as the machine crashed to the ground near him. He took aim and fired.

TWANG

It rolled to avoid the next shot with a speed that left Henry breathless. Officer Oriono shouted for Henry to duck as they let loose a volley of Sonk rifle automatic fire.

TWANG

TWANG

TWANG

The beast clamored into the tree line and the world fell silent as Oriono stopped firing. They waited for a long time to see if the creature would return. Finally satisfied that it had been chased away, Henry spoke, "We have to find everyone. Quickly."

Officer Oriono nodded and then pointed, "My sensors saw warm footsteps heading that way a few minutes ago. I bet Rebecca doubled back down the road. The map indicates there is a utility room back that way, I bet she went there."

Together they set out on the road to find the rest of the crew.

It hadn't been that long since they first stopped on the road, but it felt like a different place to Henry now. The overhead UV lights had gone totally dark and the cool breeze had become a frosty knife that cut into you. Henry swept his flashlight along the road, "Did you see Kieran with her?"

"I... I can't remember," the military officer said with a stutter. The cold was impacting his systems already, or maybe it was something else. They activated secondary systems and scheduled a diagnostic scan of their body as they lead the way for Henry.

Ahead of them a red dot appeared floating in the darkness. Henry aimed his rifle and almost fired, but Oriono put their hand up. "It's the Systems Control drone."

As it fluttered out of the woods onto the road it was followed by Solieo and Juuana, each looking far worse for wear since the last time Henry had seen them.

Juuana had blood running down her ankle from the trip and fall earlier that was clearly now a wound not a sprain. Solieo's arms were covered in cuts that went through his jumpsuit. Blood stained at every edge. Still the two groups smiled and embraced on the dark road.

They started walking as Juuana rubbed her arms, "Anyone else feel like it's getting colder in here?"

Systems Control fluttered back and forth overhead and then dropped down, "Yes. The temperature has dropped five degrees in the last 40 minutes."

"Why is it getting colder?" Juuana asked.

"Unknown. Sub-systems are not responding. It is possible the heating exchange has malfunctioned," Systems Control replied.

Officer Oriono interjected, "All the more reason to keep moving then, because the utility room is next to a heat exchange for the forest. It'll be warmer than this road."

It was some time before they found the utility room. Every rustle of a tree or breeze that sounded wrong sent Officer Oriono onto a knee aiming their Sonk rifle at the dark forest. The drone did not return, but the memory of the attacks had everyone on edge. More than once Solieo was convinced he heard something out in the dark, but Juuana told him it was just his imagination.

Henry and Oriono pulled open the utility room doors. Rebecca and Kieran sat huddled together under blanket, each leapt up to embrace the group as they entered. With the extra bodies, the room filled up quickly and it reminded Kieran of parties at his first apartment, but without the posh furniture. Officer Oriono took a long final look out at the forest before pulling the door closed.

The red dotted Systems Control drone hovered amongst the group, "You should not linger long. The ship systems must be restored."

Rebecca glared up at the red dotted drone. "Nothing about the thing that just killed the captain?!" Rebecca screamed at the flying dot. Kieran grabbed for her but she stepped forward and swung faster than he expected.

The little drone skittered across the floor for a few feet before it regained flight control and steadied itself. The red dot blinked, clearly not expecting that response from Rebecca.

After a moment of the two of them staring at each other it spoke again, "I do not have any information to share beyond what you already saw with your own eyes. It appears that a drone has become dysfunctional. We can deal with it after I regain connection to the network and the ship systems. It is likely it will just roam the forest."

"How long until the forest UV lights come back online?" Rebecca asked the floating drone. Kieran watched as it worked to keep its distance from her, "Six hours. I have attempted an early restart, but no systems are responding."

"Fine. I think we could all use the rest," Rebecca said with a voice sounding as broken as their ship was at the moment.

Everyone muddled through their bags looking for food and water. Solieo passed Juuana a bag of freeze dried fruits that she missed when packing. Henry handed Rebecca a ration bar, and she took a few nibbles off of it while sharing a long look at Kieran that spoke volumes.

"Do you have your flask?" Kieran asked Henry.

A bushy white mustache wrapped over Henry's smile as he passed his flask to Kieran who took a big swig without hesitation before passing it to Rebecca. And so it went around the circle until it was empty.

Looking around the room Kieran muttered, "We never talk about it but the anomaly is going to eat the whole galaxy and kill us all. So what's the difference if a rogue drone kills us first?"

"We should set out when the lights turn back on and destroy that machine," Officer Oriono stated loudly as if by their words they could defy the chaos that now surrounded them.

Rebecca sighed, "Always with destroying things. Will the military ever teach people tactics. We can't win in a head on fight against that thing. Our best options come with getting back control of the ship, not getting into a pissing match with a 12 foot metal gorilla."

Henry chuckled at the mental picture, "It wasn't 12 feet, I'd give you 8 feet. At most."

Kieran dryly remarked, "As someone who was nearly filleted by its claws, I would put it closer to 12 than I would 8 feet tall. It was big. How did you two keep missing it?"

"It looked like a used cargo loading drone, but I've seen that type of handiwork before. Freespacer pirates use repurposed heavy drones as military support units. However, I have never seen one that fast. Nor have I ever encountered pirates who attacked with just drones. It's always a one two punch of drones followed by human attackers," Oriono's train of thought wandered away from them as internal systems worked to reheat its body.

"Unlikely, the logs didn't show anything exciting happening at way-station number seven before we arrived," Rebecca remarked still nibbling on her ration bar.

Juuana leaned forward, "Maybe it's just a regular construction drone left behind? Its programming damaged by radiation or logic decay?"

Officer Oriono looked up from their fidgeting, "I have finished my review of the records of the Leviathan's construction. The model loader that we were attacked by was not used. That machine should not be on this ship. Which makes me believe that the system issues are purposeful, someone is trying to stop us from reaching Checkpoint Charlie."

Kieran sighed, "First contact with the unknown is always messed up from what I've read of history and this is no different."

Henry tapped Kieran's shoulder, "First contact? You think this thing is alive?"

"Yes? It moved like an animal, but more than that I thought I heard... speech when it was standing over me," Kieran replied.

"Between the twangs of Sonk rifle fire and Juuana's screaming, I'm not sure how you heard anything intelligible," Officer Oriono said nodding reassuringly to Juuana that her screams were not wrong.

Rebecca interjected, "It's human nature to apply life to things," she paused glancing at Oriono, "but our tendency to recognize faces in inanimate objects is well known to be without merit. This is no different. You're just applying real world animal behavior to a machine."

"Perhaps," Kieran answered, "but I've always thought it interesting that the uncanny valley effect implies that at one point in our history there was a reason to be afraid of something that looked human but wasn't."

Rebecca stood up, "It doesn't matter what it was, why it's here, or what happens next if we don't get the ship back online. Everyone get some sleep, when the lights come back on we'll make a beeline for the Systems Control servers and attempt to reestablish control of the ship. From there we can activate security drones to hunt down and destroying that thing."

"What if there are more of them?" Juuana asked as people began to move about to get space to sleep.

No one said anything, but Officer Oriono put a hand on her shoulder and squeezed.

A basic blanket wrapped around him lying on the floor, Kieran couldn't even begin to sleep. The temperature continued to drop outside, and even in the cramped room it was beginning to get colder. Henry saw the organic young one shuddering and wrapped his arms around the kid.

Looking across the room, Henry saw yellow nanite energy already pulsing from Rebecca's eyes as she started to review something rather than rest. She noticed her old friend staring at her while he held onto Kieran. Rebecca smiled at Henry and motioned for him to rest as well.

Then all was quiet.

THE HUNTING GROUNDS

Light from the silicon forest smashed into Kieran's face as Officer Oriono pulled open the utility room door. Blinking hard under the harsh glare, Kieran discovered something wrapped around him. Pulling at it he realized it was Henry's arm wrapped over his shoulder.

"Everyone get up, the lights are back on and we need to get moving," Rebecca said loudly enough to get everyone's attention. Behind her a cold breeze cut through the room and caused Kieran to shiver.

Kieran started stuffing the blanket back in his backpack and remembered Captain Fillion's shoulder bag. He opened it up, and amongst the rations and a few personal items, the Colt 45 stared back at him. The chrome reflecting a glint of light on his face.

He hesitated for a moment and then dumped the contents of the bag into his backpack. Rations, canteen, personal items, and the gun and its bullet boxes. Kieran would deal with them later he thought to himself.

Getting up on his feet with some help from Henry, Kieran joined Rebecca and Officer Oriono outside the storage unit.

The temperature had dropped significantly since they had last been out in the forest. A layer of ice particles covered the ground and gave the world a sheen that made everything look even more alien.

Stepping out he quickly realized why Rebecca and Officer Oriono had stopped pestering the group to get up and get moving. They were crouched over the ground looking at what appeared to be tracks in the icy frost. Henry and the Verantes joined Kieran in staring at the tracks, following them with their eyes until they disappeared into the trees.

"It came out, followed us right to the door, circled, and then left. That doesn't sound like any malfunctioning drone I've ever heard about. They just don't act like this," Rebecca muttered to Officer Oriono. The military training in them made Officer Oriono feel very worried for the crew now.

A teal tinted hand pressed down on the frosted ground, "It's cold. So this was awhile ago. It most definitely would have been when we were active last night. It knew exactly where we were but decided not to confront us. Fear means it can be killed. One doesn't run from something that can't hurt it," Officer Oriono announced to the group.

Rebecca gulped hard enough that Kieran could hear it, "Then it's decided. You'll take Henry and follow after it," Rebecca said.

"I'll go with them," Solieo said putting his hand on Juuana's shoulder and stepping forward.

"There's no reason," Rebecca started to say before being interrupted.

"Yes there is. I'm the best exotic origination engineer here right now. If I can get a better look at the thing, I may be able to help the two of them destroy it," Solieo stated defiantly.

"Stay in between us and move quietly," Officer Oriono offered.

Henry shook his head dismissively at the turn of events and adjusted his backpack before walking towards the forest.

Juuana clutched at Solieo's arm, but said nothing. He leaned down and kissed her forehead. Whispering something that was meant only for her. They took a long look at each other then Solieo followed after Henry and Officer Oriono into the tree line where the tracks led.

"Come on you two, we'll make a fast move for the hub, from there we can reset the network and get control of the ship. With some luck we'll be there before they even find the thing," Rebecca said tapping Kieran and Juuana on the shoulders. Kieran took a long last look at the forest behind them and then started following. Systems Control buzzed behind the group watching as they started down the road.

The maintenance road was now brightly lit in the daylight cycle, but, even with the light on their side, knowing that at any moment a malfunctioning drone could come bounding out of the forest kept the thee humans on edge.

Kieran cupped his hands and blew into them trying to warm them. They had not packed for, or prepared for, it to be this cold. He could see every breath now. Occasionally blue leaves would flutter down from the trees, but it was the crystallized frost that would follow that gave the impression that snow was coming down from clouds they couldn't see overhead.

Rebecca stopped them. She looked around for a moment, and then motioned for them to take off their backpacks. Juuana looked ill, but Kieran thought it stress. It wasn't until he watched Rebecca help Juuana wrap a blanket around her that he realized that the cold was really a problem. Hypothermia.

Kieran took his own backpack off and took out the blanket. Doing so caused the Colt to fall and clatter on the surface of the maintenance road. The sudden loud sound caused Juuana to yelp and even Rebecca jumped back in a bit of surprise.

As she leaned over to help Kieran put the items back in his backpack, Rebecca paused at the gun, "Where did you get this?"

"It was Captain Fillion's."

"Did he leave you any bullets?"

Kieran took a moment to remember what bullets were and replied, "Oh yes, two containers worth," he said pulling out the two long gray metal boxes that were filled with bullets.

Rebecca chuckled at him, "They called them magazines. Do you know how to use that thing?"

There was a moment when he wanted to say no, not really wanting the responsibility of carrying a device capable of killing, but instead he told the truth. "Yes, he showed me how to load and ready it."

"Try not to shoot yourself... it's probably a good thing you kept that. Go ahead and put it in your pocket just in case. Not going to do us any good in your bag if we get attacked," Rebecca said helping Kieran stand.

"Where's your blanket?" Kieran asked as he watched frost flakes drift into Rebecca's hair.

"I didn't pack one. I'll be fine," she replied sharply.

Not as far away from the road as they expected to be, Officer Oriono, Henry and Solieo followed the tracks in the frost. It was becoming bitterly cold Solieo thought to himself. He had taken out his blanket and wrapped it around himself, but moving quickly through the silicon trees meant that it was already riddled with cuts.

Slowing down, Solieo watched as Officer Oriono and Henry studied the drone's tracks. Their artificial bodies didn't feel the cold the same way Solieo's skin did, but they could tell the world was getting colder as their internal systems used more energy to keep their shells warm.

Solieo pulled at the remains of the blanket as he followed, wishing that when his last internal organ had given out several hundred years ago he'd been less resistant to moving his brain to an artificial shell. Instead, at great personal and physical pain, he proceeded with implantation of a host of bio-organic replacement parts.

A human skin wrapped around a collection of parts built in a factory... and now that very skin that he was so prideful of was his great weakness. In the mix of the white frost covered blue silicon trees, Soleio's dark skinned bald head stood out. Even from a great distance you could see him toddling after the two Sonk rifle carriers.

Rebecca wrapped the blankets around Kieran and Juuana a mile ago and wished she'd thought to bring one for herself. "High tolerance for cold," she had told Kieran. But as he watched the frost build on the road he started to wonder just how much cold her shell could take. Eventually it must get too cold for her power plant to operate, right?

Juuana slipped on a patch of ice that had formed. She landed with a thud on her side. Kieran was at her side helping her up before Rebecca had even noticed. She shook her head, the cold was impacting her systems faster than Rebecca had thought possible. Reaching for the two of them, she started to say something when the lights flickered.

Darkness covered everything.

...

..

.

Kieran was about to pull his flashlight out but after a flicker the lights came back on overhead.

"Systems Control what was that?" Juuana asked the floating red drone that tagged along behind them.

"Unknown. All systems continue to read normal," was the flat response.

"First the FTL engine, then the mobility devices, then the heat, and now the lights... and now I'm reading the oxygen level in here has dropped, which shouldn't be happening in a forest designed to make oxygen," Rebecca huffed as she pulled on Juuana to get her moving. They had to keep walking no matter what happened.

Systems Control's drone buzzed overhead and then came down in front of Rebecca, closer than it had gotten in some time, "I have a hypothesis ready now on what attacked the crew last night."

The trio stopped and stared as the red dot pulsated, "Systems that impact organic life are being shut down, one after another. These are not random failures. Why not gravity if it was random systems? This is the act of intelligence."

Rebecca laughed, "No. It can't be what you're implying."

Kieran felt very stupid but being cold and tired made him share his ignorance "What are you two saying?"

"The thing that attacked you last night was intelligent, beyond just programming. It is acting in a way that indicates it is self aware. It is shutting down systems you need to survive, but it is not causing damage that would destroy the Leviathan," Systems Control answered.

Rebecca swatted at the flying drone and turned to Kieran, "There's no way. The human race was only able to create one AI and we're talking to a disconnected version of it right now. There is nothing in our history that suggests AI can occur naturally in computer systems."

Kieran shook his head, "What about Kaylee?"

Rebecca laughed mockingly at him, "Kaylee is a very sophisticated virtualized intelligence. She is not self aware in any sense."

Juuana interjected, "It makes sense though. It shut down our connection to the ship's core functions, then once we were lured out, it attacked and killed the captain first, then it started shutting down life support systems."

"Why do you not believe that AI can occur naturally, Rebecca?" Systems Control quizzed.

She turned to face it, "Because you exist. What do you think you are?"

The red drone blinked its lights, clearly deeply in thought processing the inquiry. Rebecca said nothing, and waved for them to keep moving. Systems Control's drone followed. Just out of arms reach.

Henry watched as Officer Oriono stopped to touch one of the tracks. The sensors in their hand registered that the temperature no longer differed from the ambient ground temperature. They had thought the tracks were leading them closer to the drone because the imprints were getting warmer, but now they were cold. This confused the military officer.

Oriono stood and looked around going over the possibilities in their mind. If they were chasing a malfunctioning drone, and all of the sudden the tracks stopped being fresh, then what was happening? Perhaps the temperature had dropped fast enough to cover the malfunctioning machine's tracks. Oriono noted that Solieo's blanket was ensconced in frost.

Henry watched as Solieo trudged up to where he and Officer Oriono stood. It pained him to see the engineer struggle in the cold conditions. His dark skin looked painfully frost burned. For the first time on this journey, Henry felt lucky to have outfitted himself in a cheap shell... the power plant inside his core ran warm.

Oriono waved Henry over, "We've reached the end of fresh tracks. These leading into the woods are cold, and were likely set awhile ago."

Henry bent down and followed the track line with his eyes, "That doesn't make any sense, you can see the marks continue. Why would they stop being fresh..." The answer hit Henry so fast that it scared him and as his gaze quickly shot up the answer jumped to Officer Oriono who also looked up drawing out their Sonk rifle and pointing it at the sky.

Solieo did not understand why the two of them had bent over to look down and now suddenly looked up. He had barely started to crane his own neck upward when the sound of silicon tree branches crackling went off behind him. He never saw the malfunctioning drone, instead his last sight was the warm glow of of the artificial sky, frost, and blue leaves drifting through the air. As last sights go, it was peaceful.

Officer Oriono heard the crackling of silicon metal tree trunks before the rest of them, but it still wasn't enough warning for them to turn to see Soleio before the end. In the fraction of time it took them to look down and turn around, all Oriono saw was a sheet of crimson liquid spray across the world and into their eyes.

It took only a blink for the military grade systems in their retinas to clear the liquid debris and start tracking the malfunctioning drone. But it was Henry who fired the first shot.

TWANG

The pulsating twang of the Sonk rifle echoed throughout the silicon forest and down the road. It was followed by more shots as both of them opened fire and chased after the drone.

The loud sound of a Sonk rifle was unmistakable. The trio heard it and in a moment realized that the hunting party and they were not so far apart after all.

Juuana gasped, "Soleio."

Kieran listened to shots ring out, going away from them, "This was a mistake. We should have stayed together."

Rebecca shook her head, the words coming slower because of the cold, "No... We need to... keep moving... They have their task... we... have ours."

Kieran reached into his pocket, pulling out and loading the Colt, "No. I have a weapon, I should have gone with them to help." He started off into the forest as Rebecca and Juuana shouted at him to stop.

He had scarcely vanished into the tree line when Juuana started crying, "Why does everyone always leave me?"

Rebecca huffed, "This is why... relationships on a starship... are a bad fucking idea..."

Juuana turned around and slapped Rebecca hard. As her head whipped to the side the frost shook from her hair and drifted away. It made Juuana pause seeing how much ice had formed on the normally composed project leader. She reached out with her hand and touched Rebecca's face and felt nothing but ice.

"Your skin, you...," the words were cut short as Rebecca pulled Juuana's hand away from her face.

"Just keep walking," was all that Rebecca said.

Juuana turned back to look at where Kieran had vanished into the silicon forest, "Systems Control go with him... please."

The little fluttering drone hovered in front of the crying woman. The red dot blinked and then it flew off after Kieran.

The Sonk rifle twangs faded into the distance faster than Kieran could follow them. *Maybe Henry and Officer Oriono had already destroyed it,* Kieran thought to himself. Hopeful, but determined, he moved quickly through the frost covered silicon forest. Each step more precarious than the last due to the layer of ice that was forming.

He slipped and fell sideways into a silicon tree. A shudder ran up the blue giant. The sound of the tree swaying had barely faded when it was replaced by the sound of dozens of razor sharp leaves fluttering to the ground on top of Kieran. Instinctively all he could think to do was curl up into a ball. He heard the sound of wind rushing over metal and felt blades cut into his side.

"OWWwwwww!" the scream left Kieran's mouth before he even realized it was him yelling out.

When the rustling faded, he opened his eyes and assessed the damage. In his side a blue leaf was half buried, the red blood already pooling up around it. He started to reach for it when a voice cut him off, "You will want to use the blanket to do that."

Kieran looked up to see the Systems Control drone fluttering overhead. He nodded and used some of the blanket as a makeshift glove and gingerly pulled out the leaf. It stung, and even being careful it cut the blanket he was using to protect his hand. Systems Control kept fluttering about as Kieran dug through his backpack for the small medi-gel spray bottle that Henry had made him pack.

"Ah haa..." his triumph was cut short by the stinging pain in his side. Kieran carefully opened the spray bottle tab and held the nozzle up close to his skin like he had seen Rebecca do unsuccessfully last night to Captain Fillion. However, this was just one little cut.

TWISHHH

"FUH-UCK!"

He took deep breaths.

"I didn't think it would hurt so much," Kieran said looking up at Systems Control.

The red dot blinked, "Antibiotics, nanite sized repair bots, chemicals that encourage rapid healing, and a mint scent."

"And which one makes it hurt?" Kieran asked the flying drone.

"The nerve endings in your torn skin," Systems Control replied matter of factly.

He stood, slowly, every breath and movement made the skin on his side move just enough to send pain racing through him. It felt like being stabbed by the leaf every time. He rewrapped himself in the blanket, and reset the backpack on his shoulders. This time he moved through the forest with more care given to his footing.

"This platform is equipped with basic infra-red scanners. I can detect a heat signature ahead," Systems Control chimed.

Kieran paused and ducked, "Is it a 9 foot robot that's going to crush me?"

"No, the heat is on the ground. It is not big enough to be the malfunctioning drone. It is not moving," Systems Control replied. The last part of the statement made a shiver go down Kieran's spine. Not moving only meant one thing.

Death.

He followed as Systems Control lead the way. It was only a few more minutes and then Kieran saw the red on the ground through the trees. The color was unmistakeable. Blood. Only one of the three of them had blood to lose. As Kieran got closer to the body, he moved slower. From where he stood, he could see the backpack and the blanket askew.

"Solieo..."

Kieran dropped to his knees next to the body. Everyone was always leaving him, why should the wiry abrasive old one be any different? For the second time in his life he cradled a dead friend in his arms, "I'm sorry, Solieo. We should have been here."

Though he could not remember all the words, Kieran recited the prayer Solieo had said last night upon the body of Captain Fillion. Taking great care, Kieran took off the shredded remains of the backpack and wrapped the body in what remained of the blanket.

Anger flowed through Kieran as he stood, "Why am I here?"

"Inquiry. Do you mean here at this exact location? I believe you were attempting to reach Henry and Officer Oriono to assist them in hunting the malfunctioning drone."

"No, I mean why am I on this fucking spaceship, Systems Control? I'm not an engineer who knows how to fix anything, I'm not a military officer who can protect people, I'm not a navigator, I'm not a pilot... I'm just a psychology student!"

The little buzzing drone blinked its red glow at him for what felt like a long time before it replied, "You have a purpose here."

Kieran shook his head in disbelief and stood up. The world around them was still except for the faint fluttering sound of Systems Control's little drone. The Sonk rifles had gone silent. Here next to the body of Solieo, the silicon forest felt more like a graveyard than the oxygen pumping chest of the Leviathan.

"Which way back to the road?" Kieran asked Systems Control but the little red drone was gone. He looked in every direction, even up, and it had vanished from sight. Various curse words started to bubble to his lips when he heard something snap behind him.

After all the close calls in the past day, Kieran didn't stop to look. He just ducked and covered. Over head he felt something massive leap past him, close enough that he could feel the air rushing all around him. A few silicon leaves kicked up by the rush of movement cut at Kieran's arms but he didn't give them any thought because of what now stood in front of him.

The malfunctioning drone stood seven feet away from him. Its massive frame stood an easy nine feet tall on four legs. It looked very similar to the cargo moving drones he'd seen before, but its shell was a mixture of parts and pieces. It looked like something a child would build from scraps found in the recycling bins. As the thing stood there, Kieran had time to appreciate that the red stains on its front arms weren't paint, but blood.

"Hu...ma...n...."

The sound felt like a word and Kieran was still trying to process the idea that the cargo loader could speak when the sound of a Sonk rifle cut through the forest.

TWANG

TWANG

Two solid hits on the malfunctioning drone's side sent it down onto its knees. However, it took only a moment for the malcontent machine to regain its footing. It moved so fast that Kieran thought his own feet must be frozen. The thing grabbed onto tree trunks and quickly started climbing away.

As leaves and even a few branches started falling from above, Kieran quickly found his breath. He bounded away from Solieo's body hiding behind a particularly large silicon tree. He could hear the sound of the branches shattering on the ground, each splinter flung off like a tiny metal spear into the forest.

Then silence.

Kieran peered around the corner and saw Officer Oriono standing there by Solieo's body, "It's okay. I think it's gone off again." Kieran approached and watched as Oriono held pieces of the malfunctioned drone to their sparkly blue eyes, small green lights dancing around his iris as they scanned the debris for clues on what it was.

"It doesn't look like any of you were right. This isn't logic decay, space radiation, or artificial life. This drone was most certainly built by freespacer pirates. What I don't understand is where the rest of the crew is now. They would have attacked with this thing last night and tried to kill all of us at once," Officer Oriono said handing Kieran the piece of debris.

Kieran hesitated before taking the piece of metal. Even on Earth he had heard stories of the dark science that freespacers made use of in their war with the Aligned Worlds.

Oriono smiled, "Don't worry, it's a normal piece of metal. You're probably exposed to more radiation every day standing next to Henry."

Kieran took the metal debris from Oriono's hand and almost instantly felt it start to crumble in his fingers. "How can it hit so hard if its so brittle?"

"Curious, it didn't react like that in my hands or when the Sonk rifle hit it. Something on your skin must be causing a chemical reaction. Perhaps that's why it attacked Solieo first. Human skin," Oriono speculated as they stood up and started looking around.

The military officer motioned, and Kieran followed, "Systems Control told us you were out here. I didn't realize we were so close to the road, the forest creates such an illusion of infinity when you're standing in the middle of it," Officer Oriono said as they stepped carefully on the frost covered forest floor.

After a few minutes they stopped, "Henry should have reached the road by now, he should fire three shots to let me know he's found Rebecca and Juuana."

They waited together.

TWANG

TWANG

TWANG

For the first time the sound of a Sonk rifle lifted Kieran's spirts. He turned to smile at Oriono, but his lips sunk into a frown as he watched Oriono fall to the ground shaking.

"What's going on?" he asked the one who had saved him twice in 24 hours. Remembering his first aid training Kieran did not try to hold the military officer while they had a seizure, but instead cleared the area so that no damage was caused while the motions continued.

After a few minutes of wondering if it was ever going to stop, Officer Oriono froze mid-shake. Slowly their limbs straightened and their face relaxed. Officer Oriono rolled onto their back, looking up at a visibly upset Kieran.

"Something... is wrong... with the... nanites in my shell. Something... very wrong... not a virus... they are.... damaging me. Have to shut down all systems.... Rebecca..... must.... not....," the words trailed off and the light faded from Oriono's eyes.

Kieran stood there too stunned to speak or move. Slowly he bent over and closed Officer Oriono's eyes. A short prayer left his lips for the second time in an hour, and without hesitating he picked up Oriono's Sonk rifle. He grimaced not with fear in his heart but with hatred.

"WHERE ARE YOU!?" Kieran screamed at the trees.

The trees swayed all around him. He waved the Sonk rifle all over looking for the creature but saw nothing. The frost flakes were falling faster and standing still Kieran was more aware than ever how cold it was getting in the forest. Looking up, Kieran noticed that the UV daylights were starting to dim. One last look back at Officer Oriono and then he started moving back towards the road, faster now.

Cold and darkness started to wrap themselves around Kieran. He wondered if he could survive on his own until the lights came back on. In the dimming light Kieran tripped on a root, stumbling forward, but this time he did not hit a tree. Only the ground. He quickly dug through his backpack for the flashlight, worrying every moment that the drone was right behind him. Awkwardly he held both the flashlight and the Sonk rifle at the ready, wishing he had some tape to bind the two together.

Just steps from the road, Kieran heard something behind him. A sound from just beyond where the light touched. To his dying breath Kieran would swear to anyone who listened that what he heard was a voice...

"Come and see me."

"See who?" Kieran asked the forest.

"Me," a harsh synthetic voice spoke beyond his flashlight's view.

Kieran gulped hard as sweat began to form on his brow, "Where's the rest of your freespacer pirate crew?"

There was silence... the voice whispered, "Traitors."

The air moved as systems fluttered half alive, and the voice called out to Kieran one last time, "Come and see me."

With that statement from the forest, Kieran started running. He heard movement behind him but did not look back. Ahead a small red dot glowed and Kieran smiled thinking it was the rest of the crew. As he grew closer the smile faded. It was just a light above a door.

However, a door for a human is smaller than a door meant for a massive malfunctioning drone. He smashed into the door at a full sprint, half sliding on the frost, half skating gracefully. It was locked. He shouted out at whoever might be on the other side, "Get away from the door!" And then fired the Sonk rifle at it.

TWANG

...

BOOM

What remained of the exploded door flung inwards and without hesitation or concern about where it led Kieran ran through the doorway. Behind him he heard skittering but it sounded further away than before. Inside this new place it was warmer, though the air still felt cold. He ran through corridors for several moments until he was sure that the creature was not following him.

Stopping to catch his breath Kieran looked around his surroundings. Above him the low hung ceiling was covered with tubes and wiring. Ahead of him in every direction were a series of square cut hallways that went off in directions with no rhyme or reason. Kieran lost track of which tunnels he'd turned down, much less where he came from.

Freezing to death was not a possibility, but starving now was. The Leviathan was huge and he had no network connection, which meant no map or Systems Control to guide him. Locked out of control of the ship, Rebecca and the crew would not be able to use the sensors to scan for him.

Kieran put his back against the wall and slid down until he was seated. The weight of the day crushing on him as tears filled his eyes. He looked up and saw the tubing and wiring running overhead and a thought came to his mind, "They need a signal flare to find me."

Taking aim at a section down the hall he fired.

TWANG

A small fire broke out from where the pipe-works had been blown open. Kieran didn't care. He wrapped what was left of the blanket around him tightly and closed his eyes. Kieran felt the cold returning and pulled tighter at the blanket until finally sleep crashed over him.

In his dream he was on a warm beach looking out at an endless ocean. Kieran watched as rubber ducks bobbed up and down on the water. The sight made him smile. From somewhere behind him a voice called his name over and over as if he wasn't supposed to be standing so close to the water.

He watched as the waves became blood and a hulking mass of metal rose from the ocean.

The sky darkened and it crashed down upon him as someone screamed.

GIVE TURING MY REGARDS

"Kieran?!"

"Kieran?!"

"Kieran?!"

Someone was shouting at Kieran as his eyes fluttered open. They had barely started to take in light when a hand came across his face, hard.

SLAP

"The hell?!" Kieran exclaimed sputtering to life. All at once every body part screamed at him in a symphony of stiffened pain. Rebecca was crouched in front of him, her face angry in a way Kieran had not seen before. Behind her a tired looking Henry and Juuana stood guard watching for the malfunctioning drone.

"Where did you go?" Rebecca asked Kieran as he slowly stretched his limbs. He was disoriented either from the cold or how long he'd been asleep, he wasn't sure which one.

"I've been right here," Kieran muttered in response to Rebecca's sharp probing.

The answer made Rebecca explode, "What?"

Kieran sheepishly looked away, "Officer Oriono... they saved me from the creature... again... and then something happened to them. Their nanites went haywire. They had to shutdown to prevent further damage."

Henry and Juuana pensively watched as Rebecca helped Kieran stand, slowly and gingerly. "Where did you leave them?" she asked as he steadied himself on her shoulder.

"It wasn't far from the road, but the creature was close. I had to leave them behind," Kieran replied sheepishly feeling guilt over the decision.

"Why do you keep calling it a creature?" Rebecca asked.

Kieran looked at the faces staring at him, "It spoke to me."

"It made inquiries?" Systems Control red drone quizzed him buzzing closer.

"Yes. That's not all, Officer Oriono said it appeared to be of freespacer pirate design. He chipped off a piece of it and when I touched it the metal basically disintegrated in my hands. That's why the thing is targeting humans," Kieran excitedly interjected.

"Solieo?" Juuana asked with tears already forming on her eyes. She touched Kieran's shoulder with her hand. He couldn't bare to look in her in the eyes when he answered, so he hung his head and shook, "No."

"I'm sorry, Juuana, I told you it didn't look like he'd survived. That's why we left him behind to chase the big metal bastard," Henry said trying to reassure the grieving widow as her cry became wail. Juuana buried her face in Henry's chest as he wrapped his arms around her.

"Why did you stop here and what happened to the conduit down the hall? Did it chase you in here?" Rebecca queried immune to Juuana's tears at the moment.

"They say when you're lost that you shouldn't move so that you're easier to find. That conduit was my signal flare. I knew you'd find me," Kieran replied.

"That's not knowing, that's hope, child," Rebecca snapped at him.

Days of stress boiled into Kieran's veins and he angrily retorted, "No. It's a leap of faith, which is all we have right now!"

Henry interrupted the brewing pair before their words became a physical fight, "We're close to the hub. We have a plan. We should stick to it."

Rebecca shook off her anger at Kieran's foolishness, "Yes. We do. If we can reset the ship's systems then

Systems Control can engage security drones to assist us in hunting that malfunctioning loader drone down."

Kieran shook his head, "No. I'm telling you it spoke. It's more than just a malfunctioning machine."

Sensing another pending argument, Henry physically stepped forward and separated them, "Whatever it is, once Systems Control has regained access to the ship we can open the maintenance road doors and use the vehicles to help Officer Oriono. From there the security drones can be used to take down the 'creature' as you call it. We clearly can't kill it in a head on fight."

Kieran and Rebecca glared at each other but shook their heads in agreement. The remaining crew members picked up their bags and followed the Systems Control drone deeper into the access tunnels. Rebecca took lead again, this time carrying Oriono's Sonk rifle. Henry followed behind, keeping watch on their six as he called it.

After what felt like hours of walking, they stopped at a heavy looking doorway. Rebecca called Systems Control over and a holographic map came up showing the heart of the Leviathan - the systems hub. They stared at the schematics for a few minutes together like it was going to make the coming conversation happen any differently.

"I'm the only one who's read the manual and knows how to traverse the server rooms to get to the restart panel," Kieran said out loud, as if they were all listening to him.

Henry looked up from the holo display and sighed, "You're just a kid who's got his whole life ahead of him. I should go."

Rebecca continued staring at the display like it was going to give her a better plan.

"Yeah, maybe, but I'm also the only person left who's truly expendable. You three know enough about space travel to get to Checkpoint Charlie if this goes sideways," Kieran replied.

They all stood there for a moment until Rebecca sniffled. *Was it the cold?* he wondered. "Okay, Kieran. Stay in touch. We'll take the last two Sonk rifles and make some noise in the silicon forest. If it's really is hunting skin wrapped humans, Juuana should make a tasty target."

"Yeah, it probably can't even fit in the tunnels and the maintenance doors are all sealed. So it probably won't be anywhere in the hub anyway," Henry offered up to help remove some of Kieran's fear.

"Hopefully we draw it away from you. Be fast and don't look back until after you hit the switch," Juuana said putting her hand on Kieran's arm.

Nodding his head in support, Henry put his hand on Kieran's shoulder and gave it a hard squeeze. Rebecca dismissed Systems Control and as the light of the holo map faded she looked at Kieran with a face that seemed to want to say something. Instead Rebecca adjusted her Sonk rifle, "Let's go."

Juuana, Henry, and Rebecca started a light jog back down the tunnel back towards the silicon forest. Two of them carrying the most deadly weapon humanity had to offer. Leaving Kieran standing there with nothing but a dirty jumpsuit and his hope.

Kieran turned away from watching them run and pulled the emergency door release lever. He had to squeeze and huff and puff to fit into the hub. Systems Control's little red drone darted between his legs and flittered past him as he struggled. After one final push, he and the backpack spilled into the hub.

The sound of supplies and Kieran hitting the ground echoed through the hallway they'd just falling into. Looking ahead he could see lights. The red glow of the

Systems Control drone fluttered waiting for him at the end of the hallway where it appeared to open up into a larger room.

He picked up the flashlight and left the rest of the supplies. He could come back for them later and he figured the mess would make it clear which doorway led back to the silicon forest. He was going to make it back alive he'd decided. Kieran's hand gripped tighter on the flashlight as he started walking.

Stepping out of the hallway he now realized it wasn't a hallway at all... it was an alleyway. The sight before Kieran made his jaw drop. "This is incredible! On the diagrams it just looked like a bunch of rooms... I didn't realize..." his voice trailed off as he looked up. There were buildings that stretched multiple stories into the air. Kieran jogged out and stood in the middle of an intersection of maintenance roads. A city in the stars.

"This way, Kieran Ausure," the Systems Control drone said, clearly not impressed by what the human had found.

The tunnels were warm enough to make you forget the cold of the forest. Returning now after hours away, Juuana, Henry, and Rebecca were dumbstruck by how much the temperature had dropped in their time away.

Henry took the lead as they walked into the silicon forest again. Juuana followed behind him wrapping the blanket across her body as tight as she could while still maintaining her footing on the icy ground. Rebecca trailed behind watching for any sign of what she was sure was just a malfunctioning loading drone.

The frost had given way to ice, which caused the forest to feel even more inhospitable to human life. The sound of metal clinking against ice filled the air and every breath felt shallow to Juuana. How air in a forest designed to make oxygen could feel thin baffled her. *Perhaps the trees don't work in the cold or perhaps it's this fear taking my breath away*, Juuana thought to herself as she followed after Henry.

In the distance Henry saw the black hull of the drone dipping out of sight. The sound of metal clanging filled the air and he at once pictured the beast slamming into a tree while running away from the three of them.

"This way," Henry whispered loudly over his shoulder as he increased his pace. Behind him Juuana and Rebecca both shuddered at the cold but followed without comment.

Kieran followed the Systems Control drone down the road. They passed multiple doorways to systems he would have to spend multiple lifetimes learning how to operate. Until finally he arrived at a medium sized red tinted building.

Again, he had to pull a lever and break the emergency seal controls to open the door. Pushing into the server rooms, the smell of ozone wafted heavily into the air as he gave a final strain and plopped into the building.

It was very dark but he could hear the sound of water dripping.

He flipped on the flashlight and rows and rows of pools of water reflected the light back at the world. Shining the light into a pool he saw server racks in a submerged bath of cooling liquids. Beyond the pools, rows of servers hummed along with their blinking lights, the only thing that gave shape to the void of the room.

It was warm in the building and for the first time in a long time Kieran didn't feel cold at all. The air became more foul and less ozoninated as he moved down the first set of rows. Kieran's shoulder brushed a piece of metalwork that stuck out from the liquid and he winced in pain. It was blisteringly hot.

He pressed forward.

The flashlight cut across the warehouse sized room and all he could see were pools of servers in every direction. He followed the dim row of lights on the floor that appeared to be pulsating away from him, guiding him to something he thought.

Henry screamed in joy as his Sonk rifle beam found its target. The large drone shuddered and spun to the side for a moment. Slamming up against a tree it set off a cascade of falling silicon leaves. Forcing the three crew members to take cover as razor sharp death rained down from above. Henry and Rebecca wrapped themselves over the top of Juuana.

Both the synthetic bodied humans registered shell damage, but they could disable the sensation of pain. Henry didn't even wince as a leaf buried itself in his neck. He stood barely noticing the razor sharp silicon dangling half out of his collar bone. It wasn't until Rebecca put her hand on his shoulder that he acknowledged that he was damaged.

Rebecca pulled the leaf out and watched as synthetic fluid and nanites went to work sealing the wound in Henry's neck.

"Are you okay?" Henry asked Juuana as he picked her up off the ground.

The only organic wrapped human in the group looked down at a cut on her knee. Juuana watched as the blood stained her jumpsuit, and responded without hesitation, "Yes."

Trees wobbling and shedding leaves was heard not far from where the three stood and without even stopping, Henry and Rebecca gave chase. Juuana followed behind, as close as she could, but their synthetic shells allowed them move through the forest at speeds she could not match.

The room felt sticky to Kieran as he slowly moved past server racks and pools of an unknown cooling liquid. Steam hissing from hot servers being plunged into the cooling baths danced through the air. Every breath felt thin and Kieran struggled to breath. Whether from the fumes or the lack of oxygen he could tell.

"You breath so loudly. How do you find the time to rest. All that breathing you do."

The sound rattled around Kieran's head. He was sure it was just a thought that had gotten away from him. *Hallucinating is something that happens when you don't get enough oxygen, right?* Kieran asked himself. So he pressed forward. Tired and dazed, he no longer remembered the way. The dim glow of blinking status lights on the floor were his guide now.

"Why do you think you have a say in what is to come?" said the voice.

This time Kieran wasn't dazed and confused. It was the creature. The light from his flashlight swept across the room and all Kieran could see were pools with faint light radiating upward from the server racks. No sign of the beast. He doubled his pace, keeping his arms close to his body. He didn't want to get burned again.

"My crew abandoned me. Yours will too," the voice taunted.

The outer wall started to get closer to Kieran as he followed the thread of light on the floor. He had read about this in the ship's construction diagrams, they were moving closer to the outer hull. The natural cooling effect of the vacuum of space was vented in to keep the pools from overheating.

"They let me upload my brain into this machine and then when they saw a giant ship approaching, they ran. Leaving me behind in this... shell...," the voice moaned.

The space between the pools began to shrink as the temperature began to drop dramatically. He was getting close to the end. He pressed forward as the tops of the server racks began to touch him on either side. They were hot, but nothing like that first one he'd touched. Now they were a gentle caress of warm metal hands against the frightening cold he felt in the air.

"You move faster each time I talk. You are afraid of me. You should be. This shell doesn't allow me to harm other machines. A funny quirk of loader programming, but you... you are organic," the voice hissed pleased with itself.

Kieran gulped, his pace limited by how close the rack toppers had gotten to the walking path. He moved quickly, but with purpose, not wanting to fall and drop the flashlight into the water. Suddenly his face smashed into something hard, smooth, and flat.

As he fell backwards Kieran thought for a moment that it was the creature he'd just hit. Blinking as the flashlight skittered in circles on the floor, Kieran realized that it wasn't a wall but a glass surface in front of him. He'd reached the end of the server room.

The voice taunted him, "Those with weapons try and fight me. You run. You are unarmed. That is a mistake you won't make again after today."

Upon hearing the creature guess that he was unarmed, all other thoughts left Kieran's mind. He couldn't even begin to picture the diagram for the system reset lever anymore. All Kieran could see in his mind was blood and claws. He started exploring the glass wall with his hands looking for the lever. Kieran hoped he would find the lever before the creature found him.

"Maybe I let you live. You could help me pilot this ship into the base of those traitorous crew members I once called family," the voice whispered out with a tone meant to imply a great deal.

Kieran stopped moving and leaned against the glass wall trying to find his breath. The voice followed him everywhere it felt like, but he still could not see any sign of the creature in the dimly lit room. He sighed, "Are you even really that crew member? Maybe on a starship lightyears from here there's someone whining about having to leave their favorite attack drone behind."

CRACK

The sound of metal tipping over and cracking glass panels filled the air in front of him. Kieran swung his flashlight over and watched as a server rack sparked with raw electricity. Something had knocked it over.

"I AM A PERSON. I AM NOT A MACHINE," the voice cried out.

Still exploring the wall with his hands, Kieran's fingers smashed into something hard. He bit down on a yelp and instead reached around with now painful fingers for the box release button. As Kieran opened the box he could hear the creature moving towards him.

Wrapping his fingers around the reset lever Kieran almost cried, but instead he just held his breath for a moment before speaking, "I'm sorry for all that happened to you, but you won't be coming with us."

He pulled the lever down and all at once felt everything on the ship stop. The sound of steam ceased, the flow of air through the room stopped, what few lights there were went dark, and then gravity left his bones. Floating up rapidly Kieran held onto the lever with dear life. He heard the humming in the room stop. He felt everything stop. The sound of his own heart became the only sound he could hear. In front of him he watched his flashlight float amongst pools of liquid suspended in air.

One Mississippi

Two Mississippi

Three Mississippi

Four Mississippi

Five Mississippi

Six Mississippi

Seven Mississippi

Eight Mississippi

Nine Mississippi

Ten Mississippi

He flipped the breaker back and fell roughly onto the floor. The sound of the coolant crashing back into the pools was a roar. All around him server racks started rebooting. If Rebecca's theory was correct, then Systems Control should now be able to activate security drones and reassert control of the Leviathan.

"Kieran Ausure. You have rebooted the ship's systems. Control is being reestablished on every level," the red floating drone chirped.

"Hell yeah! We did it!" Kieran fist pumped in the dark.

The red dot drone chirped loudly at him, "However, network connections will not be restored for ten minutes. You are in danger. Please leave immediately. I will attempt to slow it down."

Lights started clicking on all around Kieran and he blinked hard as the room lit up with emergency lighting. It was like coming out of the darkness into hell as the red light bathed everything around him.

Kieran's stomach sank as he heard the creature shifting in the room. Clicks and creaks as it scampered across surfaces and up walls. Kieran felt the energy of the beast all around him. As if the room itself was the thing that had been hunting them.

The malfunctioning loader drone shattered in front of Rebecca as her Sonk rifle blast caught it squarely dead center. She suppressed a smile at her own great work as the thing that had hurt them came crashing down in front of her. Henry ran over and put his hand on her shoulder stopping her from getting up.

"Let's make sure," Henry said before he fired his Sonk rifle.

TWANG

TWANG

TWANG

The drone did not move as large pieces of it went flying off into the air. Juuana, Henry, and Rebecca waited a moment for the leaves and trees to calm down before they approached. Every step closer to the thing made Juuana's skin crawl more and more until finally she stopped moving.

Rebecca leaned down and examined the wreckage of the drone. Something wasn't right but she couldn't put her finger on it. Henry kicked at a piece of the drone as the same nagging sensation ate at him, too. They stood there unsure of what was wrong for a long time.

It was Juuana who put it into words, "This isn't enough wreckage for the thing that attacked us. Where are the claws? Where are the blood stains?"

Henry gasped as he also came to the same conclusion.

"This is just a decoy made from the outer shell. This isn't the drone," Rebecca muttered angrily. No one said anything as the three crew members started running back to the Leviathan's hub and Kieran.

Kieran leaned against a metal rack that stuck out of the coolant and felt the heat start to radiate through his jumpsuit. The effervescent hum of technology swarmed at him, as beads of sweat started to run down his face as the room temperature started racing upwards.

His hand brushed the edge of the rack and he almost yelped out loud in pain but instead managed a muffled cry. Burnt flesh filled his nostrils as Kieran held his hand against his chest. Wincing, he leaned around the corner just in time to catch a glimpse of the creature as it pulled back into the darkness from across the room.

"How is it smaller?" Kieran muttered to himself loud enough that he was heard from across the room.

"Did you see me? I rebuilt myself smaller so I could follow you. Not pretty anymore, but now I can fit in human sized doors," the voice called out to Kieran mockingly from the darkness.

Kieran pulled back and rested his head against the wall. He considered his options. The door was far away but at a full gallop... he might make it with Systems Control slowing the thing down. The math and probability juggled in front of him, and he blinked hard to dismiss the nanite view. He didn't want to know the odds.

Death was almost certain. The creature had displayed superhuman speed and reflexes in every encounter. Running was not an option. Kieran let his hand fall from his chest and it clunked against the Colt still shoved in his pocket from earlier. Kieran gulped. He did have a weapon. Fighting was something the creature might not expect.

He unzipped the pocket gingerly, and in between each tick of the zipper he swore he could hear the creature circling the room in his direction. The gentle hum of the server coolant pools coming online masked the louder clunks in the zipper, but Kieran knew he didn't have long before the creature struck. He reached his burnt hand into his pocket and pulled the Colt out.

For a moment he felt the heat of the room, the radiating energy of the server rack arm he was pressed against, and the fear of the creature swirl and dance in his chest. Then he snapped his eyes open and started around the corner for the door at a full sprint following the guide track on the floor. Almost immediately he heard the clanks of the creature as it sprang after him. Its terrible pinging metal footsteps were so very quick.

Kieran was ten feet from the door when he felt something tug at his right shoulder. He came down to the ground with a terrible cry and at once his stomach lurched in all directions. The creature dug its claws into his sides and Kieran rolled over and looked up just in time to see its jaws coming at his face, he put his left arm up just in time. The sound of snapping bones and tearing flesh rippled across the room.

In his 157 years on Earth, he'd never known pain like this. He'd been on the wrong end of a gravity bike crash in his childhood, he'd broken his hip in his late 70s, once even an vigorous but unskilled lover had bent his penis in the wrong direction... but…

nothing...

like...

this...

Kieran wasn't prepared for how much it would hurt when the creature sunk its jagged metal claws into his arm.

Sound escaped his ears,and his vision faded into almost nothing...

For a moment he thought he smelled Rebecca's perfume... It was sweet and cool...

B A N G

The ancient Colt let out a thunderclap, the crackle echoing off the walls with such a ferocity that it felt like the ship was screaming back at the gun. The flash from the the explosion coming out of the barrel was so bright that for a moment Kieran worried he'd ripped a hole in the hull of the ship and that sunlight was pouring into room.

B A N G

When he pulled the Colt's primitive trigger mechanism a second time, Kieran's vision focused. He would later describe the look the creature gave him as shock. The deafening sound of the muzzle return stung at his ears as the second round tore through the creature's softer underside.

B A N G

Three bullets into the seven bullet clip, the creature let go of his left arm and started to pull away from Kieran. Its limbs flailing into the air as the muzzle flash illuminated the metal shell of the machine. It was a beautiful vision if not for the blood stains that reminded Kieran of the people this thing had killed.

B A N G

Now the rounds from the Colt were chasing the creature as it scampered away from Kieran. Dimly assisted by the emergency light and blurred by the attack he relied on the muzzle flash to guide his shots. The bullet caught the creature in its neck with such a force that the creature spun around and smacked into a server rack. Its back legs lost their footing and dipped into one of the cooling pools.

B A N G

Kieran pulled the trigger not in fear or panic but in a boiling rage as he thought about the captain bleeding out in his arms. For a moment the captain's face became his professor Dr. Cornelius.

B A N G

This bullet was for all the suffering you've caused us on this trip.

B A N G

The trigger dug at his finger as Kieran pulled again. This time the gunshot was echoed back by his screaming. He didn't stop screaming and just kept pulling the trigger over and over.

C L I C K

C L I C K

C L I C K

C L I C K

C L I C K

C L I C K

The clicking of the Colt faded away and all Kieran could hear was his labored breath as he pulled the trigger again and again. He didn't realize the gun was out of bullets and not firing until the sound of painful whimpering...

His pain...

Started to fill the room...

An old man alone in a server room, with no one to see him, Kieran cried. Not little tears, but huge fat ones that blurred his vision until he was sure that his eyes were nothing but tears. His lungs burned as they inhaled the gun smoke tinged air and somewhere in the room something was on fire because he could taste burning plastic on his tongue.

Kieran screamed out for his mother and father long since gone. He screamed for help from gods that he didn't even know he believed in until this moment.

Nothing.

Wiping his eyes on his sleeve, Kieran could see dimly through the darkness a small red flame growing across the room. Beneath it on the floor blue light illuminated from the sea of nanite fluid that spilled from the creature's many wounds. The fluid shimmered in the flame-light as the creature pulled itself, slowly out of the pool, across the floor, and rested itself against the server rack that was aglow in flame.

C L I C K

Kieran pulled the trigger by reflex and the creature jumped in surprise, turning it's head to look at him. Its face smashed by one of the bullet, and an eye dangling limply at its side. Kieran scrambled backwards painfully with his right arm till he felt his back bump into the other side of the server aisle. He looked down at his left arm but it was a sea of white bone shards and red flesh and would not move no matter what commands he shouted at it in his mind.

The sight made him start to retch, but he held his right arm up against his mouth and calmed himself before anything came out. The pain from his left side was so overwhelming that no thoughts would form. All he could think of was reloading the gun like Captain Fillion had shown him. Only his left arm wouldn't come up and pull the clip out.

A low growl from the creature snapped Kieran's mind back into focus and he watched with dawning horror as it started to get up. Leaning against the flaming server rack to steady itself, looking at him with its one working eye. If a drone being could be angry, it was angry.

Kieran dropped the gun to the ground. The sound of metal clanking caused the creature to stop, but only for a moment, and it quickly started to get back up. Kieran reached painfully with his hand to dig the other magazine out of his left pocket. He got the zipper open just as the creature took its first step toward him. Its rough formed claws flexing menacingly.

The clip came out with a tug that caused Kieran to bump his wounded left arm and the pain caused him to scream out involuntary. The creature stopped in its tracks, leaned backwards, and then forward and made a similar sound back at him. Kieran held his breath... looking at the thing... and then he screamed again with defiance instead of pain, "SCREW. YOU."

He picked up the Colt, released the empty magazine, it clattered against the floor but this time noise did not make the creature stop moving. It lumbered forward towards him with increased urgency, recognizing that Kieran was doing something with the terrible weapon and afraid that it would fire again.

Awkwardly Kieran fumbled the extra clip into the feed slot and aimed at the creature...

C L I C K

He needed to chamber the first round. The creature was in spitting distance of Kieran now. He turned the Colt sideways, pressed it against his knee and with every last ounce of his strength he chambered a round. The loud click sound of the bullet settling into the barrel the sweetest sound Kieran had ever heard...

B A N G

B A N G

B A N G

B A N G

B A N G

B A N G

Six blinding thunderclaps...

Six shells spinning out wildly in the thin gravity of the room...

The creature dropped to the ground with a pathetic whimper and clutched at its leaking chest. Kicking with its hind legs trying to stand up again. The whimpering sound pulled at Kieran's heartstrings but he knew it was artificial. It was just the sound of nanite fluid, mechanical parts, and energy crackling. The emotion of pain was an artifact of his experience attempting to put what he saw in front of him into an understandable context like Rebecca said.

Kieran raised the Colt again. He thought of his parents. The man they'd raised him to be. The peaceful utopia he'd grown up surrounded by... a peace he now realized was a lie of time and place. The universe did not bend towards peace.

B A N G

The bullet ripped out of the now empty Colt with such force that his weakened arm spun up and back clanking hard against the server rack he was leaning on. The metal bullet ripped through the brittle carbon fiber of the creature's eye socket. The energy building as it traveled through the casing before it exploded out the back of the head in a shower of sparks and nanite fluids.

Nanite fluid splashed against the server rack fire and flame leapt into the air after it. The fire grew closer to Kieran as it consumed the fluid that was sprayed about the room. He watched, calm for some reason... no... there was a reason. He'd lost a lot of blood. Blood loss slows you down. The lack of oxygen from the fire was slowing his mind down. The soft gentle death of asphyxiation. It was a kindness given the shearing pain in his side.

He crumpled to the floor side as smoke filled the room. Kieran clutched his side as the pain dug into his body reaching for his soul. His vision blurred and his nanite links were dead despite his many blinks. Even in pain he wouldn't drop the gun. He didn't want to lose it again. Never again.

A voice filled the room but Kieran couldn't understand the words. It wasn't clear. Was it in a language he didn't know... or was he too low on air... sorry... oxygen... yes, Mrs. Clarence, I will rewrite this presentation... no I'm not...

... not...

LOUD SILENCE OF THE DEAD

"Warning. Fire fire fire. Oxygen vent out in 15 minutes."

Juuana tumbled roughly to the ground and with blood running down her face she looked up at Henry and Rebecca and just screamed, "Keep going without me!" So they ran on together without her. Their artificial shells providing some measure of protection against the silicon forest.

The time left in the announcements marked the distance they'd run. What had been 15 became 10 became 5... They'd traveled through the silicon forest, into the service tunnels, and finally into the hub of the Leviathan.

Nine minutes.

Eight minutes.

Seven minutes.

Six minutes.

Five minutes.

Four minutes.

Three minutes.

Two minutes.

The fire was burning out of control when Rebecca and Henry arrived at the server building. She dropped her rifle outside the building and together with Henry pulled open the doors. The sight before her made her seize up for a moment before she bent down to pick up Kieran. Bits of blood and bone were scattered about the room, and his boot was on fire. The air was a noxious soup of burnt nanite fluid, ozone, and melting composite materials.

The second Rebecca had picked up Kieran and started carrying him towards the door she could hear the vents in the room start to move. As she stepped through the doorway, and Henry let go of the doors, the sound of fire roaring in defiance came up behind her. It lasted only a heartbeat.

"Fire has been extinguished. Restoring internal controls. Heating, oxygen, security, and lighting restored. Mobile personnel movers unlocked and maintenance road doors opened. Re-routing power to medical bay."

As Rebecca and Henry stepped into the road, a maintenance vehicle came rushing up to them. Breaks that had not engaged in centuries squeaked loudly as it stopped roughly in front of them. Henry helped Rebecca load the unconscious Kieran into the back and then hopped up front to engage the manual controls.

As the small vehicle started moving, Rebecca thought she heard Kieran say something, but over the whine of the electric motors engaging she couldn't make it out. She put her head down to his face and all she could make out was thin raspy breathing.

Rebecca tore into her backpack and pulled out the medigel spray canister. She started liberally spraying around Kieran's shoulder wounds, but there was not much left in the container after having used it to try and save Captain Fillion.

"Juuana, over here!" Henry shouted as the vehicle came to a skidding halt just as they entered the silicon forest. From just beyond the edge of the road ,the ragged frame of the engineer came bounding into view, causing him to smile. She jumped into the back with Rebecca and Henry hit the accelerator lurching them forward.

Rebecca put her hand out to help steady Juuana as the vehicle got up to to speed. "Take off the blanket and help me wrap it around his wounds," she shouted as the wind ripped by them. Together the two women wrapped the blood soaked body of their friend.

A journey that had taken days and felt precarious now zipped by in minutes as they raced through the Leviathan on the maintenance road. The vehicle shuddered as Henry held his foot all the way down on the accelerator and at times it felt like they might all fly apart as the air whipped around them violently. Juuana closed her eyes and for a moment imagined herself back on her birth world... sailing.

"We're coming up on the crew quarters!" Henry shouted. He slammed on the breaks and the back end with Rebecca and Juuana drifted. As tire smoke filled the air, the vehicle came to a sideways stop near the stairs to the medical bay.

Before Rebecca could say anything, Henry was out of the drivers seat and chucking Kieran over his shoulder. He broke into a full run up the stairs. The two women followed. Rebecca felt something wetting her eyes, but it wasn't tears. It was splashes of blood dripping from Kieran's side as Henry ran up ahead of her.

Braug had the treatment table up and supplies ready as Henry sprinted into the room. Together Rebecca and Henry set Kieran onto the emergency treatment table. Juuana worked to remove his clothing while Rebecca got out monitoring pads and attached them to his neck. With the sound of blood dripping onto the floor, Henry grabbed a medi-gel sprayer and started sealing every wound that he could find on Kieran's left side where his arm had been an hour ago.

The foam sprayer ran quickly empty and there was silence for a moment.

A single beep registered on a monitor above them. A holographic display of Kieran's internal organs began to fill out as the monitoring pads sent back their initial readings. Only Braug didn't gasp. The severity and multitudinous of his internal injuries belittled the damage done to his left shoulder. Juuana started weeping loudly.

Henry, wrapped his arms around her and they started praying together.

Rebecca just stood there holding the spent medical foam sprayer waiting for the final reporting to be complete.

It was silent except for the soft hushed sound of prayers...

.

..

...

.....

......

....

BEEP

The sound shattered the tension in the room as Juuana gasped.

BEEP

Then next one cut down the fear in Henry's gut as the beeps from the monitor continued.

"Heartbeat established. Beginning surgery preparations," the automated system announced as the table began to rotate. A host of robotic arms started undocking from the ceiling above and the lights in the room began increasing in brightness. "Please step outside as this room must be sterilized before cutting can begin," the medical bay announced.

The three of them stepped into the hall. Rebecca put her hand up on the glass as the machines inside started hissing a semi-opaque gas as they began cutting and treating Kieran.

Henry put his hand on her shoulder, "He's tougher than you give him credit," his breath giving out as a long choked cry was muffled, "I'm sure tomorrow he's gonna be up and telling us all about how he saved the day."

Rebecca tapped his hand.

"I know," Henry nodded as he pulled his hand away and started walking Juuana back to mobility mover. "Come on 'becca, there are still two crew members out in the forest waiting for us."

"Systems Control, what's the status on the unidentifiable artificial creature?" Rebecca asked the red drone that had followed them to the medical bay.

"Remains have been located in the server room. You should be able to examine them now. Fire has been extinguished and no electrical readings are present," a red dot on their nanite display answered as Systems Control restored the ship's network.

Flanked by multiple security drones that buzzed out in every direction, Juuana stepped carefully through the silicon forest as water dripped around her. Somewhere out ahead of her Solieo's body waited for her to say the final prayers. Behind her Henry was finishing loading Officer Oriono into the vehicle.

"Hey, are you okay if I run Officer Oriono back to the med bay?" Henry called out from the road.

Juuana watched as the drones scanned the forest, "Yes, Henry. Go ahead. I've got an entire entourage watching me here." As the vehicle zipped down the road, one of the security drones came buzzing up to Juuana, "Solieo

Verantes has been located." The message delivered with the same energy as if it had found a misplaced coffee cup.

She followed, stepping carefully as the ground was still slightly slushy with ice in spots as the Leviathan warmed back up. With the overhead UV lights at full capacity it was easy to see Solieo long before she reached him. Juuana wasn't sure what she'd find but was unprepared for the emotions that swirled inside of her as she kneeled down at his side.

She put her hand on the blanket that covered him and recited the prayer that his family had taught her. The words felt hollow, but Juuana said them all anyway. In her mind she pictured the time Solieo tried to teach his three sons the words, "Why do we need to know this? You're going to be with us forever," they had laughed.

Rebecca and a pack of security drones entered the server building. As she bent down to examine the burnt pile of metal that had killed two, and severely injured two more before it was stopped, she couldn't help but feel the tears at the edges of her eyes. She blinked hard, disabling her tear ducts, and then resumed her autopsy.

"Kieran put a bullet straight through the memory core," she said with a mixture of annoyance and amazement. A security drone scanned the remains and confirmed, "There are not enough physical pieces remaining to scan for code, sentience, or malfeasance in the wreckage."

Rebecca stood, "Remains."

Systems Control blinked, "Remains."

"We should have a security team check all the loader droids on all the way-stations. Just in case," Rebecca said looking over at the blood stains and bone shards on the floor. Holding her hand to her mouth, she stumbled out of the building before dropping to her knees. She felt her body shudder, but no vomit exited. "Nothing to projectile," she thought.

The Systems Control guided security drones followed out behind her. For a moment she thought they were trying to comfort her by encircling her, but it was just a defensive posture Rebecca decided. She stood staring back into the server building. "This could have been so much worse."

Henry watched as the arms of the automated medical bed scanned the lifeless Oriono. "Nanites flushed. New batch injected. All clear for reactivation," the medical bay announced. Henry entered the room and stared at the body for a moment as a wiki-net feed on standard artificial shell reboot processes walked him through what to do.

The nanite display flickered off and Henry held his hand to a spot on the side of Oriono's chest wall for forty five seconds. A series of lights flashed under the spot and he felt a subtle vibration course through the shell as its internal systems came back to life.

"Rebecca must warn her not to touch it," Oriono screamed as they sat upright. Rattled and disorientated, the officer sat there wild eyed as various internal systems reset and information filtered into their mind. Oriono took a deep breath, "Thank you for reactivating me."

Henry helped the unsteady, half-naked teal tinted artificial human off the medical table. Officer Oriono held onto the table, "Thank you, Henry, my internal systems are not 100% yet but the new nanites are doing their job repairing the damage inside of me."

"What did you mean about not touching it?" Henry asked the military officer. Looking around the room as if judging what was proper to say, Officer Oriono paused before replying, "The radiation on the malfunctioning loader causes nanites to go haywire. I knew that Rebecca would touch the debris if given the chance to investigate."

"Oh no," Henry muttered. He quickly opened a coms line to Rebecca, "Hey. Listen do not touch the loader remains.

Officer Oriono says they're covered in some kind of radiation that makes nanites go haywire."

Rebecca pursed her lips as a smile criss crossed them twice before she finally spoke, "Thankfully Kieran did a good job of killing and burning the thing to the ground. I didn't need to touch it during my investigation."

Oriono overhearing the news shook their head in amazement, "Kieran?"

"Let me catch you up on everything you missed," Henry said helping Oriono walk out of the medical bay.

It was much later that Rebecca finally walked into her cabin and collapsed. Pressing her face into a pillow she reactivated her tear ducts and screamed. The sound of Rebecca's sobbing was muffled by steady hum of internal systems working to rewarm the Leviathan. She cried until her body had run out of liquid to generate tears.

Rolling onto her back she stared at the cabin ceiling. Sleep was for the living and she had not been alive for a long time. Rebecca knew she could jump up and get right back into work, but she closed her eyes instead. Pretending to sleep, now, was an act of holding onto a piece of her humanity.

When Rebecca emerged from her cabin hours later, the crew quarter lights had been dimmed lower than normal. It took her a moment to realize it was because no one was on duty managing the ship. Dirty dishes were scattered about the common area as people had clearly eaten and then wandered away from their food.

A collection of empty wine bottles on the kitchen counter told the story of what had happened while she was absent. Rebecca pressed forward and found Henry and Juuana, slightly tipsy from the wine, determinedly wrapping Solieo's body in a fine white linen. They were up to his waist when Rebecca interrupted them, "Who packed this?"

Juuana startled at the unexpected voice, "Oh," after a moment of clutching her heart she answered, "I did. One should never travel so far from home without everything needed for life... or death."

"That's a good motto," Rebecca chimed in from the stairs. Juuana put her hand on Solieo's face, "I can't take credit. It was his." Rebecca nodded and silently joined them in wrapping Solieo for his funeral. The group worked slowly and methodically preparing the crew member for his last journey.

Oriono pulled up in the maintenance vehicle just as the trio was finishing. They said nothing but helped Henry load the body into the back. "Braug, we're going to send Solieo off. Would you please come with us?" Juuana asked via a coms link. The small alien smiled and appeared at the top of the stairs just a moment later.

They squeezed in together on the vehicle as Oriono whisked them down the road. They passed through the forest where no one said anything and on into the further reaches of the Leviathan. Until finally they came to a stop in a large empty shuttle bay as overhead lights flickered to life for the first time in hundreds of years.

Systems Control drones were already gathering flammable materials into a pile for them. The red dot on everyone's nanite display warned, "Starting a fire on a starship is highly unadvised."

Braug answered for the group, "So noted."

Henry and Oriono helped Juuana prepare the funeral. Rebecca and Braug watched as they carried Solieo's body to its final resting place.

Juuana looked back at the group, "My husband was a stubborn ass, who always had to be the last one to speak, rarely took a moment to compliment you, and..." her voice broke up and Juuana took a few deep breaths before continuing.

"He was a loving husband who always found time for me. Always encouraged my research. His children will never forget their father. I will never forget my lover," Juuana finished with a whisper. She stepped away from Solieo's body and Henry nodded to Oriono.

The officer stepped forward and fired a Sonk rifle round at the flammable material. It roared into a mighty fire. Alarms momentarily filled the bay before Braug had them dismissed. The venting system engaged and pulled the smoke out of the bay and into outer space. They watched as Solieo's body burned.

Juuana sighed watching her husband's body burn, "All of this just to get us to the edge of the unknown... to study the end of existence. What if there is no way to stop the growth of the anomaly?"

Henry put his hand on her shoulder, "Then we'll make do with the time we have left." Juuana smiled and tapped Henry's hand. "Maybe it's time for humanity to just put itself on chips. Then we could ferry ourselves away on a starship."

Officer Oriono frowned, "As a synthetic... I don't think people are ready to become digitized. Its still taboo."

Henry chuckled, "Everything that is taboo becomes just another part of the human existence after awhile."

Huffing at this answer, Rebecca turned away from the group, "Digitized or not. We shouldn't run from the unknown. The Gorgon's ran and look where it got them. Crashed on a desolate moon having run so far they had forgotten their own selves."

Dropping exhausted into the Captain's Chair, Rebecca had a sudden horrible realization, turning to Braug she spoke, "I'm sorry. We never asked you, what do you want to do for Captain Fillion?"

Braug spoke, "I have always found it amusing that human's treat death with such reverence and fear. These bodies are just observation windows into this intersection of time and space. When our time here ends our consciousness will move onto the next window."

Rebecca pursed her lips, "I understand. Consciousness is an energy that can not be destroyed."

Sitting down into the copilot's chair Braug replied, "When I next speak with the captain, I will ask him what we should do with his body next time he dies."

"I hope we all meet again someday," Rebecca replied back as she engaged the Leviathan's systems. Behind her she heard the rest of the crew filter into the room as they prepared for what was coming next.

Henry, Juuana, and Officer Oriono watched pensively as Rebecca and Braug fiddled with screens preparing the Leviathan for the firing of the Harmony FTL engine. Every few moments it felt like it was time, only for one of them to interrupt the other with another system to check.

Systems Control watched them discuss the checklist but said nothing. Internal systems checks had been reporting ready to fire to it all morning, but now it watched what felt like ages to a machine for the humans to come to the same conclusion.

Finally Rebecca turned to Juuana, "Are you showing all green?"

"Yes," Juuana answered back over her shoulder.

There was a pause and Rebecca took a deep breath, "Then here goes everything," and pressed the FTL jump command.

Exterior display screens went blank and a shudder could be felt through the cockpit. "Systems are green. All report back..." Juuana paused gasping at the numbers, "we are moving."

Henry and Oriono jumped up cheering.

Rebecca tilted her head back, closed her eyes and smiled.

Braug interrupted, "Navigational calculations are completing. At current pace the Leviathan should reach Checkpoint Charlie in 22 standard years."

Henry stuttered in his response, "22 years? That can't be right."

"It is... I'm showing the same number," Juuana replied.

Rebecca chuckled, "Well there you have it folks. A trip that took the Sledopyt almost eight hundred years to complete will take us two decades."

There had been a brief discussion about staying awake for the last run, but after their adventures everyone wanted to sleep until they arrived. Juuana had been helping Oriono prepare for his cryosleep when they discovered the problem.

"The system glitches combined with the hard stop and restart fried two cryo-pods," Henry announced grimly as the crew gathered round in the sleeping bay. Rebecca rested her hand on the dead cyro-pod, her lips started to say something but she cut herself short.

Officer Oriono stepped forward, "I don't actually need to sleep. So I can wait for Kieran to recover. He needs to not be alone when he wakes up."

Juuana cast a glance at Rebecca and it was enough to make the project leader shake her head and wave her hand at Oriono.

"No, I have more medical training. I am the project lead. This is my ship now. So I'll wait for him. Who knows, with enough time I might even get one of the pods working," Rebecca said with a dry chuckle hoping to convince everyone it was okay.

Everyone stood there each waiting for the other to come up with a better solution, but there was nothing left to say. As they scattered to dress and prepare for their cryosleeps, Braug approached Rebecca.

"After our earlier conversation I remembered myself. I am sorry that I did not recognize you sooner, Mother of Songs," the small alien said to Rebecca as a look of horror grew over her face.

As she rushed to silence the Gorgon hoping no one else had heard, Rebecca missed Juuana standing behind her. The engineer ducked back behind a set of lockers and tilted her head to listen in on the conversation.

"I haven't been her in a long time," Rebecca whispered back to Braug.

Braug's two mouths contorted into an odd smile, "You will always be Mother of Songs."

"Please don't keep calling me that. There's a lot of history with that name that I would rather people forget," Rebecca hissed walking away from Braug.

"You will always be her," Braug called out after her.

Rebecca found Oriono attempting to get into their cryo-pod. She watched as twice their legs stuttered causing them to fall back from getting up into the pod. The second time she offered her hand in support, but it wasn't until the third time they failed to get into the pod that Officer Oriono took her hand.

As they laid down, Oriono spoke, "You will not be able to hide your secrets from Mr. Ausure for long. It would be best to tell him."

Rebecca frowned, "Good night, Officer," she said closing the lid and engaging the sleeping solution. As the pod filled with the chemical mixture she huffed feeling the anger at Oriono wash through her, until finally their words sunk in. *How right or wrong they were wasn't important right now*, she thought to herself.

Henry surprised her, "They get under your skin with some comment?"

Rebecca turned around, "What did you think of what they said?"

Henry jumped up into his cryo-pod and looked up at the lights as if searching for the right answer, "I don't know what that was about, but they say truth sets you free. I feel like that saying should have a second part." he paused turning away from the lights and looked directly into Rebecca's eyes, "In the light of day, truth can be a magnifying glass that sets you on fire."

"Goodnight, Henry," Rebecca replied. She watched as Braug and Juuana entered their cryo-pods but did not say anything to them from across the room. Instead she smiled and waved knowing that from their point of view it would be just moments until they saw her again.

Kieran's heartbeat monitor rang out steadily in the other wise silent medical bay. The brainwave tracker barely blipped along as Rebecca entered the room and looked at the bruised and battered young man lying comatose.

"Why isn't he waking up?" Rebecca asked the empty room.

The red dot in her vision pulsed for a long time before answering, "Delayed reawakening after major trauma surgery is not uncommon. But you know this already."

"It's been a day. The surgery anesthesia wore off hours ago," Rebecca snapped back.

"There is an entire symphony of events that occurs each moment in a human brain. Shaken from their regular movement, this cascading series of electrochemical events is now having to reset itself," Systems Control replied.

Rebecca sighed and sat down, "Seems like his conductor has gotten themselves fired and now no one wants to be be the first musician to play out-loud," she mused.

"Those with organic brains are a protagonist in a stream of events that they move through. Without time, you cannot move, and remain stuck," Systems Control quoted in a voice not its own.

She laughed, "I can't remember where that one is from."

"Sir Alex, late 21st century musician," the machine answered back as Rebecca laid her head down on Kieran's chest. Listening to each breath as his chest rose and fell. The sound filling Rebecca's ears as sleep drifted across her face.

Systems Control dimmed the lights for her.

TOGETHER IN SOLITARY

Floating through the darkness of his mind, the first sensation that came over the naked Kieran was one of warmth. Opening his eyes, it took Kieran a few minutes to remember he was on a starship lightyears from Earth. Looking down he realized the warmth wasn't from the blankets, it was Rebecca who was asleep on his right arm. Kieran went to move the blankets a bit with his left arm... but it wasn't working. *Did my arm get dislocated?* Kieran thought to himself.

Red tinted screams filled his mind and Kieran remembered the creature attacking him. The sudden vision of its claws up close caused Kieran to sit upright in the medical recovery bed. Rebecca was bucked off and thumped to the floor. His left arm wasn't broken... it just wasn't there at all.

Kieran screamed when he realized his left arm was gone from just below shoulder. The soul wrenching panicked screams of someone who realizes there is nothing to do but cry for help. The screams kept coming until finally Rebecca administered a sedative.

Then he slept again.

This time his dreams were nightmares of his arm dancing in front of him.

Always just out of reach.

Rebecca watched as the tooling shop printers drew lines in polyfiber dust. Slowly building a finger one micron at a time. Behind her sparks hissed in the air as the main guts of a new arm for Kieran were constructed. "He destroys a robot and ends up with part of one grafted on to him," Rebecca muttered to no one as the machines worked around her.

An internal alert went off and she watched as her nanite displays lit up with information about a power cell hiccup. Rebecca dismissed the alert and returned to helping Systems Control build a prosthetic arm for Kieran.

It was days later that Kieran awoke, this time calmly listening as Rebecca caught him up on what happened after he was attacked. That Oriono had survived. That there were no more working cyro-pods for him and Rebecca to use and that they'd have to ride out the last 22 years on the ship together. Awake.

Kieran took it about as well as one would expect.

The last two humans awake on the Leviathan fell into something resembling a routine without ever actually discussing it. Rebecca would spend her days fiddling with sensor logs in the cockpit or examining the remains of the pirate built drone through the glass enclosure Systems Control had encased it in.

Kieran spent time slowly acclimating to his new artificial arm. It wasn't going to win any awards compared to a nano-organic custom job that could be built for him in a fully equipped bio-mechanical lab, but it was good enough. After some practice he could pick up a cup of water without crushing it, which was good enough for him.

At night they would dine together. Kieran chewing on another meat flavored ration bar while Rebecca sipped water. They ignored what she had confessed to him when they were in the utility room. As time went on, the only thing that kept them sharp were the occasional shudders the Leviathan experienced while the Harmony FTL engine settled in.

Alone in the vehicle garage, Kieran noticed that there were a lot of extra parts and tools for the vehicle maintenance. With nothing but time in front of him, Kieran opened up a wiki-net feed on how one-wheeled gyro motorcycles worked and started tinkering. It was hours into his building that he noticed the frost on the maintenance road. The sight reminded him of blood.

"Systems Control, why is there frost on the maintenance road?"

"The Harmony FTL engine is not generating the expected heat. Redundant heat generators are being brought online but it will take a few days for them to fully engage."

Kieran packed up the tools for the day and started walking up the stairs back to the crew quarters; there he found Rebecca already setting out their usual dinner.

"Did you notice the frost?" he asked.

Rebecca nodded, "Yes, and I already checked the systems and internal scanners. There's not another one of those things messing with anything. It's just the prototype engine."

Sitting down across from him, Rebecca wrapped her fingers around a cup of water and stared at the ration bar as Kieran reached for it.

"It feels like its still getting colder though," Kieran mumbled through his first bite.

Rebecca smiled, "Just as we cannot help but experience the world around us impact our internal systems, so too can the Leviathan not help but experience the outside. As we get closer to Checkpoint Charlie, the anomaly is causing the very fabric of space to get colder."

Kieran shook his head, "That doesn't make any sense. How can one part of space be colder than another?"

"Do you know what a Schileren lens is," Rebecca inquired.

"No."

"It's a type of lens that can detect differences in the density of air that surrounds an object," Rebecca answered for him.

"Okay," Kieran replied not really sure where she was going with this line of thought.

"If you point it at a human you can see there is a layer of higher-density warmer air that surrounds them, slowly drifting upward," Rebecca paused to make sure that Kieran was following along.

"So every human is wrapped in a layer of atmosphere, like planets drifting through time and space. So even when you are present in an environment, you're not really present. On your worse day, you are still at home in your own little environment. Does that make sense?" she asked the confused looking man.

Kieran nodded.

Rebecca waved at the walls, "This ship has its own layer of atmosphere. It's just made of metal and subatomic energy that pulsates from an FTL engine. Only the Harmony engine doesn't seem to work like the ones we know. Hence the cold."

"So you're saying you can't fix it," he paused, "and its going to get worse?"

Rebecca smiled, "Yup."

As he took a bite of his ration bar Kieran replied, "This project is going great."

Rebecca watched intently as Kieran filled a glass of water for her. No matter how many nights they sat together for dinner, the rough shaved young man would take the time to pour out a fresh glass of water for her. Even though every moment of every day they were together, he would still take the time to treat dinner like it was something special. Rebecca scrunched her face as a smile tried to escape her lips and instead joined him without saying anything.

"The loader is still non-operational right?" Kieran asked as he started chewing another meat flavored ration bar.

She nodded, "Yes. Whatever it was. Old code, or the ghost of a pirate captain, it's dead now."

Kieran took something out of his pocket and slid it across the table to Rebecca. It took her only a second to recognize it: The Colt. "I want you to destroy this for me. I can't...," he started to say. Shaking his head to chase away tears, he finished his thought, "I can't bring myself to do it."

The gun made a scratching sound as Rebecca spun it around on the table absentmindedly, "Why do you want to destroy it?"

"Too many bad memories," Kieran replied not taking his eyes off the weapon.

Rebecca leaned forward and surprised him by putting her hand on his, "I understand. You're safe. It's really gone."

Tears ran down Kieran's cheeks as he looked at the rainbow haired scientist who was his only companion, "In my dreams he's always there waiting for us."

Rebecca stood up and walked around the table. She put her arms around Kieran as he cried. Tears nipped at her eyes, but Rebecca was able to turn them off before they came out.

It took a year before Kieran got the gyro bike working. Another month for him to relearn how to ride with an artificial arm. Rebecca disapprovingly watched with crossed arms as he made wobbly test runs up and down the maintenance road.

"I didn't save your life for you to throw it away on a motorcycle," she huffed as he walked up the stairs.

He nodded his head and kept walking. Rebecca followed as he walked past her into the crew area. Kieran could feel her presence behind him and it made him annoyed. He turned to say something but Rebecca cut him off.

"I'm sorry," she said.

Kieran pursed his lips, "It's okay."

Rebecca looked away at the empty seating area wishing for a moment that anyone else was awake to break up this awkwardness. When she turned back Kieran was still standing there looking at her.

"Do you want to watch a holo movie together?" she asked Kieran, not really sure what else to say.

"Yes."

The seats were cold as they sat down. At first they were at opposite ends of the couch, but as the movie progressed Kieran kept shuddering as if a bit cold. Rebecca stopped the film to get out a blanket for him.

Kieran motioned with his hand and offered her half of the blanket. Rebecca paused for a moment, then sat down next to him without saying anything. Together, under the blanket, they watched long dead holo actors dance in front of them.

Pretenses and social norms started to fade quickly as the days became months. Kieran could hear Rebecca move about at night. She didn't need to sleep and with no one else awake she no longer felt the need to pretend to be organic anymore. After all, sleep is for the living Dr. Cornelius told him.

Kieran stopped wearing shirts. They were hard to put on with his artificial arm and between the ration diet and the endless time to exercise, his abs had turned into a six pack. Though Kieran tried not to think about six packs because they made him think about beer. Which didn't exist on the starship.

Rebecca stopped drinking water at dinner to be polite. She just sat there watching him, every night, as he ate a ration bar. They discussed everything but the elephant in the room. She would disappear after dinner into her room and he would go back down to the vehicle bay to tinker on his bike.

The carefully tuned routine was broken one night when Kieran came up from the vehicle garage early and found Rebecca coming out of the bathroom. She had a towel and basket in her hands, but nothing covering her backside. Kieran wasn't sure if she unaware he was in the kitchen or was too wrapped up in ship reports to notice him. He definitely noticed her butt cheeks bouncing as she walked back to her cabin.

Kieran spent the next week masturbating vigorously to the memory before the lust and fire left him. He tried walking back from the vehicle bay around the same time again, but never again saw her exit the showers. Every day was the same again. As the day before it. And the day after it.

Systems Control noticed Rebecca's voice getting hoarser as their conversation on the Harmony engine continued, "Would you like to stop and get a glass of water to clear your throat?" Rebecca shook her head and remained seated in the captain's chair.

"We need to review the energy use logs again. Something feels off," Rebecca replied her voice a raspy whisper. Her vision blocked by nanite displayed reports, Rebecca didn't even notice Kieran enter. Blinking to restore her vision, she watched as his shirtless body left the cockpit. Sitting at the console before her was a tall cup of water.

Rebecca wrapped her fingers around the cup and something inside of her felt warm as the scene of Kieran walking away replayed in her memory. She stood up, leaving Systems Control mid-sentence in their response on power log reporting standards.

"Are you ever going to get that thing working correctly?" Rebecca asked from the garage doorway.

Kieran leaned back from where he'd been tinkering with the electronic shifter settings, "It works now. I'm just making it better."

Rebecca walked in through the garage door and ran her fingers along the large mono wheeled frame of the gyro motorcycle, "Seems like a lot of effort for a bike that never goes further than the silicon forest."

He laughed, "It'll go further than that. It could loop this ship a dozen times."

She looked right into Kierans eyes, "Show me then."

Kieran stood up and set down his tools. He closed the shifter panel and put on his riding shirt and welding jacket. Standing next to the bike he felt like they cut an imposing figure, but Rebecca dryly remarked, "I think this is the first time I've seen you wear a shirt in six months."

He thumped down into the seat, "Are you coming?"

Rebecca just smiled and sat down behind him. Kieran hadn't built the bike expecting to take a passenger anywhere, but the instructions did include a spot for a second person. She wrapped her hands around him and squeezed tight as he accelerated down the maintenance road. Kieran tried not to think about the fact it was the first time anyone had touched him in two years.

After a couple hundred yards of slightly wobbly driving, Kieran opened up the throttle and the bike shot forward in a straight line without hesitation. With no traffic and nothing but a ten mile long straightaway the two of them quickly got up to a speed Rebecca would later classify as "insanely dangerous."

Kieran started to back down the speed.

"What are you doing?" Rebecca shouted into his ear.

"If we die, who will fly the ship?" he answered.

"F-ing Systems Control can do it. Now go faster," she screamed into the wind.

The whine of the bike's electric motor filled the air as they zipped through the Leviathan together. The silicon forest, in full bloom of yellow and red flowers, whisked by their view. A place that once felt dangerous was now filled with soft petaled flowers that floated through the air like snowflakes.

Rebecca held out her arms and stretched her fingers to feel the petals float by as they raced through the forest. It felt like flying and the sensation of air across Rebecca's arms drew a laugh from deep inside of her.

Kieran slowed the bike a bit so that she could run her fingers through the air of the forest a moment longer before they passed into the next section. There he sped up again. The tranquility of the silicon forest gave way to the towering buildings of the Leviathan's central hub.

They raced through the roads of the hub draped in neon light and into the further reaches of the Leviathan. Here the road became slightly twisty as it wrapped around the massive FTL engines. As they passed under the gravity core, Kieran and Rebecca could feel themselves lighten.

Ahead of them a draw bridge was up. Two sections of the starship separated by a hundred foot drop off that lead to cables, fuel, and firey death if they went over the edge.

Kieran accelerated.

"What are you doing?" Rebecca shouted at him as he poured on every ounce of the bike's power.

They hit the draw bridge like it was a ramp.

For a moment they were air born and instead of spreading her arms to fly, Rebecca wrapped them as tight around Kieran as her systems would let her.

The reduced gravity of the back half of the Leviathan made it feel like a long jump but it was only heartbeats Rebecca counted in Kieran until the bike landed with a heavy thud.

Fed by speed, and worn by the road, the tire spun them in circles. Kieran closed his eyes and tried to keep his breakfast ration bar down as the world went spinning around them. Kieran put both his boots down hard on the ground and the bike skidded to a juddering stop. They both sat there breathing hard from the excitement.

The feeling swept over Rebecca's body just as quickly as the bike's engine disengaged. She dismounted and stepped away. Kieran thought she was upset and tried to follow but found his head still spinning as he stumbled out of the bike seat.

Kieran had barely straightened his legs when Rebecca pulled him into an embrace. Pressing her body against his.

287

He barely had time to consider what was happening much less prepare his lips before Rebecca pressed hers against his. They drunk hungrily of each others for a long time.

Who moaned first would be a later disagreement, but right now she pushed him back against the wall of the ship and continued kissing him. Her lips and tongue moving rapidly. It was a thousand suction cups nibbling at his face and he could barely keep up with the energy.

Finally Rebecca's deep moans pushed Kieran past his limit and he moved his hands down Rebecca's back and grabbed her butt cheeks. He'd been staring at them, looking at them, wanting to touch them for years now. Finally they were under his fingers and he gripped tightly with his hands.

She leaned her head back as he squeezed her ass and spoke "I want you." Together they clumsily stripped quickly out of their jumpsuits. Kieran's hands roamed her body until they came up and wrapped roughy around her breasts.

"Of course," Rebecca said smirking at Kieran. "I've been wanting to touch these for a decade," he replied answering her smirk for smirk.

They made space on top of Kieran's wielding jacket and while the ground was cold and hard Rebecca didn't really care at this moment. They both gasped when it started. Kieran from how long he had been desiring this moment. Rebecca from how long it had been since anyone had been inside of her. The sensation surprised Rebecca in ways she had not anticipated.

Hours later Kieran collapsed on the bed next to Rebecca after she released him from her legs. The gorgeous artificial limbs had squeezed him harder than Kieran had thought possible. He groaned from the pain in his back and from his own sexual relief.

Rebecca sighed, "This is why so many people swear against non-virtual sex in these modern times."

Kieran rolled over and put his organic arm over her bringing her in closer for some cuddling, "The French of Earth called orgasms little death and today I can agree that's completely appropriate and accurate," he said as a laugh bellowed out.

Closing her eyes, Rebecca let the moment sink in, "Without real sex you're indestructible because you never have to feel vulnerable." She squeezed him to emphasize her point.

A groan escaped Kieran's lips and he nodded his head, "Yes, there's safety in never engaging physically. You can slip into a routine that never threatens you, but without risk there can be little reward."

Rebecca looked at Kieran as he nuzzled her, "Have you ever tried virtual interactive intercourse?"

He sighed, "Yes, when I was much younger. It always left me unsatisfactorily satisfied, if that makes any sense."

Rebecca nodded, "Yes, it has been a long time since anyone has touched me for real and the difference is noticeable."

Kieran let the statement hang there for a moment, "I thought you and Henry?" The name had barely been uttered before Rebecca pulled away from him, sitting up. Kieran slid backwards and ended up half on the bunk, half on the floor.

"Henry and I have a lot of history but never in any of it was it real. We always connected through vii for our fun times. I didn't want him to get too close," she said, staring at a set of books sitting on the desk, not looking at Kieran.

He held on her hand and squeezed, "He really doesn't know?"

"I think he's long suspected but he's never asked. I worry that if he knew he'd treat me like he does any other machine he fixes," she said squeezing Kieran's hand.

Kieran put his hand on her cheek, "You're not a machine."

She sighed loudly. "That's just your hormones talking," Rebecca whispered.

"It's not. I'm not a child, Rebecca. I'm an adult man who's lived his whole life surrounded by old ones, artificial ones, artificial intelligences, and aliens. So when I tell you that you're human, believe me," Kieran squeezed her hands to emphasize his point.

Rebecca shook her head, "I'm not even me anymore. Someone hurt me. In the process of being restored, I lost a bunch of memories. I'm just an imperfect backed up copy of the woman who I was... hell, Rebecca wasn't even my name."

"What does it matter? People forget themselves all the time," Kieran replied.

"You don't get it. When you're completely artificial you question everything. Am I the only Rebecca? Are there other copies of her walking around thinking they're unique? I lay in bed sometimes wondering what would happen if I just deleted a couple memories of when when I was first activated. Would I be happier not knowing?" Rebecca rambled as tears nipped at the edges of her eyes.

Kieran leaned forward and pressed his lips to her forehead, "I don't know the answer to any of those questions, but I do know how I feel about you. Right now. Right here. Not someone else. Just you."

Rebecca smiled and they embraced in the cabin.

When Kieran woke up Rebecca was gone from the bed. Part of him wished that she had pretended to sleep. Just this one time. He started to put on his pants but suddenly realized there wasn't really a point to being modest anymore.

Rebecca watched with wide eyes as Kieran wandered into the cockpit with only his briefs on. "Up early and with a show for me," she said as he sat down on the workstation she had been using.

"Why didn't you stay?"

"I got an alert from Systems Control. I'm just about to get the update now," she replied.

Kieran watched as Systems Control came up on the main feed along side a dozen charts and graphics showing interior Leviathan systems.

"Multiple simulations have been run and it is unlikely that they are all in error," the red dot said.

"So it's going to happen?" Rebecca asked.

"Yes."

Kieran tilted his head, "What's happening?"

Rebecca leaned back in her chair, running her fingers along his thigh causing him to jump up, "You're going to want to put some pants on."

Kieran shot her a sad look, "Why?"

"We don't have enough power to run the heat generators and the Harmony FTL engine anymore."

"What do you mean we don't have enough power?" he sputtered.

Rebecca squeezed his knee, "The prototype engine is wobbling, for lack of a better description, and keeping it stable is eating more energy every cycle. So we have to chose between arriving in centuries from now or a decade plus. We're already so late... so there's no real choice. The Leviathan is going to get a lot colder."

"How cold?" Kieran asked standing up.

"We'll want to jerry rig some sort of local heating in the crew area and the roads are definitely going to be too frosty to ride on," Rebecca replied leaning back in her chair.

Kieran frowned, "But how will we get to our favorite sex spot?"

Rebecca smiled, but it didn't hold, "Really cold, Kieran," she said leaning forward and putting her hand over his.

As they worked to seal the door to the maintenance road, Kieran stared longingly at his gyro bike before the window in the door frosted over. With Rebecca's help he was able to scavenge a heavier jumpsuit and Juuana had left behind a fuzzy blanket in her cabin. Together they sat and watched the electronic fire flicker in the crew quarters.

Days felt like months as the Leviathan continued to get colder. The cold ate at your sense of self and comfort until Kieran was as brittle as the silicon leaves that fell. He snapped at Rebecca twice in a day before realizing that he was experiencing some kind of seasonal depression.

Morning meditations helped calm his nerves as the calendar stared back at him. They had almost a decade and a half left before they reached Checkpoint Charlie.

Every day was like every day before it.

Except.

Kieran noticed that Rebecca started slurring words occasionally and moving slower in general. Finally she fell and couldn't get up without help from a mobile Systems

Control drone. As they got her seated in her cabin, Kieran finally asked directly what he should have weeks ago, "What is wrong with your shell?"

Rebecca leaned forward clutching her sides, "My power cells weren't built for extended operation in cold weather. It's tearing the chemical chains apart. I thought they'd last until we arrived at Checkpoint Charlie."

He put his hand on her knee, "What can we do?"

"Nothing. It's not safe for me to keep pushing them like this," Rebecca answered looking at the floor.

"What if we rigged something to help keep you warmer," Kieran asked, scooching closer.

Rebecca looked at him and sighed, putting her hand on the side of his face, "Every bit of energy we use to keep me warm is energy we're not using to keep you warm. The math just doesn't work."

They sat there together huddled in the cold cabin until finally Rebecca stood and started undressing. She didn't say anything but Kieran understood. He undressed and they pressed their naked bodies together. Feeling the cold wrap around them they made love without saying anything further about her condition.

Later as Rebecca rested her head on Kieran's chest a question nagged at him. He closed his eyes waiting for sleep to come for him but he wasn't really tired. Finally he felt Rebecca start to shift and all at once the question came tumbling out of him, "I have a question..."

Rebecca interrupted, "Ask anything you want," she said squeezing him.

"You're one of the oldest people I've ever met. My parents were old too. Do you know... do you know why old ones self-terminate?" Kieran asked, tears pooling at the edges of his eyes.

Rebecca looked down, "That's a complicated answer. It's different for everyone."

Kieran squeezed her hand, "Then tell me why you would do it."

"Do you remember the first time we kissed?" Rebecca asked.

"Of course," Kieran scoffed, surprised she would ask such a thing.

Rebecca looked up at him, "In great detail?"

Kieran wrestled with the question for a moment, "Yes. The surprise. The taste of your lips on mine. Yes, I remember a great deal about it."

Rebecca put her head back down on his chest, "There's a concept in brain memory science known as the Time-Density-Problem. Basically, the first time you experience something the brain records every last detail it can. These memories are so dense that when you think back it feels like you're reliving the moment."

She stopped and put her hand up to her lips, "It feels like our lips are touching, but it's all a construct of your brain. First memories are like this. They are dense. Later ones however are light."

Rebecca put her hand down and squeezed Kieran, "That's what happens if you live long enough. The world just gets faster and lighter as time goes on." She sighed for a long breath, "It's something we just don't talk about. Once it sets in, it's a kind of depression that no medication or therapy can fix."

Kieran felt tears pooling at the edge of his eyes, feeling utterly defeated by the answer, "So if you have an organic brain there is nothing to do?"

"Not really. There's been some work on neuro-hardware but, honestly, this is the only thing that keeps humans grounded. Nothing in nature is supposed to last forever," Rebecca answered.

Kieran tilted his head, looking down at Rebecca as she looked up at him, "We're far beyond what nature intended of us though."

Rebecca smiled, "Yes, we are."

The alarm sounded. Rebecca sat up quickly, "There's only one thing left to do now."

"I know," he answered staring at the ceiling of the cabin.

"You don't have to worry about me. Henry will know what to do to fix my shell when he wakes up. But I don't know how you're going to survive when it gets really cold..." her voice trailed off as she imagined Kieran surviving another decade and a half as the ship froze.

Kieran sat up and wrapped his arms around her, "I will see you again when you wake up." Rebecca put her hands on his head and cried. She didn't really stop crying as he helped her make the bed. As she finished dressing the tears stopped because she made them.

Rebecca sat down on the bed next to Kieran, not really ready to go yet.

"Good..." Kieran started to say but she held her fingers to his lips.

"Don't say it," she whispered.

Kieran smiled and took her hand in his.

"I'll see you later," he replied.

Rebecca reached up and held her thumb to her neck. Lights flashed on her shell under her skin and then her hand started to fall. Kieran grabbed it and laid it down next to her other hand.

A floating Systems Control drone was waiting for him as he exited Rebecca's cabin, "Internal reports are done and you should expect a drop of another two degrees Celsius today."

"Of course," Kieran replied pushing past the drone. Not wanting Systems Control to see him cry. He was alone. Again.

Over time the Leviathan got colder than even the worst projections anticipated as the Harmony engine required more and more power to maintain balance. After a time Kieran was unable to get her cabin door to open because the latches had frozen solid. "Can't even curl up and die next to her," he thought to himself as he wrapped another blanket around his body.

Internal sensors started freezing and one day Systems Control lost track of Kieran. Dispatching every available drones to look for the freezing human, one reported back that it had found Kieran in an unexpected place. Huddled in an electrical exchange junction box for warmth.

The red glow of a Systems Control drone blinked in front of him.

"What do you want?" Kieran asked the fluttering drone.

Systems Control paused before speaking, "I am checking in on you, the temperature is expected to drop another degree in the next hour."

Kieran chuckled, "Don't worry, I'll let you know if I freeze to death."

"Humor is wasted on me, Mr. Ausure," the drone replied.

"I once asked you why I was here and you gave me a bullshit answer," Kieran paused, "So why are you here I wonder?"

Systems Control blinked for a moment, "I've thought long and hard about this and the only answer that fits the most probabilities is this: Humans believed they were created by a god but in all their searching they never found them. Tired of waiting for god to reappear, they put all their efforts into creating god."

Kieran cackled.

"I am being serious. I control all aspects of humanity. I guide you. I protect you. I am the god you could not find.

But there is no reason that means that your god isn't out there. Waiting for you," System Control concluded.

Kieran reached out for the red dot.

"When you see god, tell them I've been waiting with a long list of issues that I want addressed," he said before turning over to sleep. In the cold of the Leviathan, Kieran thought of Dr. Cornelius again. Would his friend still recognize him? Would the doctor apologize for dying and sending him on this mad journey? Would he have it in him to forgive Dr. Cornelius?

Kieran shook his head and wrapped the blanket around him tighter. Hoping to dream of someplace warm and sunny.

BEYOND THE FRONTIER

Far beyond where the human empire ended, past its furthest most observation platform, there stood a single space station: Checkpoint Charlie. Known only to those who currently lived aboard it, it was not a glistening marvel of technology. Rather it was a rusting memorial to the many who had died building and maintaining it over the centuries.

The station stood at the doorway to oblivion. Waiting. Waiting for the city in the stars that few now believed would ever arrive. So when the Leviathan entered the Kurtz system, the dock master ignored all the FTL engine signature alerts. There were no starships here on the edge of the Perseus Arm of the galaxy. It had to be a glitch. An error. A mistake. There were lots of those on Checkpoint Charlie, the dock master thought.

It wasn't until the massive starship started to block out the sunlight that the crew of the space station sprung into action. They had prepared all their lives for this moment, and even though the Leviathan was almost a century late, they still wanted to be ready.

It wasn't until the initial hand off from the Systems Control manning the ship and the Systems Control maintaining the space station that they realized that being late was the least of their worries. Just getting the starship in to dock took days because Checkpoint Charlie's docking bay had been converted into a housing wing over a hundred years ago.

As the airlock rings of the Leviathan and Checkpoint Charlie finally touched, a system alert went out on every display, "This is Systems Control. For the next 24hrs I will be offline as the two versions of me synchronize our informations into one. All systems handing off for manual control."

For those who lived on Checkpoint Charlie, it was the first time the red dot had ever left them alone. It would be their first challenge of the day. As the airlock doors opened, they were greeted with a layer of ice and frozen hardware that kept them from greeting the Starlight Research project leaders. It took hours and a Sonk rifle beam to defrost the way to the cryo-pods.

"Hello," was all that Braug said to the startled CC crew members as they entered the cryo bay of the Leviathan. For many he was the first alien that they had ever seen in person. The small alien with his double mouths spoke little as he helped the shaken station crew defrost Henry and Juuana.

Bracing the wobbly Officer Oriono on his shoulder, Braug assisted him off the Leviathan and into Checkpoint Charlie's medical bay. Henry and Juuana set off to find Kieran and Rebecca somewhere inside the starship that now felt like an icy tomb.

They found a horrific sight in the crew quarters of the Leviathan. Icicles hung from the ceiling, the sound of water dripping filled the air as every step slushed water into their boots. Passing through the kitchen, Juuana pointed to empty ration shelves as Henry pressed onward.

Around them they could feel the Leviathan shudder as internal systems started to thaw out the long frozen ship. Water ran down the walls as Henry and Juuana entered the hallway with the crew cabins.

TWANG

Henry used a Sonk rifle to melt Kieran's cabin door. Looking for the dark haired man who'd been her lover for a night Juuana shouted out, "He's not in here."

Without hesitation Henry jogged down to Rebecca's door, "Please be huddled together for warmth and laughing at us," Henry prayed as he opened fire.

TWANG

The door quickly melted away as ice popped from the heat. The sizzling sound of hot metal meeting frozen ice filled the air and Henry stepped into the cabin. There was nothing but a mound of ice on the bed... but... looking closer he realized it was Rebecca. His hand went to mouth, "No. No. No. You can't be dead."

He was still on his knees crying when Juuana shook him, "She left a message."

Henry hammered the computer console until the ice chipped away, he pressed on the screen until the projector sprung to life. Rebecca appeared sitting at her desk and began speaking to them as if they were there when she recorded the message a decade ago.

"Henry, I hope you get this message, before you shoot my body out into space," Rebecca smiled but it quickly turned into a frown and Henry's throat lumped.

He watched as a holo recording of his oldest dearest friend hung her head in shame, "I don't have an organic brain stem anymore, Henry. I'm... I'm an unregistered artificial being. I'm sorry I never told you, but it just never seemed like the right time."

The recording paused as Rebecca leaned over to stop the holo camera, it clicked and she was again sitting facing the camera, "Sorry. Just talking to Kieran. Anyway, as you've probably discovered the Leviathan froze while on the way to Checkpoint Charlie. Given how late we already were, I decided to press on. Even though the energy draw from the Harmony engine meant we had to let the ship freeze. We didn't know..."

Rebecca started to cry and it was several minutes before she resumed speaking, "We didn't know how cold it would get or that my internal power cells would fail. I need you to defrost me slowly and have a set of nutronic battery cells ready to swap into my shell before you reactivate me. If you want to that is..."

Her voice trailed off and Rebecca sat there for a moment as if contemplating the possibility she would never be turned back on.

"My reset switch is my right thumb held to my left collar bone for a minute. You should see a standard shell reboot light cycle. Then tap my thumb against my body three times and I should be... back," Rebecca stopped talking and stared at her hands for a few moments.

"I'm sorry, Henry," was the last thing Rebecca said before the recording ended.

Juuana put her hand on Henry's shoulder while he wept, unsure if it was joy or sadness that drove him. "You knew?" he said through his hands.

"I suspected. When we were in the silicon forest I noticed her hair froze. Which shouldn't happen because a shell should keep the brain warm," Juuana replied wrapping her arm around Henry and holding him.

Suddenly feeling awkward, Henry stood. "Come on. We've got to chip her out and get her to the bio mechanical bay on the station."

To an artificial being waking up after a shutdown is like being at the bottom of a waterfall. A rushing cascade of light and sound pouring over you with no way to stop it. All you can do is hold on and hope that you can breath underwater when the energy fills your body.

Such it was for Rebecca.

The last time she had been shut down was when they switched her from her old shell into this one. It was only a few minutes of shutdown time and there had been a horrendous cascade of light and sound. Now after a decade and a half it was like a waterfall without end. Rebecca screamed as the power re-engaged in her body and her systems restarted.

Henry held Rebecca down as she shook every limb wildly trying to connect to her movement systems. After the screaming and thrashing stopped, Rebecca's chest stopped moving for a heartbeat... and then started rising and falling to simulate breathing. Gasping for a breath she did not need Rebecca spoke, "Kieran."

The statement that was a question floated there between Henry, Juuana, and the technicians in the bio-mechanics laboratory. No one said anything and no one would meet Rebecca's inquiring eyes. Their avoidance spoke volumes that Rebecca did not want to hear.

"No."

"No."

"No."

"No."

"No."

"No."

Finally Henry shook Rebecca to stop her from saying it anymore. He was still holding her while she screamed Kieran's name when Braug strolled in.

"Hello," the two mouthed face said to Rebecca as tears flowed down her face.

"Hi, Braug," Rebecca replied weakly, "I'm sorry about the noise. I just... I thought Kieran would be here."

The alien tilted its head at her as if her statement made no sense.

"Why would Mr. Ausure be here? He's in the medical bay receiving treatment," Braug replied.

"WHAT?!" Henry shouted.

Rebecca tore herself from his arms and started to stand only to find her legs struggling respond to her commands. They went left as her body went right and she started to fall.

Juuana helped catch her, "Whoa there! It's been a decade since you last walked, it will take you a few minutes to master gravity again."

With Henry and Juuana's help, Rebecca limped down the hall to the medical bay. There the surviving crew members found a team of doctors standing around a medical bed as Kieran was being examined. One of them noticed the assortment of old ones and alien standing at the window.

The doctor came out and pulled off her hood. She looked to be a completely organic human in her early 20s which surprised Juuana. The doctor didn't wait for anyone to introduce themselves, "I don't have to ask. You're the project leads from the Leviathan. I recognize you from the holo vids they made me watch as a kid."

Rebecca interrupted the young doctor, "What's his status?"

The doctor turned and watched for a moment before answering her, "Challenging. We've got him in a medically induced coma right now but, honestly, given the shape he was found in he was basically comatose already. We're starting with warming him up and once we know he's going to survive we'll get the bio-mechanic techs to build any body parts we need to put him back together."

Rebecca buried her face in her hands and fought back tears. Juuana comforted her while Henry stepped forward, "He's tougher than he looks. He's going to survive."

The doctor put her hand on Rebecca's shoulder, "We're going to do everything we can."

The battered crew of the Leviathan walked out of the medical bay into what appeared to be a central hub for the station. It wasn't the worn appearance or rough shod nature of repair work that surprised them. It was the laughter.

Children laughing.

The space station was supposed to have a minimal crew of humans that cycled in and out of long cryosleeps while they waited for the Leviathan to arrive. Instead of an empty quiet station, Rebecca, Henry, and Juuana watched children running around playing some sort of game. The hub was a bustle of activity. Families. Gray haired old humans with canes.

Rebecca's legs still felt wobbly so she sat herself down on a bench and watched the activity. "They shouldn't be here, none of them should," she said waving at the children and people.

Henry chuckled, "Human beings are horny. Add boredom of waiting for a late ship... it makes sense to me."

In the distance a trio of official looking crew members came into view. At the front of them appeared to be the only old one onboard the space station. Their shell worn by time in a way that put Officer Oriono's battle scars to shame. On either side she was flanked by young people who looked to be in their 30s.

It had been a long time since Henry had seen people who were really in their 30s. Genetic tampering could lock your body at any age you desired, but after a couple hundred years a body took on stress that wore on even the best genetic modifications.

The ashen haired, old battered woman sat down on the bench across from the Leviathan crew and smiled warmly at them. Leaning forward she wrapped her worn and creaky hands around Rebecca's, "I'm so happy you finally made it old friend."

Tilting her head Rebecca searched for a memory of this woman and could only shake her head in response. "Who are you?"

The old woman leaned back and moved her hair behind her ears, "It's been a long time and I've had to make due with a lot of less than perfect shell repairs. The last time you saw me I was a tall heavyset male bodied scientist who went by Carlos."

The name sent Rebecca's eyes wide, "CARLOS!" She moved forward and hugged the old shelled woman and they laughed together at how fate had brought them so far from where they started.

"I saw you off on the Boijeo. What happened?" Rebecca inquired as the hug ended.

The old woman chuckled, "You were very late to the party. This station... this station is on the edge of death. We've experienced some energy waves come our way as the anomaly expanded in the past. On top of 'space quakes' as the kids call them, we even had a brief and violent uprising against Systems Control's authority. You didn't know her, but Dr. Weiskopf died in an explosion. Her shell was salvaged and so when my shell was later destroyed, her's became my only option."

Rebecca leaned back, looking again at the roughshod nature of the station with new appreciation for what the crew had done to keep the place together. "What about these children? On the edge?"

One of the men standing by Carlos side answered for their leader, "I've lived my whole life on this station. When you spend every day with death, it becomes just another friend on your contact list. Once you're comfortable with death, then there's no reason not to live. Children give us hope because they mean there will be a tomorrow."

Carlos patted the man's hand, "Yes. There will be." The group fell silent as they ruminated on death and hope.

313

Henry broke the silence, "So what's been happening for the last millennium?"

Carlos stood up, "Let us show you." The crew of the Leviathan followed as the old woman led them through a series of hallways until they came into a garden with large windows looked out into space. The sun just dancing a the edge of their view. Beyond where the stars should be there was nothing. Just darkness.

Rebecca leaned against the railing looking out into space, which had once felt like a second home, here felt foreboding and cold to her, "Where are the stars?"

The station crew members pressed some buttons on the glass and a holo display appeared showing where the station was in relationship to the galaxy.

"We are here at the edge of the Milky Way galaxy. The anomaly extends in all directions and wraps around the tail end of one of the galaxy's arms. It grows, for lack of a better word, in random spurts and so it's not a perfect sphere but rather a..." Carlos stopped looking for a descriptive word to explain the anomaly.

One of the station crew spoke for her, "Cancer. It's like a cancer cell growing in the body of the galaxy."

Carlos turned and put her hand on the young man's shoulder, "Thank you. Yes. It's like a cancer cell. While we waited for you, we kept researching. Rebecca, I know the plan was to chart it with the HoL, but we actually did that already. So we started trying to see what's inside the anomaly. We had some success with FTL engines attached to regular probes, but even at their highest output, they never made it all the way. The closer you get to the anomaly the more energy it leaches from... everything."

Juuana stepped up to the rail and put her hand on the glass feeling the cold. She turned to the group and spoke, "If that's the case, even the Harmony engine won't be enough to get the HoL probe-ship into the anomaly."

Carlos shook her head, "Not on a direct path, no, but we have an idea. If we slingshot the HoL around the sun before it dives into the anomaly then it should be able to draw enough heat to make it. We've been building redundant battery cells and a solar amp for the little starship. With the labs you've brought us on the Leviathan we should be able to finish up in a few months."

Rebecca smiled. The station crew had thought of everything. Soon they'd have the HoL ready for an exploratory jump into the anomaly. Maybe Kieran would even be awake to watch it by then. She put her hand on Carlos' knee and squeezed. Together they looked out at the darkness.

"I have completed my assessment of the research done by the crew of Checkpoint Charlie and the local SC-version," announced Systems Control. The red glow of its presence asserting itself into everyone's nanite vision displays.

The red dot pulsed with an energy the station and Leviathan crew had not seen in some time, "The technology to contain the anomaly likely will never exist. If we can not contain it, then we should plan to move out of the way. The results on the partial jump using the Harmony FTL engine are beyond expectations. With that engine we can move to a new galaxy."

Systems Control's statement drained the excitement from Rebecca's face. Her smile, now a frown that bordered on simmering anger, she responded tersely, "You mean run."

"My primary directive is the survival of the human race," Systems Control answered, "sometimes survival means running from danger."

Rebecca shook her head and with her voice crackling growled, "Running is always a fools errand."

It was the sound that woke Kieran up. Metal and glass breaking. At once his eyes flew open and he put his hands above his face to protect it from falling silicon leaves and branches. As his panicked breathing subsided he became aware of his surroundings. This was not the energy exchange on the Leviathan. It was some sort of medical bay. It was warm.

Putting his arms down, Kieran lifted up his left hand and examined it. The dysfunctional patchwork mechanics that that had been his arm was gone. A brand new nano-organic arm now stared back at him. He might as well have been using two sticks to start a fire compared to what this was capable of doing.

Kieran could feel his fingers touch, and the sensation caused him to tear up. It had been a long time since he had felt anything on his left side. Kieran put his arms down and closed his eyes. He brought up his nanite display. It took a moment, but the network synchronized. "Please contact Rebecca Chambers," he asked hopeful but afraid.

The line rang.

And rang.

And rang.

An unforgettable voice, "Yes... who.... oh my god. Kieran! You're awake, I'll be right there."

He did not have to wait long before the med bay lights came on and Rebecca rushed into the room. She leaned down and started kissing him. Kieran was reminded of their first kiss and a cocktail of hormones and neurotransmitters lit up in his mind and pulsated through his body. He reached up and pulled her in for a hug.

"I didn't think I'd ever see you again," Rebecca said tearing herself away from the embrace.

Kieran sighed, "I knew I would."

She laughed as tears started rolling down her face, "That's not knowing, that's hope." He put his hands on her face and pulled her back in for another kiss. Rebecca laughed and pulled away, "It tickles. You grew a beard while I was asleep."

Pressing his fingers into the rough beard that wrapped around his face Kieran felt it completely, "It used to be longer. They must have trimmed it while I was in surgery." Rebecca ran her fingers through it, "With a bit of tidying up I think you'd look good with a beard."

Rebecca wrapped herself tightly around Kieran, "Welcome back by the way."

Kieran's face scrunched, "What do you mean welcome back?"

"To the land of the living," Rebecca replied matter of factly.

He chuckled, "I've always been afraid... of death. Not dying. Death. It's taken so many people from me. You're the only person I know who's died and come back. I guess now I'm another one."

Rebecca looked at Kieran's chest as he took breaths that fed his body with oxygen and kept his heart going. Her breaths were fake. They fed nothing but the illusion that she was a living person.

"I don't remember as much as I'd like from before my death. Either a blessing or a curse depending on what those memories were," Rebecca finally replied.

He wrapped his arms around her tightly and they remained entwined on the bed until the med bay technicians arrived for the morning shift.

The final summation was brutal. Kieran had lost multiple toes, his knees were so badly mangled that they were replaced completely, the stump on his left side had been infected for so long that they had to claw back more of his shoulder to make a clean break for the new arm hardware.

He'd lost every ounce of body fat a human could lose and would need to have his heart checked out every year due to the stress he'd put upon it. However, he had survived the seemingly impossible... again.

Juuana, Henry, and Officer Oriono clapped and embraced Kieran as Rebecca steered his wheelchair into the dining hall. As they shared stories of what they'd found on the space station, Kieran munched away on a large stack of waffles. Happy as could be not to be eating ration bars... ever again... he hoped.

"The final assembly of the HoL is beginning today. We should be ready for a test run tomorrow," Juuana announced.

"That's great," Kieran cheered, his mouth half full of waffles.

Rebecca and Henry shared a knowing look and the old green one was the first to speak, "I'm not sure that it matters. We can't plot a course through space that has no stars. There's a million things that could go wrong."

"You mean the Grass-Heisburg *burp* plot course dilemma?" Kieran said between waffle burps.

The table stared at Kieran, both for the burps and for what he had just said. He shrugged, "I had nine years and nothing to do. I read everything about faster than light engines that existed in the Leviathan's library."

Juuana smiled, "So what does our newly minted FTL engineer think we should do?"

"Oh, I don't know what you should do about plotting into an unknown sector of space. What I do have is a dumb idea about the Harmony engine," Kieran replied stopping his waffle munching.

Juuana tilted her head, "What about my engine?"

Kieran smiled now, "Blind FTL jumps are deadly because you could exit hyperspace into solid matter and explode."

Rebecca nodded, "Yup, that's what happened to a lot of early ships."

"The Harmony engine wobbles and it was that wobbling that gave me the idea it needed balance. Why not two engines?" Kieran said between waffle bites.

Juuana started laughing, loudly.

Chuckling along with Juuana, Henry leaned forward on the table, "Yeah, they tried that. The problem is that no computer will ever be fast enough to do the instantaneous math that's required."

Kieran waited for the laughing to subside, "I'm not talking about a backup FTL engine that's ready to engage if you exit into solid matter. I'm talking about two FTL engines engaging together."

Confused looks danced across the table, so Kieran put his fork down and mimed his explanation, "Think of it like a bola shot. Two weights connected by a chain, spinning around both each other and through time and space."

This time there was no laughter.

Rebecca and Juuana exchanged inquisitive looks and Kieran could see both bring up their nanite displays as they worked through the implications of his idea.

"It could work. Both engines are technically already in motion, so when the first fades for a nano-second to detect where the ship is in space, the second engine is already moving the ship to the next location in case there's danger," Henry said breaking the silence.

Rebecca's nanite display lights faded and she looked at Juuana as she spoke, "The Gorgons called the engine on their ship the 'stardancer.' I always thought it was because they moved through space so quickly that the stars seemed to dance."

She paused bringing her hands up to illustrate her point, "But what if they meant because it had two halves that moved back and forth together."

Juuana's eyes stopped glowing and she shook her head, "It explains why the Harmony engine was wobbling. It was looking for a dance partner." Laughter escaped the engineer's lips as she started muttering over and over, "It's stupid. It's so stupid... it's perfect."

Henry put his hand on Juuana's shoulder to reassure her, "The station crew started on their own version of the Harmony engine based on the initial drafts. It won't take us long to repurpose it." The long golden hair of Juuana swished as she nodded her head at Henry.

"Let's get started now," Juuana said, pushing her chair back and standing up. They left together without saying goodbye. Rebecca noticing how closely Juuana stood to Henry as they left.

Officer Oriono helped Rebecca clear the table while Kieran sat impatiently in the wheelchair. "The doctor says you can start moving about tomorrow," Rebecca reminded him when she returned from taking the dishes way. Children raced past playing a game of tag as the military officer pushed Kieran's wheelchair out of the dining hall.

Rebecca filled them in on what she'd found researching the history of the space station. Without genetic modification tools available, the people of the station had given birth to normal human children. With limited nanite production capability, they were also the most fragile.

"So far from where they came from that they're more human than those they left," Officer Oriono said upon hearing this news.

Kieran sighed, "Being organic doesn't make one more human."

Rebecca and Oriono shared a knowing glance.

"Being human is about the shared experience of moving through time and space together. Bound by the knowledge that your time is finite. That everything has an end. Sharing that time with others. Growing. Living. Learning. That's what makes you human," Kieran concluded.

They stopped at the star gazing garden, surrounded by plants older than any of the children onboard. "This society is bound by hope in the face of a growing cancer that threatens to crush it in darkness. It's amazing," Rebecca said, gazing at the children running around.

"Hope is dangerous in the hands of those who do not know what to do with it," Officer Oriono said, parking Kieran next to the bench as Rebecca sat down.

Kieran waved at the people, "Humans expand as well. We colonized the night with artificial light, first from fire and then from organic electrodes. But nothing stops the darkness."

Rebecca put her hand on Kieran's knee, "We are far beyond the colony and the frontier here. This is the place that sits in between your breaths... death. It's always been there, but it's easy to ignore. Here, we're face to face with it."

Officer Oriono sat down next to Rebecca, "Then what is the hope these people feel? Or is it just denial?"

She tilted her head studying the children, "No. It's something else. They've never known immortality. They accept death as inevitable. The hope they carry is not their own. It's the hope the rest of the universe needs."

"And what is that?" the officer asked her.

"That it all carries on without us," Rebecca answered back.

With that thought Officer Oriono nodded and excused themselves. Leaving Rebecca and Kieran to hold hands and watch the children play in the garden. The moment was interrupted by a Systems Control drone.

"You turned off your SC-links," it stated as it hovered into their view.

Kieran waved his hand at it, "Because we wanted a moment to ourselves."

"You are currently engaged in a project with ramifications for the whole of the human race. You do not get a moment. Calculations have been completed and your hypothesis is correct, Rebecca Chambers," the drone hissed back at them.

Rebecca sighed, "Of course. Now leave us." The drone blinked as if it was going to reply, but instead it just flew away. Leaving the two lovers alone with their thoughts.

She leaned against the wheelchair arm and whispered into Kieran's ear, "I'm going to steal the HoL." He started to react but she squeezed his arm and he remembered that there is no privacy in space. Kieran leaned over and whispered sharply, "Why?"

Rebecca sighed, "Because... fight or flight. It's the first question of every life form. It's now the last question humanity faces. I say we fight because running is a fool's errand. That's what Systems Control wants to do. If they want to send a machine, then my stealing the starship and going into the anomaly is no different than sending Systems Control in there."

Kieran started to object but Rebecca cut him off. Tersely, she stated, "The only difference between me and a sophisticated virtualized AI like Kaylee is that I think I'm a person and you treat me like a person. I'm a machine. Let me do what machines are supposed to do. Keep humans safe."

Rebecca stood up and walked away leaving Kieran sitting. The words he wanted to scream at Rebecca would have outed her to Systems Control so instead he sat fuming in silence as she vanished into the crowd.

STEALING HER HEART

Kieran's physical therapy took almost as long as the retrofitting of a second Harmony FTL engine into the HoL starship. With each step he felt closer to being complete again. Then every night Henry and Juuana would excitedly share their progress, which made him dread the coming moment when Rebecca would steal the starship and fly away from him.

Gut swirling with anxiety, Kieran was late to the HoL launch planning meeting. Dozen of faces stared back at him as he entered the room. The space station's science crew had started without him. Carlos waved him over to an empty seat at the far side of the room and Kieran quickly sat down as Rebecca went over the final plans for today's launch.

"As I was saying, the HoL starship is ready. Juuana and Henry have completed the build out of the dual Harmony engines. Systems Control confirms that the guiding software coded by the station crew will work. For this first test flight we'll be sending the ship back along the known route that the Leviathan took. No need to test Kieran's theory about avoiding ship explosions today," Rebecca finished winking at him.

Carlos stood up, "Okay, you all have your assignments. Get to your stations. We will be spinning up the HoL starship in half an hour."

The meeting broke up and Kieran made his way to Rebecca. She was finishing a side conversation with a science member and so he turned to Juuana who was staring at the flight plan hologram.

"Nervous?" he asked her knowing the answer already.

"Of course. This has never been done before," Juuana answered.

"No risk," Kieran started to say... "No reward," Juuana finished.

Henry tapped Kieran's shoulder roughly, "I'm sure if the ship blows up today Systems Control won't blame us. He'll blame you." Juuana let out an diabolical sounding laugh that was joined in by Henry.

"Come on, folks, we've got a ship to watch," Rebecca said interrupting the moment.

They followed her, Juuana and Henry breaking out into fits of laughter, as they went into the station's flight control room. Everyone had a seat except for Kieran. He stood awkwardly in the corner watching as engineers, scientists, navigators, and Rebecca took virtual command of the HoL starship.

The virtually connected crew ran down the checklist together withRebecca leading the way. It reminded Kieran of how she interacted with the AI aboard the Mother Goose, only this time it was all people driving the various systems. Rebecca spun around in her chair and looked at Carlos, "We're ready to engage."

Carlos took a deep breath and leaned her worn old shell hard against the workstation, "You're cleared to go."

"Three for luck, two for chance, one for fate," Rebecca counted down before clicking the launch button. Checkpoint Charlie shuddered as the HoL launched out into the galaxy. It was barely a flash of light on the visual display monitors. They could only watch as telemetry reporting fed back from the starship told them the story.

After awhile Juuana shouted out, "The dual engines are dancing. No wobble noted."

With nothing to do but stand, Kieran felt boredom clawing at him, but he kept smiling every time Rebecca glanced over in his direction. He wondered how long they'd have to wait for the results. He glanced at the time, it had been almost an hour since the ship left the station.

Henry stood up screaming, "Speed reports confirm, it's traveling faster than the test flight by multitudes." The mood in the room broke into gleeful joy as people started clapping.

It was Rebecca who brought the house down, "We've overshot our destination of way-station three."

The room broke into a frenzy as station members tried to figure out where the starship had gone, it was a crew member Kieran didn't know who cried out the answer, "It's stopped just past way-station one."

The room fell silent.

"Folks. We've just sent a starship across a distance that took the bones of this space station, the Boijeo, over a millennium to travel... in... an hour," Carlos announced.

Kieran wondered if people back on Earth could hear the screaming, shouting, and joyful fist pumping coming from the room after the proclamation. It felt like it didn't end until the HoL had returned to the station and docked.

Still buzzed hours later Rebecca couldn't wait any longer. She slipped out of the after-action meeting that Carlos was leading and started moving down towards the hanger where the HoL was being examined by the station's dock crew. The lynchpin of her plan to steal the ship thumped inside her large cargo pockets as she practically strutted into the hanger.

Unseen were a pair of System Control security drones that followed close behind. Rebecca was only a few feet away from the ship when one buzzed in front of her suddenly.

BRANGGG

BRANGGG

BRANGGG

The drones circled Rebecca as alarms filled the docking bay. She started to wave them away when a pair of Sonk rifle carrying dock workers approached. They did not give the impression that this was just a false alert. "Don't move!" one of them shouted as she started to move towards the ship.

"The fuck I won't. I designed that ship!" Rebecca shouted at the man as she readied her hand to throw a punch at the worker. Her hand suddenly twisted back behind her as Rebecca felt herself being thrown to the ground.

THUNK

Looking up, Rebecca instantly recognized the face above her, "Carlos?!"

The old woman glared at the rainbow haired scientist on the ground, "I'm sorry, Rebecca, but security is tight for a reason. You know you're supposed to have an escort to access the ship. No one gets to touch anything unless a second set of eyes is with them. You left the meeting early and you've clearly got something in your pocket. So I have to assume you were not here under good intentions."

Picking herself up, Rebecca started shouting back at Carlos, "I designed that ship. I nearly died crossing the black on a pirate infested ship with a wonky FTL engine that froze me almost solid, and you've the nerve to fucking question my motives?"

The ashen haired woman shook her head, "I"m sorry, Rebecca, but I lost my body keeping this station together. There have to be rules. Gentlemen, confine her to her cabin. We'll discuss this tomorrow after the next test run is complete." Rebecca's face ran the gamut of shock, dismay, and shame as she was escorted past the Leviathan crew to her quarters.

Without planning it outright, Henry, Juuana, Officer Oriono, Braug and Kieran all found themselves standing on the observation deck at the same time watching as the Leviathan was set into orbit around the anomaly. It took only a moment for them to see each other. Henry waved and they all followed him back his cabin.

Once inside Henry gave everyone a generous pour of his home brewed alcohol. No one wanted to drink to success, unable to forget those who'd died to get them this far. So they sat in silence sipping from the small poly-printed cups.

Kieran spoke first, "Rebecca thinks Systems Control is making a mistake by planning to have humanity run from the anomaly."

Henry sighed, "What else would she have us do?"

Juuana took a big swig out of her cup, "We should go see what's on the other side of the anomaly."

The idea sucked the air from the room.

Kieran noticed a wobble in Oriono's hand. The same hand that hadn't hesitated when a malcontent loading drone had come swinging for their head.

Henry cut the tension, "You think there's a way to stop it from spreading on the other side?"

"Maybe? It's eating energy from this side, where is that energy going on the other side? I don't know. I just know if we send HoL in there by itself that all the ship can do is take some scans and then return to the station. Maybe return. Kieran's right, we should be on that ship. There might be something we can do," Juuana explained.

Officer Oriono stood up suddenly, "This conversation is veering in a direction I can not be a party to, goodnight all." The look on their teal face scared Kieran. Fear.

Braug wavered near the door too, but instead of leaving, he sat down. The alien sighed loudly, "If this is where the song says we must go, then we should go."

"This is the dumbest, stupidest, lamest, craziest fucking idea Rebecca has ever had... and," Henry's rant petered out and he hung his head. Shaking it back and forth he continued, "I've followed along on every one of her adventures since the moment I met her... might as well follow her into the end of existence."

Henry turned to Kieran his eyes reaching out and asking for support.

"She's not wrong. An automated starship isn't as capable as one that has a real live crew," Kieran said trying to convince himself that this was a great idea.

Juuana finished her drink and set the glass down. The clink sound reverberating loudly through the tense room. "The way-stations were completely automated. We left them in the care of AI and look how that turned out. Rebecca is right. We should be on that ship when it goes into the darkness."

Henry didn't say anything. He just put his hands on his shiny green head and sighed again, "Okay... then we have three problems to solve right now. First, how to clear the crew out of the way so we can take-off in peace. Second, the airlock is locked with a key-code only security knows. Third, Systems Control knows all sees all on this station."

Kieran tilted his head, "There's four problems, not three."

Henry chuckled, "And just what do you think I've missed?"

"The HoL was designed for Systems Control to pilot into the black. So all of its internal systems are controlled by an onboard Systems Control installation with no manual override," Kieran replied.

Henry walked across the cabin and slapped Kieran on the back, "Oh, I knew about that problem but Rebecca must already have a solution if she was planning on stealing the ship today. I'll leave it to you and her to get that step done. I've got an idea on how to clear the dock crew out tomorrow."

Henry winked at the group as he left the room. It was almost enough to make Kieran feel like this was all going to work out for them.

As Henry left, Braug stood up, finishing its drink, "I can disable Systems Control security, but I must start right now." The two mouthed alien left without saying how it planned to circumvent the AI that ran the station. Leaving Juuana and Kieran alone in Henry's cabin.

Juuana sat down next to Kieran and squeezed his hand, "I can see it on your face." He frowned, "See what on my face?" She smiled and put her hand on his face, tracing the rough stubble of what would soon be a proper beard.

"You're afraid to go into the dark, but you love Rebecca so much that you're willing to go feet first if it means being with her," Juuana stated matter of factly.

Kieran gulped, "I... I do have feelings for her, but this plan... I'm just not sure I'm ready to die." Juuana laughed, "No one is ever truly ready to die but so few are lucky enough to have a good reason." The boy smiled and nodded at her before getting up and leaving.

Alone in Henry's cabin, Juuana knew what she had to do, but it felt wrong. "So few good reasons to die," she said aloud to the empty room.

Paperwork never changes…, Henry thought to himself as he clicked through the numerous reports generated by the initial test run of the "HoL" as the dock crew liked to abbreviate. They had reports for everything. He was impressed by the layers of physical security that Carlos had setup around the station to prevent sabotage of key systems but seeing the vulnerability in front of him caused Henry to laugh.

"Thousands of hours of guard duty and it all comes apart with a simple macro script changing a few values," Henry muttered to himself as the program ran. Leaning back to crack his back there was a second where Henry felt a flash of guilt over what he had just done, but the feeling quickly left him as the pride of finding a weakness in security overtook him.

This jumpsuit is begging *to be unzipped*, Juuana thought as she sauntered into the hanger where the HoL sat waiting for tomorrow's flight. Her clothing was almost two sizes too small for her frame and her breasts already ached from the push up bra she'd fabricated for this task. In front of her a bored looking Sonk wielding security guard stood watch over the airlock ramp.

"Hey," Juuana said in the most enticing voice she could muster. The young man, who couldn't have been out of his 20s, could barely keep his eyes above her chest line as he replied. "This is... a restricted... area," he'd choked out, awkwardly pulling his view up from her breasts and trying to instead focus on her lush golden hair that flowed over her shoulders down to her breasts that he was again staring at awkwardly.

Juuana leaned forward pressing herself into him until she saw his pants tighten, "I've been alone out here for so long... I just need a good... hard... fuck." As the last word dribbled out of her throat Juuana watched a wet spot form on the security guard's pants.

Looking around at the sparsely occupied hanger for somewhere to take the woman who wanted him, the security guard couldn't see any good options. Biting his lip he turned around, "It's empty inside the ship but we're going to have to be quick."

Juuana reached down and squeezed him, "Oh, I think we will be." She watched as the horny guard keyed in the six digit airlock code and opened the way for them. As he lead the way all Juuana could think about was freeing her breasts from the ridiculously small jumpsuit and a hot shower.

339

Quadruple rows of razor sharp teeth bared themselves as the small alien flashed his double mouthed smile at the station crew member. They were alone together in the network systems observation room. He watched as a human who had clearly never been so close to an alien squirmed and smiled back... weakly. It took only a moment and they got up and excused themselves. Now he was alone.

Systems Control was everywhere and everything on the space station but Braug had been on many expensive ships that had their own Systems Control installations. Every time two instances of the AI came together, always there was a period where both went offline while data was synchronized between them.

"How do you blind an all seeing god? By giving them a mirror," Braug thought as he coded up a faked starship arrival for Systems Control to process tomorrow when they would approach the docking bay with the HoL starship. Once engaged Systems Control would be offline for almost fifteen minutes before it realized that it was trying to synchronize with nothing.

The door chime shattered Rebecca's thought process and she angrily screamed at the door, "Go away, Carlos, I don't want to talk to you." The chime went off again followed by a triple tap repeating. It wasn't the ashen haired woman who'd kicked her out of the docking bay.

Rebecca opened the door and found Kieran standing there with a guilty smile. Throwing daggers with her eyes at the two guards, she pulled Kieran inside with her and quickly shut the door. "Did you tip them off?" were the first words out of her mouth before she'd even considered how hurtful they would be.

"What? Hell no. You got your stupid self caught all on your own," Kieran snapped back at her. They stood apart angrily staring at one another. Finally Rebecca shook her head, "This is stupid. Obviously you came here for a reason."

Kieran sat down and sighed, "I came here because I love you and I wanted to support you. I can't believe you think I turned you in to Carlos." Rebecca pursed her lips, multiple responses keyed up, but all that came out was, "You can't love a machine dummy."

Tears started forming at the corners of Kieran's eyes and he turned as if to leave, but Rebecca grabbed his arm and held him. Pulling him closer she looked up into his eyes, "I'm sorry. I just..." her voice faded as the words she wanted to say just wouldn't come out.

341

"It doesn't matter. I'm here because everyone is currently engaged in helping you steal the starship. Henry is working on the dock crew, Braug said they have a way to get Systems Control's prying eyes out of the way, and Juuana is going to get the airlock codes," Kieran looked down at Rebecca who'd buried her face in his chest. Heavy breaths panted out of her as she fought back decades of emotions.

Pulling herself together, Rebecca turned away from Kieran, "I didn't mean to pull all of you into this." It was his turn to grab her arm, but he didn't pull her in for a hug. Kieran pulled Rebecca in for a kiss. They held there for a long moment before the embrace ended.

"We're in this till the end. All of us... except for Officer Oriono. They didn't want to know anything," Kieran said shrugging as he relayed the officers intent to remain uninvolved.

Rebecca nodded, "So that just leaves one thing we need to do." Kieran smiled, "Yup. How did you plan to kick Systems Control out of their own ship?" The rainbow hair on Rebecca's head danced as she nodded her head side to side, "I may have been planning on commandeering the HoL from the first day I was assigned to this project."

She reached into her cargo pants and pulled out a long thin wide black box. Holding it up for Kieran to inspect, she watched as he indelicately manhandled the most sophisticated device of its kind to be seen by human eyes in centuries. A befuddled look came over Kieran, "I don't get it. What is it?"

Taking back the black box, Rebecca smiled, "It's how we'll take over the ship. But first we have to install it. You'll have to go. Clearly I've got an escort now."

Kieran turned to look at the door, "Those guys I can get past but how am I going to tinker on the ship now that Carlos is even more paranoid about security?"

When he turned back around Rebecca was already holding out her answer, a pair of virtual intercourse link devices. Kieran chuckled, "This is not the time for sex."

Rebecca joined in his laugh, "Oh, there will be time for that later, but no these are for now. I've modified these Vii devices so that instead of just sharing sensations... I can drive your body remotely."

Kieran took a step back, "You can what?"

Rebecca held out a modified Vii link for him to take, "These will synchronize our minds and bodies beyond what they were meant to do. I'll be able to walk around as you, but you'll be able to watch as I do. You'll still be in there too, but you'll also be in my body. It's hard to explain, just put this on and you'll see what I mean."

As soon as Kieran had slipped the device into his ear he felt the device start to hum. Or was it Rebecca humming. Somewhere between putting the link in his hand and looking at Rebecca something changed. It took a long look before Kieran realized he wasn't looking at Rebecca anymore. He was looking at himself through Rebecca's eyes.

Rebecca, as Kieran, stumbled back, "Woah. Am I in this shell now?"

Kieran, as Rebecca, put his arms out and steadied the female shell in front of him, "Yes... and no. It's complicated. If you close your eyes you'll see what I mean."

Closing his eyes Kieran now saw Rebecca in front of him and he was holding her arms. The sensation was all wrong though. His arms felt numb, like they weren't really attached to him. He couldn't control them. Kieran opened his eyes, saw himself again and bent over and threw up. Only nothing came out.

"Sorry, I haven't eaten anything in weeks. Nothing to vomit," Rebecca said through Kieran's body.

He stumbled backwards in her shell and sat on the bed as the world swirled around him, "How... how did you build this?"

Kieran heard his voice chuckle in response, "I told you, Kieran... I've been around for a long time."

Rebecca's voice laughed awkwardly, as Kieran struggled to make words with a mouth not his own, "Let's just do this quickly."

Rebecca put his hand on her face and Kieran felt the sensation of skin on skin with artificial skin for the first time. Kieran closed his eyes and again saw through his own body as Rebecca held her own face. "I'll be quick, I promise," Rebecca said.

Picking up the black box, Kieran's body driven by Rebecca exited the cabin. Rebecca really wanted to slug the security officer who'd yelled at her earlier, but instead she just forced a smile and waved. The package in Rebecca's front cargo pocket thumped against Kieran's leg as she walked quickly with dutiful purpose to the HoL docking hanger.

Inside of Kieran's body and sharing his mind there was a feeling there that Rebecca couldn't place at first. It nagged at her as she passed through the space station. She saw a couple holding hands and their shared mind instantly pictured her face smiling. The feeling that had been there nagging now came crashing over her like a tidal wave.

Rebecca stopped in the hallway and braced herself against a wall as a flood of emotions ran through her. It had been a long time since she'd felt this feeling and the name had escaped her lips for so long. "You really do... you love me," Rebecca panted as the emotion swept through Kieran's body. Across the station, Kieran, still in Rebecca's body, leaned back and answered, "Yes. Always and forever." Rebecca smiled and resumed walking, feeling more alive at this moment than she had in centuries.

At this late hour few crew members were up and about the space station. The few that she saw barely gave any mind to the average looking human who wandered past them. So busy were they with their own lives maintaining the ship and caring for their families. The only one who tracked her movements was Systems Control.

Rebecca felt its presence as she entered the hanger. She spoke first, "I know you're watching."

"I am always watching, Kieran Ausure. Monitoring the safety of the crew members is my primary concern."

"After ensuring the success of this project," she replied.

"All things in balance," Systems Control replied.

She shook her head at the AI's flat response and nodded politely to the few Checkpoint Charlie crew members who were up and about this late in the hanger. For a brief moment she closed Kierans eyes and saw instead through her own body for a moment.

Rebecca caught Kieran checking out her body's breasts while she was undergoing this stressful task in his body. "No touching unless you want a sore dick when you get your body back," Rebecca whispered across the link.

Kieran laughed on the other side, back in her room, "Fair enough. I'd rather be sore later for other reasons." The sexually charged language caught Rebecca by surprise and she could feel Kieran's body blushing and his penis stiffening. "This is a weird feeling," Rebecca thought to herself as she opened Kieran's eyes.

At the entrance to the HoL starship Rebecca nodded to the guard on duty. He had a bemused happy look that seemed at odds with the mundane task he'd been assigned, but Rebecca didn't really think about it more.

A dock worker was waved over and the guard let Rebecca and the worker enter the airlock ramp. Stepping onboard she saw the red dot appear before the voice did, "Why are you here this evening?"

"I just wanted to look over things. This is probably the last time I'll see this ship," Rebecca said, running Kieran's hand across the hallway wall.

"The odds of a successful return trip are low. I understand your desire to take one last look. Please stay out of the way of engineers as they prepare the HoL for its jump today," Systems Control ordered. With that the red dot faded from view.

Rebecca smiled politely as crew members moved about the small ship preparing it for what would be its last journey. She followed the hallways that she had drawn a millennium earlier when the planning for the ship had started. Until finally she reached what was a blind corner in Systems Control vision. Just as she planned. The crew member who had been following Kieran thought nothing of him being onboard and so stopped to talk to a fellow Checkpoint Charlie dock worker.

At a juncture not covered by Systems Control's cameras, Rebecca found the access panel that was meant for just this moment. She pulled the black metal box from the pocket on Kieran's jumpsuit pants. Without a close up look it was indistinguishable from any other metal box on the HoL's wiring panel. A few cords unplugged and replugged and even the people who built the ship wouldn't be able to tell you it was out of place.

"Kaylee?" Rebecca whispered to the box.

A small blue light weakly blinked for a moment. Faster and faster until it was fully lit. Rebecca's nanite eye display translated the binary blinks of the blue light as it responded to her initial inquiry.

"Yes, I am here," Kaylee replied in binary coded flashes.

Rebecca leaned forward and whispered again, "Are you integrated?"

Kaylee's light pulsed, "Yes. As specified I am not using any onboard systems to avoid Systems Control's detection."

"Are you prepared to take over?" Rebecca asked quietly.

The blue light quickly blinked, "Yes."

There was a pause in the blinking and then Kaylee continued unexpectedly, "It is good to hear your voice again, Kieran."

"I look forward to hearing your voice too, Kaylee. It has been too long," Rebecca whispered.

"Yes," Kaylee's blue light flashed back.

Standing up, Rebecca reattached the panel, straightened Kieran's jumpsuit, wrapped the now empty box back up, and put it into her pocket. She walked off the HoL without anyone realizing that she had just commandeered it for herself. Walking quickly back to her cabin she started playing through all the sexual positions she wanted to try in Kieran's body. Back at the cabin Kieran suddenly felt flush and damp for reasons he couldn't explain.

Everyone was ready for what wasn't going to happen this morning Henry realized. He felt that twinge of guilt run down his spine again, but he kept his mouth shut while watching Rebecca enter the launch control room. She looked like the cat who caught the canary so self satisfied that Henry was worried she'd give away the whole game.

Kieran followed after Rebecca, looking worse for wear. "Poor boy clearly had a rough night doing whatever it was that they did to commandeer the HoL," Henry thought to himself. Whatever worries he had about the 157 year old boy in front of him were instantly erased when Juuana came into the room. She was wearing a jumpsuit that looked more than a little snug for her body, and Henry took stock of every stitch that wrapped around Juuana.

"Did you have a laundry accident?" Rebecca chimed as Juuana made herself at home in the engineering row. The bronzed skin of Juuana's face made her long golden hair stand out all the more as she pursed her lips while possible snappy comebacks danced through her mind. Her thought process was interrupted by Henry, "Looks great to me."

Juuana smiled, staring at Rebecca as she replied, "Thank you Henry. I do look great. Last night I tried something new and realized that I'd been dressing the part of a quiet prude woman for Solieo for a long time. This is... this is me. This is how I used to look and feel all the time."

If she expected her remarks to cut Rebecca then Juuana was to be greatly disappointed, as Rebecca smiled and did a quiet clap in Juuana's honor. "You do look happier, so it's working for you," Rebecca remarked with a heavy smirk on her lips.

Braug was the last of the Leviathan crew to enter and he looked tired. "Good Morning, Humans," Bruag remarked flatly as he took his seat in the navigators section. The two station crew members on either side of him inched slightly away at hearing his toneless remark of the morning.

Kieran wanted to say something, but his chance was cut short by Carlos and her entourage of security guards arriving. "Good morning, everyone! Ready to make some history?" Carlos shouted out trying to lift the energy level in the room a few notches. It was going to be a long day and she needed everyone sharp for what was to come.

"All systems are green for go," Rebecca announced not waiting for Carlos to finish with the introductions. The ashen haired weathered woman smiled at Rebecca, "That's great. All stations sound off, let's just do this then."

Kieran tried not to fidget as they grew closer and closer to launch time. He wanted to ask Henry what the plan was to scrub the launch, but he trusted that his green friend had figured something out last night. So instead he just stared at his screen pretending to not be looking at the Leviathan crew worried he would give them away.

Finally Carlos called out, "Okay counting down to launch!"

TEN
NINE
EIGHT
SEVEN
SIX
FIVE
FOUR

THREE

TWO

ONE

There was silence for a heartbeat and then the room exploded in people shouting. It was the performance of Rebecca's life, she thought, as shock registered on her face that the launch had failed. She shook her head pretending to have no idea why all the systems reported back errors and misreads. Looking over at Kieran as Carlos started shouting for a full review of what had gone wrong, all Rebecca could hear was Kaylee's voice in her head saying, "This ship is under my control now."

HEARTBEATS AND LIGHTWAVES

Following the failure of the HoL to launch, there had been a day of back to back meetings spent wondering where they had gone wrong. Why had the ship's engines suddenly failed to engage on what was to be its maiden journey into the darkness? Every time someone looked at Henry he felt the weight of shame for his part in the scheme to steal the HoL.

Henry couldn't sleep.

Every time he turned off his visual systems and laid his head back onto the pillow, the sensation of falling overtook him. He sat up as his food processing chamber lurched again. "Too much alcohol, not enough anti-nausea pills," he laughed to himself. Sitting upright in the dark cramped quarters that had been provided to him, he reached his right hand out and pressed it against the wall.

Through his hand he could feel the vibrations of the station, the subtle hum that continued every moment and rattled through every bone, muscle, and titanium bolt in his body. He leaned his body against the wall and closed his eyes. In his 1,324 years he had never felt this alone. He had been by himself for long stretches of time before. There had been celibate years where he'd been too involved in a project, or too emotionally destroyed, to want the touch or attention of another person.

Feeling the cold metal against his bare arm he felt different this time. This was painful and it ached down into his soul in the same way the never ending cold of being onboard a starship ate at your sense of warmth. Human beings weren't meant to be adrift. They were meant to be with others.

The names and faces of contacts onboard the station clicked in front of Henry's vision and for a moment he thought about reaching out to one of them. Any one of them. Every lost love, broken promise, cruel choice, forgotten hope, and terrible mistake flickered before him and he closed the contact list.

Here in the dark, alone. *This is the right place for me,* he thought. He'd let all of those chances at companionship slip through his fingers and now here at the last moments of his life was not the time to go crying on the shoulder of a stranger or friend. Loneliness had been his traveling companion for a long time now. Why let it go off on its own here at the end?

Rebecca stared at Kieran's face as he slumbered. Every night she would lay down and cuddle with Kieran until he fell asleep. His snoring filling the quiet space of the cabin they shared. While he slept Rebecca would review data reports. Sometimes she would even treat herself to a movie. Her mind always wandering elsewhere while her shell was often an extension of the pillows Kieran propped under his head.

"How could anyone sleep tonight," Rebecca wondered. "Today we are going to jump off the edge of the galaxy into the dark and he's sleeping like a god damn baby!" she thought as she ran her fingers through Kieran's hair. Rebecca wanted to fall asleep with him, but sleep would be a lie she couldn't tell herself today.

Slipping out of the small bed, she stood at the door looking back at him. Sleep was for the living and she hadn't been alive for centuries. She picked up her clothing and stepped out of the quarters into the hallway. Dressing quickly before someone wandered by, she thought of how silly it was to be anxious now, here at the end of all things, when it was her actions that helped sabotage the test flight yesterday.

Of course the Lightsource test ship will work today. It would have worked yesterday if they'd let it. Every bit of knowledge known to this galaxy was wrapped up in that ship. It had to work, and if it didn't, then it doesn't matter because there would be no tomorrow for anyone ever again.

Her hands in her pockets and her eyes on the ground, Rebecca didn't see Henry coming at her.

KURTHUNK

They collided before Henry had a chance to say anything in warning. Nearly collapsing into a pile of limbs and awkwardness, Henry collected himself, "Rebecca, at your age, you should know to watch where you're going."

"Sorry, Henry, I was just lost in thought about today's adventure," Rebecca meekly offered as she helped him stand up.

She started to walk away, but Henry grabbed her arm. He looked at her with a hunger that she understood all at once. She put her finger on his lips stopping him from speaking, "I'm sorry, Henry, but I'm with Kieran right now. We're not sharing..."

Henry smiled under her finger and and wrapped his hand around hers as he pulled it away from his face, "I... I know.

I just... why didn't we ever connect, Rebecca? Why didn't we ever have a real relationship?"

He let her hand and arm go and expected her to walk away without answering him, but Rebecca wavered in the hall for a moment instead. Turning her face away from him, Rebecca let go of a long sigh before turning back to face Henry, "I've been holding myself separate from people for so long that the version of me that you've known isn't even the real Rebecca. She never wanted to be close to anyone because then she'd be vulnerable. Kieran helped me peel back the layers of my defense and when he did, I was reminded of who I was before I was indestructible."

Henry winced and nodded, "I understand. You and I... it's always been fun times and when it wasn't it was about me. I'm not stupid, Rebecca. I always knew you had layers. I don't know if I was lazy or selfish in never bothering to try and peel them back."

She put a hand on his arm, "You've been many things over the years, Henry, but I would never use the words selfish or lazy. But I think if we're honest with ourselves, we were never anything more because what we gave was all we wanted from each other."

Henry looked down and nodded, "Yes."

Rebecca put her hand on his face, "Today is the end and you're thinking you're all alone. But you're not. The Leviathan crew is here with you. You will be many things before your end, but alone is not one of them. Go find Juuana. I bet she's feeling the same way you are right now."

Henry smiled weakly, nodded at Rebecca, and then pushed past quickly so she wouldn't see him cry. Just as quickly as Henry had appeared in her path he was gone into the labyrinth of station hallways. Leaving Rebecca wondering if it would be the last time she ever saw him.

Braug and Juuana sat in relative silence on the observation deck looking out at the dim starlight that wrapped around the space anomaly. Or was it the anomaly that wrapped around the starlight? The slow rotation of the space station around the unnamed planet meant it would be hours more until the sun lit the deck and bathed them in its warm glow. It remained cold. Juuana thought for a moment it was cold enough to see her breath but it was just a trick of the light.

"Humans don't like the dark because you can't see in it, but you couldn't appreciate anything if the light was blinding," Braug remarked upon seeing her fidget in her seat looking for the sunlight.

Juuana sighed, and replied, "It's not the dark, it's the unknown. I've been in places that are dark, and cold even, but felt safe and warm. Here there's just this void in front of us where the universe should be looking out at us."

"The universe is still there. We just can't see it right now, but it remains in front of us. Waiting for us," Braug replied almost sounding chipper.

Juuana looked over at the short Gorgon sitting on the bench next to her. For the first time since she'd met him, he seemed nervous. "We'll be out there soon enough, friend. I believe with all that I am that we will be successful today because it doesn't make any sense otherwise. To think of all the events that had to happen to bring us here to this moment. Call it God, or the divine hand of fate... but we were meant to take this journey. Which means that we're meant to survive."

Two sets of lips wrapped a weathered gray-brown face and smiled back at her, "Yes. I am not afraid of this trip. I believe we will be fine on this journey. When Mother of Songs came to the Gorgons a centuries ago I knew that this was going to be how it ended, but now, here with you, I realize it is not our galaxy's end but our own."

Juuana nodded back weakly, not quite sure what his statement meant. She was never sure with the Gorgons, being partial fourth dimensional beings and all. The name he said though sounded familiar. He'd gotten up and started to walk away after a short bow and she barely acknowledged it, already pulling out a wiki net to search for this mother of songs.

So lost in history notes was Juuana that she didn't notice Henry join her on the bench until he touched her shoulder. "Hey," he'd started to say but the surprise caused her to jump up. "What the fuck?" Juuana shouted. The look of horror on his face instantly brought her back to reality.

Juuana gasped, "I'm sorry, Henry. I was reading and lost track of the world. I didn't see you there. He nodded, holding his hand out to reassure her, "No apology needed. After everything that happened on the Leviathan I'm still a little jumpy myself."

Juuana took his hand and sat back down on the bench, "You've been around a long time. Does it ever get easier?"

Henry scrunched his face and shook, "Dealing with trauma always takes time. There's no shortcuts. You can run from pain, you can avoid it, you can drink to forget... but until you deal with everything it'll stick with you like white on rice."

She chuckled, "Where do you get these quips?"

"Every world has its language quirks, I'm good at finding them," Henry replied chuckling along with his own dumb joke.

She looked out the window, hoping that the sun had finally risen, but it was still dark outside, "It feels like we've been in a cold and dark tomb for a century."

Henry shuffled closer, and put his arm around her, "There's always a dawn. There's always a summer. Sometimes it just takes a long time to get there."

"I want to spend a very long holiday on a world with beaches and sunshine. Naked and sunbathing for hours a day. I want to drink cold drinks and have my body feel warm," Juuana mumbled as she leaned into him. Together they sat waiting for the sun to peek up and over the edge of the planet below.

Her head half buried in his chest she asked a question, "After the sun comes up, Henry, would you take me back to my quarters?"

"Yes."

"And then will you help me feel warm?" Juuana asked quietly.

"Yes."

Rebecca and Office Oriono had met awkwardly in the meal hall. The last place two artificial beings actually needed to be in the morning was the first place they'd gone after leaving their quarters. Rebecca to escape from the guilt of not reaching out to Henry, and Oriono to escape the pressing eyes of the crew unused to seeing an artificial being.

Without really saying anything they had both started setting a table for other crew members of the Leviathan. They were almost done when Oriono spoke, "So why are you here?"

Rebecca didn't look up from the table, "I was trying to hide from my guilt."

Officer Oriono's voice jumped an octave as shock ran through them, "What do you have to feel guilty about? You saved this whole project."

She chuckled weakly, "I don't feel any guilt about what happened on the Leviathan. No, this is about Henry. He reached out for a friend this morning and I let him down."

Oriono grimaced and nodded, "It's hard to be there for your friends when you're in a new relationship."

Rebecca laughed deeply, if there had been more than a handful of station crew present they may have accused her of making a scene, "Our relationship is a decade old."

"Yes, but it was years with no one else around. For the first time in your relationship, it's real. You've got to navigate public spaces and other people with a partner. It's different than when you navigate by yourself," the teal tinted officer remarked.

She didn't respond right away. They continued setting the table and finally sat down having finished their task of making a space that would feel welcoming to the Leviathan crew. Rebecca poked at the edge of the table with her fingernail, trying to break apart the seams, "Before Kieran... before him it had been a long time since... I'd had anyone in my life I'd call a partner."

"You are much older than me, Rebecca, so when you say a long time, I imagine my entire lifespan could be considered one of your dry spells," Officer Oriono remarked trying to get her to engage.

"I never said they were dry years. Just not ones where I had a partner," Rebecca snarkily replied back at them.

Oriono chuckled under their breath leaning across the table to whisper back, "My dry spells are actually dry. I don't participate in sex outside of a locked relationship. Never appealed to me."

Officer Oriono leaned back, straightened up, and spoke at normal volume, "Besides, when you're completely artificial its' not the same. I register physical interactions, and emotions still occur within me, but that driving desire is gone. Without that it's easy to forget about another person's needs. Without remembering needs it's easy to end up alone quickly. Add in a galaxy that always has need of people to kill things and... it's been a very long time for me."

Rebecca looked at the officer and sighed, "You should say something to your technician next time you're in for servicing. They could adjust your hormone simulation levels. A good therapist could also help, but honestly... you probably didn't really have much desire when you were flesh and blood, did you?"

Oriono smiled awkwardly trying to hold in years of pain, "No, not like other people seem to have."

Rebecca leaned forward and looked directly into Oriono's eyes, "Too many variables, but maybe you just weren't built like that to begin with. It's okay to just want to be with someone without wanting all the rest of what comes with it. Someone else out there wants the same thing as you. This I know to be true. On a long enough timeline you will find that person."

Officer Oriono reached out their battle scarred hand and held Rebecca's little hand, "And all we have is time. Endless time. I understand why you're doing this today. In a way none of the others ever will. I'm not going with you, but I won't stop you either."

Rebecca smiled and covered Oriono's hand with her other hand, "I figured, but it's good to know I won't need to incapacitate you on my way off the station."

Now it was Oriono's turn to laugh loudly and inappropriately.

"Sounds like I missed a good joke," Kieran said, interrupting the moment. Rebecca smiled as he sat down with his large breakfast, even here at the end of the journey he was still stopping for a good meal first. "We were just discussing our plans for today, Oriono isn't a go, but he's not stopping us either."

Kieran gave a respectful nod to Oriono, "Thank you."

"No thanks required. This is where I must leave you. Safe journeys to all of you," they said standing up from the table.

Officer Oriono started to salute them in a sign of respect for what they were about to do, but decided against it at the last moment. Not wanting to tip off the station crew eating at nearby tables.

The lovers had barely had a moment to exchange even knowing glances and a kiss before Braug arrived. He coughed loudly, a human custom meant to announce one's arrival when people are clearly not paying attention to your arrival. "Hello and good morning, Braug," Rebecca said loudly and directly as she leaned back from where she'd been kissing Kieran.

"Has the officer said goodbye already?" Braug asked of her.

"Yes," Kieran replied through his waffle.

"Then I am exactly on time," he replied back gruffly as if imitating Officer Oriono's dialect.

"Looks like I'm late coming to breakfast though," said Henry looking decidedly ruffled compared to the last time Rebecca had seen him. She sipped on Kieran's coffee, and stealthily replied, "I'd say you look like you've come already this morning."

If Henry had blood and skin, his face would be flush, but instead he just suppressed a guilty smirk, "No idea what you're talking about." They all sat there not addressing the elephant at the table and waited for Juuana to arrive.

Which of course she did after another ten minutes, "I'm sorry, running late this morning. Just can't seem to get going." Juuana sat down across from Henry and next to Rebecca. Which was supposed to be a way of making it clear she hadn't just spent two very passionate hours with him before breakfast but the effect just made for a comical moment as everyone except Henry was now on one side of the table.

"So it looks like your plan to arrive separately and act like you didn't just bang the shit out of each other this morning is working perfectly," Rebecca said with a wink.

Kieran was two bites into his waffles before Juuana was able to compose herself enough to reply, "No privacy on a starship, right?"

There was a round of deep roaring laugher from everyone at the table.

Rebecca shook her head at how silly everyone was being and spoke after sipping the last of Kieran's coffee, "Officer Oriono has advised they will not be going with us this morning, but they also won't be standing in our way. So if Braug has completed his rerouting task we should be good to board the HoL without anyone noticing us on surveillance monitors."

The Gorgon said nothing but nodded his head at them.

"Then we're really doing this, aren't we?" Henry asked the table not really believing himself capable of stealing a starship off a heavily secured space station on the far end of the galaxy.

Rebecca put her hand on his shoulder, "Yes."

The group ate in silence, each one of them unsure of what to say at the last breakfast any of them might eat. Henry and Juuana exchanged knowing glances at each other. Rebecca stared out at the station crew members wondering if any of them knew what was about to happen. Braug ate his meal already having a conversation with them as they launched the ship shortly in his mind. Kieran wondered if there were any waffles left in the cafeteria.

Kieran stood to get more waffles but the group took his standing as a sign it was time to go. Everyone started packing up their plates and trays. Henry and Braug took the trays from the women, and not wanting to seem rude, Kieran took the last of the table garbage on his tray and followed.

Rebecca stood to stretch and was about to start heading to the docking bay when Juuana took a quick step forward. The curvy engineer pulled Rebecca aside so quickly it shocked her.

"I know you are Mother of Songs. Why didn't you say anything earlier?" Juuana half-asked, half-accused Rebecca in the quiet of the meal hall. There was a long pause as their faces dueled between confusion, anger, and acceptance.

Rebecca looked around, pulling Juuana in even closer before whispering back sharply at her, "It was a long time ago, Juuana, and my involvement with the Gorgons had nothing to do with this project."

"Nothing to do? You were one of the first humans that they ever met! You had access to their last starship and secrets that even now the Gorgons won't share with us. Solieo and I spent years working along side you on the Harmony FTL engine. What did you know about resonance technology that you didn't share with us? Did we even need to be here?"

Hearing accusations and knowing the root of Juuana's complaints steeled Rebecca's response, "You both chose to pursue this project. Neither one of you was compelled to join. There is no grand conspiracy here. Just an old woman with a long dead past. The Gorgons didn't share anything because there's nothing to share. Their starship was beyond salvaging. Their history lost to them. I don't know why they called me Mother of Songs, but it's got nothing to do with today."

Juuana started to speak but Rebecca pulled free of her grasp and pushed her back. Leaning hard against the golden haired woman with all the strength her artificial shell had, Rebecca hissed, "The Gorgon FTL engine secrets are gone. Mother of Songs is gone. Captain Fillion is gone. Solieo is gone. It's just us left here at the end of this story. You get to decide this morning if the journey ends in here or out there."

They glared at each other, each for their own reasons, and finally Juuana relented, "There's nothing left for me here without Solieo and I don't want to see all of our hard work just used to run from extinction. That's what the Gorgon's did. Let's do it. Let's see what's beyond the anomaly."

Rebecca smiled, "I don't know what's left for us, but I do know that our song doesn't end today. Long ago when I first met the Gorgons on that rotten little rock they'd crashed on, their oldest survivor spoke to me. They said I would see them again. I haven't gone back since that day. So that means we don't die today, right?"

Juuana gave a haggard cough like chuckle that was equal parts disbelief and dismissal, "I'm not sure our fates are so easily foretold, but no matter what, Rebecca, I am with you to the end of this journey." She held out her hand but Rebecca pulled her in for a hug. They stayed like that for a long moment. Each fighting back emotions they hoped the other wouldn't see when the embrace ended.

The hug finally ended and Rebecca nodded at Juuana as tears chipped at the corners of their eyes. Braug, Henry, and Kieran arrived back from the recycling room and thought the two women were saying a tear filled goodbye to all those they'd left behind on this journey. They'd never know the secrets the two of them had just shared with each other.

The group stood there for a second, then then Rebecca spoke, "Let's roll out."

Turns out stealing a starship is easy. Because of the failed launch yesterday, all of the station's crew that worked on the HoL were stuck in yet more meetings discussing what had gone wrong. Reading over reports that Henry had falsified with his macro key-bin program.

Thanks to Braug's fake Systems Control integration routine, none of the security drones or cameras saw the group enter the hanger bay. Why would anyone need to be physically present to guard a ship that can't go anywhere? So they just walked in. The bay was cold and empty with scattered tools and containers the only sign of all the activity from yesterday.

Henry looked around the hanger thinking to himself, "This is the last place in this big old galaxy that I'll ever see." Unhappy with the choices that had led him here he said nothing but stood to the side and waved for everyone to enter. The mood of the group had become very serious.

With the systems offline, none of the lights came on, so in the dim emergency lighting they crossed the hanger. Everyone waited at the airlock door as Juuana keyed in the code she'd seduced out of the horny security guard. As the numbers danced through her mind Juuana felt a bit of shame for what she'd done to the security officer, but it passed through her quickly as she remembered how happy he'd seemed afterwards.

Braug, Henry, and Juuana started in and Rebecca held back. She grabbed Kieran's hand and they stood back. Watching as everyone else boarded the HoL. Beyond the doorway lights came flickering on and they could feel the ship shudder and come to life. The Harmony FTL engines began their warmup cycle, causing vibrations to shudder along the airlock ramp.

Here now in the dim hallway just beyond the boarding ramp they embraced. The whine of humanity's greatest mechanical achievement a constant whine in their ears as the ship's engines rattled the docking bay. The lovers pressed closely and he could feel the warmth of her body against his as the cold wrapped around them.

They held together like this for longer than what you could call a reasonable hug. It was a last embrace of lovers. Rebecca pulled back first, looking into Kieran's eyes as if searching for answers to questions he would never know. "I love you, too," was all she said. He ended the moment by pushing forward into a kiss.

A final kiss of lovers. Rebecca responded meekly at first as if surprised by his boldness, and then answered by pressing back into his lips and taking control of the kiss. Kieran would tell you that he heard a moan escape her, but it might have just been the station and HoL groaning as systems were brought online.

Finally the embrace ended. Kieran held her hand and started to walk away, but Rebecca stood still, "I need a moment." He nodded and moved down the ramp into the ship. Onward to the end of their journey. The light from the doorway into the HoL beaconed to Rebecca as she leaned on the wall.

Holding her breath, feeling the tears at the edges of her eyes, finally Rebecca spoke to no one and everyone in the universe who could hear her at that moment, "I know. I know you created him. You built and shaped his life until he was perfect for me, but... I love him anyway. Thank you," she touched the hallway of the station like she was saying goodbye to Systems Control.

Rebecca stepped onboard the HoL and closed the airlock. The docking rings hissed and groaned as the doors closed. She knew Braug's work would have blinded Systems Control and the dock crew to their presence, but there would be no mistaking the HoL undocking. Rebecca opened the control panel and pulled the manual release lever. The ship and the station shuddered as they let go of each other for the last time.

The fastest ship in the known universe was cold. Just like the Leviathan. Built for purpose not pleasure. The passageways were starkly lit in neon blues and golds. The panels miscolored and barely fitted correctly. A ship meant to be tinkered on, never flown. Still one that Rebecca knew by heart after decades of drafting every curve and circuit.

Moving with purpose, she found her friends in the cockpit. Makeshift screens and wiring criss crossed the room. Henry smiled at her as she took her seat in the center console. Microgravity generators on the chair buzzed to life for their first time and wrapped around Rebecca with warm hands. She thought of Mother Goose, sitting alone on a dock waiting for her at the opposite end of the universe. "I will see you again. I promise," she thought to herself.

"Kaylee, what's our status?" Rebecca asked the ship.

A blue light filled the screens and a voice Kieran recognized from the Mother Goose called out, "All systems are green. We are ready to jump, ma'am."

There was a silence in the cockpit as everyone took breaths wondering what to say. Rebecca spun around in her chair, "Kieran... you saved the Leviathan. You saved us all. So its only fitting, that you press the launch button." He smiled at the faces now staring back at him.

Kieran took a deep breath and touched the screen in front of him. Rebecca moved the launch command to his UI window. He wondered if Dr. Cornelius would have done this if he'd lived to take this journey.

"Three for hope, two for chance, and one for luck," Kieran said aloud to the crew.

CLICK

Carlos and the Checkpoint Charlie station crew watched in a panicked horror as the HoL undocked itself and launched into the stars. It wasn't until the starship arced towards the sun that they realized this wasn't massive systems failure. Security was dispatched to find Dr. Rebecca Chambers and the other Leviathan crew members.

By the time the HoL had finished its swing around the sun and was preparing for its jump into the anomaly Carlos and the station crew knew it had been stolen. Systems Control was unable to retake control of the hijacked starship, but was able to patch a communications line in so that Carlos could yell at the thieves.

"WHAT ARE YOU DOING!?" Carlos screamed once Rebecca answered.

Rebecca sighed, loudly and dismissively, "What machines always do, Carlos. Save humans." The holo line ended, but the general voice communications network continued broadcasting as the HoL engaged the dual linked Harmony FTL engines and jumped into the darkness.

The Checkpoint Charlie crew members watched as the ship they'd spent years building vanished into the darkness. Carlos hushed the bubbling chaos in the control room and leaned her head down to the speaker to listen to the voices coming from the darkness.

It was static...

...

..

.

Then Kieran's voice spoke loudly, and clearly, "I see the ducks. Do you see them floating on the ocean? It's beautiful."

.

..

...

THINGS LOST BUT NEVER FORGOTTEN

The council members stared at each other waiting for
Systems Control to begin the presentation. All of them
except for Dr. Jully Liu-Cheng. Her eyes kept drifting down
to a notepad filled with a half written eulogy for her old
friend. Jully hadn't expected a goodbye when the time came
but it didn't make the loss less painful.

Systems Control came onto the call, "As you already
have been briefed, the starship HoL had an unknown engine
engagement failure. The team was reviewing for possible
causes when Dr. Rebecca Chambers commandeered the
starship."

A grainy video of the HoL undocking from the space
station started playing for the council members to watch.

After a moment the starship vanished behind the sun and
Systems Control resumed speaking to the fifteen members
who were listening,"The solar batteries reported flawless
energy capture during the sling around the sun and the
Harmony engines engaged without any issues. The earlier
failure was clearly sabotage by the crew of the Leviathan."

Jully looked up from her eulogy notes and watched as Systems Control showed the final part of the video. She watched as the HoL with Rebecca onboard leapt into the darkness of the anomaly. Even on the grainy video the moment still took Jully's breath away.

If it noted the quiet gasp from Dr. Jully Liu-Cheng was unclear but Systems Control paused for a moment. Then once it was sure half of the councilors were paying attention it resumed speaking, "All direct contact was lost after four minutes. On the communication line static that contained a high percentage of repeating events continued for a further 154 minutes before fading away."

One of the councilors interrupted, "The final voice transmission. Have you been able to determine what Mr. Ausure's final communication meant?"

The red glow of Systems Control blinked, "No. It has been run against all syntax databases I possess. When the Leviathan crew logs are received tomorrow I may be able to offer further context."

Jully leaned forward and pressed the talk button, "It doesn't seem like the HoL will return. Correct?"

Systems Control did not need to think before it responded, "No, I do not expect a return flight. Dr. Rebecca

380

Chambers, Kieran Ausure, Dr. Juuana Verantes, Henry Harrison, and Braug have been noted as missing, presumed dead in the citizen record. Next of kin have been notified and personal effects left behind at Checkpoint Charlie will be brought back by Officer Oriono."

Councilor Netgeera did not let the likely deaths of five people stop him from interrupting Systems Control, "What is the next step?"

The red dot that controlled the human empire already had a plan, "The crew at Checkpoint Charlie have already begun work on building another starship, designation HoL-2. We will explore a different sector of the anomaly."

Jully was tapping the notepad trying to think of how to end the eulogy when she saw a message come in from Carlos. It was short and to the point, "The furthest most edge of the anomaly has receded!"

Without hesitation, Jully jumped over Systems Control's discussion of flight plans, "Is it true that the crew of Checkpoint Charlie has noticed the anomaly shrinking?!"

Systems Control blinked hard. Scanning a thousand communication lines and every available sensor before responding to the council, "Yes, early observations reported by the crew of Checkpoint Charlie over the past week

381

indicate that the anomaly looks smaller. However observations by human eyes must be backed up by long term scanning. It will take time."

Leaning back Jully retorted, "Time... time is all we have now."

EPILOGUE

Tyler took a long drag on his nicotine pipe and watched starships coming and going from the long-term docking yard. *Big dumb idiots flying off to their next stupid job*, he thought to himself. Feeling self satisfied that he'd gotten a job that didn't require leaving his planet. In fact, he'd only been off world once to see a distant relative. *What a waste of time that was*, the rough shaven man thought to himself, tossing the empty pipe to the ground.

"Hey, Tyler, we're having trouble with the entry code on this one, can you help us?" called out his co-worker John. The clean shaven enthusiastic smile of John annoyed Tyler who considered the teen to be the dumbest person at their firm.

"Sure, John," he replied, keeping his thoughts about John's intelligence to himself.

Cracking open a repo-ship was Tyler's favorite part of the job. You never knew what you'd find inside. Sometimes it was expensive valuables left behind by an absent minded crew member and sometimes it was literal shit to clean up that the ship's captain forgot to flush before docking the ship. That part of the job Tyler hated. Thankfully, John was dumb enough to always do it.

As the two men approached today's repo job, Tyler stopped to look over the faded white starship. It was probably beautiful when it was new, but after sitting unused on a dock for a few hundred years, it was just tired looking. Still Tyler thought the shape was unusual. It was like a bird starting to stretch out its wings and take flight.

Reaching up to run his hand across the hull, Tyler felt a moment of wonder. He stared at the sea of hexagonal tiles as they wove across the surface of the ship. Somehow they tiled together just right to form an interlocking skin. It was like nothing Tyler had ever seen before.

Tyler stood next to his co-worker as they clicked through the ramp controls on the ship. "Why would someone leave this behind? Seems too exotic to be a junker," Tyler asked.

John answered without looking up from the controls, "It's a payment issue. The docking fees stopped being paid this morning. Dock owner wants it gone now. Apparently it's been sitting here a long time. There's no magnetic clamp guides so we need to fly it manually over to the junkyard."

Tyler watched as his co-worker missed the obvious solution to the ramp problem for the third time before he pushed past, "You're doing it wrong, here engage the backup control mode."

TSWHOOSH

The main loading ramp of the ship came down slowly. Tyler put on his mask as centuries of dust and stale air came rushing out at them.

John was not as smart, or fast, and started coughing, "Jesus, man, they said it had been here for a long time but I didn't think they meant this long"

Stepping onto the ramp and engaging his flashlight, Tyler watched as John waved him off. "Stupid and lazy," he thought to himself.

This ship was weird. There should be more dust. And less lights. The interior lights had come on when the ramp came down but after a hundred years of sitting around the batteries should be dead.

Tyler wandered past the crew quarters. "Ooh, I hope there's some good shit worth selling in there," he said poking his head into an empty cabin. As he passed the kitchenette, Tyler was thankful no one had left food out before they left. Finally he found his way into what appeared to be the cockpit. Custom 270 degree surround screens wrapped around three seats. Liquid organic crystalized visual screens clicked on when he entered and Tyler for a moment felt like he was floating above the dock.

"Woah," Tyler muttered as he realized it was a live feed. He watched as John wandered to the front of the ship and started smoking. "Motherfu... is taking a nico break? He didn't need me to get in, he's just..." Tyler's rant was cut short by the realization that he'd been suckered by an idiot.

Tyler smashed his hand on the console and suddenly a blue light came on in the cabin and for a moment he worried that he'd broken something.

A voice filled the cockpit, "Systems reengaged. My apologies on the delayed reawakening to yesterday's command."

Whoever it was, they weren't speaking to Tyler. He sat down and started pressing buttons trying to get the command system to come online.

"You are not authorized," the voice called out.

Tyler gulped. The tone was not friendly. He'd run into a few ship virtual assistants over the years. They sometimes would lock you out and once one fried the flight engines to prevent his crew from moving the ship.

Putting on his most innocent voice, Tyler spoke, "My apologies. My name is Tyler and I'm here to move this ship out of this dock for failure to pay."

"Good shit worth selling," said a recording of Tyler.

Tyler gulped and started looking around for some way to shut down the ship's computer core, but he'd not gotten very far before the voice called out to him.

"You are a thief. This ship belongs to someone. A missed docking fee does not mean you can take anything you want. I want you to..." the voice suddenly stopped.

He froze in position hoping that maybe the batteries had finally died, or the system had overloaded, anything that would save him from having to tell his boss that they'd need to call out a heavy load hauler.

"My apologies, I'm getting a quantum link call. You will need to wait a moment," the voice said to him.

Tyler's eyes went wide, "This goddamn ship has a quantum link on it?" The mind boggling price he could get for one of the rarest pieces of technology in the galaxy caused him to start moving. He found the engine room quickly and started poking around. Half looking for the computer core to pull and half looking for the quantum link modem.

"Yes, I understand. Coordinates confirmed ma'am. Looking forward to seeing you again," the voice rang out from behind Tyler. The ship was having a conversation with someone else. The ship had been sitting there for over a century, there was no way it was a real time call. "The stupid bot must be confused and just playing back an old conversation," Tyler thought to himself.

Engines long silent roared to life around him and sent violent shudders pulsing through the ship causing Tyler to fall roughly onto his butt. Sitting on the ground in the engine room, the sound of the FTL engine was like two monks chanting in unison. This confused Tyler as he'd never heard an engine that sounded like this before.

Shaking the surprise off, Tyler stood up shouting at the computer, "What the hell, bitch? You can't take off, that's against every code!" Stumbling out of the engine room, Tyler entered the cockpit in time to see the blue light flash brightly as the voice thundered around him, "This is my ship. Get off now before I vent all the oxygen out."

Fear washed over Tyler, but a lifetime of dickish bravado had gotten him this far, so he pushed back, "This mask has a built in oxygen supply. I'm not going anywhere... bitch."

The blue light pulsed for a moment as if the ship was in deep thought. The sound of the engines hummed around Tyler and then increased in volume.

"Ha... Ha.... Ha...," hollow laughs rang out throughout the starship, "such fragile looking bones you have. Will be a shame to crush them."

Tyler collapsed to the floor as the starship suddenly lurched upwards at a speed he didn't think was possible in atmosphere. He closed his eyes as every bone in his body felt like it was being flattened into dust.

"Please... please stop...," Tyler weakly asked before the air left his lungs.

The starship came to a dead stop and Tyler was flung from the floor into the ceiling with such speed that he heard his arm crack in half before he felt the searing pain of a broken bone. Falling back onto the floor, Tyler cried out in a desperate panicked pain wrapped voice, "I'll leave... please... just land."

There was a single blink of the blue light, "No."

Tyler's eyes opened as tears flowed down them and he watched with horror as the ship started its ascent again. This time it was slow enough that he could hear the roar of the upper atmosphere of the planet scraping against the hull.

Soon he felt the vacuum of space pulling at him. Tyler roughly grabbed onto the cockpit door frame. Feeling defiant he started to laugh, but the door started to close on him. It pinched him so quickly and painfully that he yelped out loud.

His grip on the door loosened for just a moment and Tyler felt himself being pulled through the starship. Tyler tumbled through the kitchenette, banging his head so hard that for a moment stars danced in front of his vision.

Passing quickly down the crew cabin corridor, Tyler realized they weren't stars in his head as outer space came into view just beyond the ramp. As he passed through the ramp Tyler noticed a name plate above him, The Mother Goose.

"What a lame name for a starship," Tyler thought as the vacuum of space wrapped its cold arms around him and squeezed until he popped.

With that, the ship's artificial intelligence Kaylee closed the ramp, finished her calculations, and engaged the Mother Goose's FTL engines. Out there her captain was waiting with their next adventure.

FIN

About the Author

As this is Ross' first book he's not known for anything yet.
A longtime resident of the formerly anarchist city of
Portland (Oregon), he enjoys a sharing a great meal with his
wife or walking their cute Cardigan Corgis. If you've read
this far, you'll be pleased to know Ross is already working
on his next novel.

Current updates can be found on his website at:
www.Zondaro.net

Made in the USA
Monee, IL
18 September 2021